"I've been waiting for this moment all damn night."

Teague ran his hands up her back, pressing her more firmly against him, and dug them into her hair. He used his hold to tilt her head back so she met his eyes. They were dark and stormy and full of too many things to name. She recognized the presiding emotion, though.

Desire.

He kissed her, the slightest brushing of his lips against hers. When she would have deepened it, he tightened his grip on her hair, holding her in place. He kissed each corner of her mouth and then trailed down her jaw. Then his mouth was on her neck. She didn't have to see the path he took to know he was tracing the map of bruises, his lips so incredibly gentle that she whimpered.

"Am I hurting you?" His voice was rough against her skin.

"No." Not in the way he meant. But his tender way of touching her was affecting her more than she could have anticipated. How was she supposed to keep her head about her when this man kept surprising her?

She didn't know if she could...

Acclaim for Katee Robert's Novels

THE
MARRIAGE
CONTRACT

ALSO BY KATEE ROBERT

THE
MARRIAGE
CONTRACT

KATEE
ROBERT

FOREVER

NEW YORK   BOSTON

Forever
Hachette Book Group
1290 Avenue of the Americas
New York, NY 10104
hachettebookgroup.com

Printed in the United States of America

OPM

Originally published as an ebook by Forever in June 2015
First mass market edition: December 2015
10 9 8 7 6 5 4 3 2 1

Forever is an imprint of Grand Central Publishing.
The Forever name and logo are trademarks of Hachette Book Group, Inc.

The Hachette Speakers Bureau provides a wide range of authors for speaking events. To find out more, go to www.hachettespeakersbureau.com or call (866) 376-6591.

The publisher is not responsible for websites (or their content) that are not owned by the publisher.

To Tim. It's been one hell of a ride so far, and I wouldn't want to share it with anyone but you.

ACKNOWLEDGMENTS

There hasn't been a single one of my books that has made it out into the world without a village supporting its journey from the initial draft to the polished story that makes its way into readers' hands, and this one is no exception. First and foremost, thank you to God for putting me on course for this crazy awesome path. I don't know that I'd be able to write the way I do if my life wasn't often stranger than fiction, and I wouldn't have it any other way.

Thank you to Laura Bradford for giving me the chance to really run with this idea, even though I'm sure that initial email sounded scattered at best. You were Callie and Teague's first supporter! And thank you to Leah Hultenschmidt for being an amazing editor and really *getting* what I was trying to do with this book. You helped me realize this story's potential and take it to the next level.

A huge thank-you to Jessica Lemmon, PJ Schnyder,

and Julie Particka for being this book's first readers and for your invaluable feedback. You've been a great support system through every step of this. I can't thank you enough! More thanks and hugs to Trent Hart, Jen McLaughlin, and Tonya Burrows for listening to me prattle on about this crazy idea I had while driving and not telling me I was nuts. You guys are awesome!

Words cannot express my thanks to my family for being there every step of the way and never complaining about the multitude of pizza nights and hours I spent glued to my computer. Alternately, for occasionally dragging me outside to actually interact with people. Husband, you're pretty much the bee's knees. Thank you for taking care of business while my head was in the clouds. Kids, I love you like crazy. No, you can't read this book until you're twenty-five. A special thanks to Little Miss for the solemn nod and approval she gave to the cover. So glad you like it!

And last, but certainly not least, a massive thanks to my readers. I couldn't do this without you. Thank you for taking a chance on something from me that's new and a little different.

THE
MARRIAGE
CONTRACT

CHAPTER ONE

Callista Sheridan pulled at the hem of her dress, wishing she'd chosen something else for this ill-advised trip. But there was no help for it. She wanted to get a peek at the kind of man this fiancé of hers was, and he'd been remarkably adept at avoiding her attempts to meet so they could get each other's measure. After two weeks of his dodging her calls and his father digging in his heels, she was forced to take matters into her own hands.

The only time Brendan Halloran left that compound he called home was to come to Tit for Tat, which was why she was here in this seedy neighborhood, in a building that was most definitely not up to code.

She wrinkled her nose as she moved down the hallway of private rooms. It might claim to be nothing more than a strip club and bar—albeit a trashy one—but there was no mistaking the sounds coming from behind those doors. Dread wormed through her, climbing higher with each step. It had been child's play slipping past the men Brendan had posted at the bottom of each stairway—they were looking for threats, not just another stripper. Wearing much more makeup than normal and a bright red wig, that was exactly what Callie looked like.

She stopped before the last door, her heart in her throat. This is where the girls had said Brendan would be. It wasn't too late to back out. No matter what kind of man he was, no matter how against the marriage she'd originally been, the truth was that the Sheridans needed the Halloran alliance—and that alliance came at the price of her marriage to the Halloran heir. She knew Brendan's father, Victor, by reputation, and it wasn't one she wanted to be associated with, let alone link her family's future to, but desperate times called for desperate measures.

And surely the sins of the father weren't shared by the son?

If there were any other option, she would have readily taken it. There wasn't. When her brother, Ronan, died, it left a gaping hole in the power structure. It didn't matter if she was more than capable of moving forward as the heir, even if she mourned the cause for the necessity. Their enemies wouldn't see that, and they certainly wouldn't care—all they cared about was the perceived weakness.

The only way to fix that perception was an alliance...and so here she was, stalling in an effort to avoid going through a battered door where her fiancé was most definitely in the middle of doing something she didn't want to witness.

Taking a fortifying breath, she cracked open the door before she could talk herself out of it. All it would take was a quick conversation to hash out their respective expectations for this "marriage," and then she'd be out of this place that made her skin crawl and on her way home. If he'd just agreed to meet her in the first place, this disguise wouldn't be necessary. But if any of his people had recognized her walking through the strip club door, they would have kicked her out—which meant her disguise *was* necessary.

She'd made it a full two steps into the room before her brain caught up to her eyes and understood what she was seeing.

The room was nothing fancy—just a bed and a small side table—but it was what was happening on that bed that rooted her in place. Brendan—because who else could it be with that massive body wound about with tattoos?—thrust into a woman, his big hands around her throat.

In those first five seconds, Callie tried to tell herself that it was some kind of kink play, but then he shifted and she saw the woman's face. Bruises blackened both her eyes, and her lip was split, leaving a trail of blood down her cheek. *Holy mother of God, is she even breathing?*

She reached blindly behind her for the door, but missed it, smacking into the wall. He froze, turning his head and pinning her with eerie blue eyes. If she'd had any doubts about his identity before, she didn't now. All the Halloran family had eyes that color. Even as she slid sideways along the wall, wanting nothing more than to escape and bleach this whole thing from her mind, he smiled. "Another present for me? You shouldn't have."

Breathe, Callie. Breathe and brazen your way through this. Her hand closed on the door handle. She had a split second to make a decision—come clean or try to lie her way back through the door. It was no contest. "Sorry, wrong room."

"I don't think so." He was up and on her before she had the door open, moving faster than any man his size had right to. Even in her ridiculous heels, he dwarfed her. "You're prettier than their norm here. You must be new." He licked his lips. "I love breaking in the new ones."

Oh God, oh God, oh God. No one knew she was here. He could do to her what he'd done to that other woman—who still wasn't moving—and no one would know. Fear tried to blank her mind, but she'd been trained better than that. *Show no weakness.* She tried for a smile. "There's been a mistake."

He laughed, hooking an arm around her waist and hauling her against him. "Then it's my lucky day twice over."

Having his big hands on her, restraining her even as he backed toward the bed with the girl she was starting to fear would never wake up, blanked out all her thoughts, her training, her years of holding perfect poise under pressure. Panic clawed its way up her throat, but she bit back the scream and fought him, going for his eyes.

The monster laughed. "You *are* new." With one hand, he pushed the woman off the bed, maintaining his hold on Callie with a hand around her neck. He stopped and watched her face, squeezing until black spots danced behind her eyes. *Do not black out. Don't you dare black out.* What had she thought she'd accomplish by coming here? Talking? Even if she had the right words to put a stop to this, she couldn't force them past his fingers digging into her throat. This was all a mistake. A terrible mistake.

He moved, pinning her against the wall, his voice detached as he looked her over. "Kind of skinny, but you got some tits on you." As if she were a cow he was considering buying.

She kept struggling, because there was nothing else she could do—giving in was not an option. Callie ignored the way he seemed to enjoy it, and kneed him between the legs like her brother had taught her years ago. Brendan cursed, but his grip barely loosened. She tried again, but he blocked her, and tossed her into the wall like she was nothing more than a pile of rags.

She hit the floor, knocking over the table. Pain lanced over her back and every breath was fire through her throat. It didn't matter. Nothing mattered but the sight of his big feet moving toward her. She pushed away from him, scrambling until her back once again hit the wall.

Then her gaze landed on the gun.

A Desert Eagle, which would have been laughable under any other circumstances. The only men who carried those guns were the ones who had something to prove— they were too big and bulky for everyday use.

But it might just save her life tonight.

She dove for it, snatching it up before Brendan got to her. The safety was so stiff, she had to switch hands to disengage it—a sign he hadn't shot this thing often. She raised it, fighting to keep the heavy weight from wavering. "Stop."

Brendan laughed. "What would a pretty little thing like you know about a big ole gun like that? Now put it down before you hurt yourself."

Hadn't he seen her switch off the safety? She straightened her arms, knowing full well that she couldn't hold this position for long. "Just back up and let me leave."

She'd find a way out of the marriage later, when she was back in the safety of her own home. Her family might need an alliance, but she'd find some other way—a way that didn't involve her spending another second alone with this man.

"I don't think so."

He reached for her, already far too close for her to escape, and she pulled the trigger. The gun practically leaped from her hands, but it was too late for Brendan. He hit the bed and went down, thrown back by the impact.

Callie didn't wait around for someone to hear the gunshot. She used the bottom of her dress to wipe off the gun and then fled, her heart pounding so loud, it was a wonder the entire club didn't hear it. She stumbled down the stairs and out the back door, mere feet from one of the men who was supposed to be guarding Brendan with his life.

Her thoughts went round and round even as she reached the car she'd parked in the back lot and climbed inside. *Oh God, he's dead. I killed him. I killed someone. But maybe he's not dead? Maybe I just winged him?* She cranked up the heat despite what had earlier felt like a warm July night. Now she couldn't seem to get warm. *Shock. That's what it is.*

She made it out onto the main street before she noticed the blood spatter on her dress. Her chest tried to close up, and she narrowly avoiding crashing the car into a light post as she scrubbed at the fabric. That almost impact jarred her back to herself. "I am Callista goddamn Sheridan. I'm better than this."

Better than what? Than murdering a man? She could argue self-defense until she was blue in the face, but the truth was that she'd gone to that club with the sole purpose to see Brendan in his natural environment. She'd been the catalyst that caused the confrontation.

Scenes flashed behind her eyes. Brendan's hands around that poor girl's neck. The maniacal gleam in his eyes at the thought of doing the same to Callie. The way the girl's body had hit the floor with a sick thump.

"*Enough*." She concentrated on breathing as she made her way across town, the tight muscles along the top of her shoulders loosening just a little as she crossed into Sheridan territory. "What's done is done. Didn't Papa teach you that? Now all that's left is to clean up the mess." Literally, in this case.

She parked in the garage, and spent the next thirty minutes scrubbing down every part of the car she'd touched with cleaner. Then she stripped off her wig, heels, and pathetic excuse for a dress, and threw them into the furnace in the basement. This early, there was no one else about, and things had been quiet on the illegal front as well, so she was able to slip on a pair of coveralls and make it back to her room without having to explain her presence.

Callie turned her shower as hot as it'd go and stepped in. Then, and only then, did she bury her head in her hands and let loose the hysterical sobs that had been threatening ever since Brendan Halloran wrapped his hands around her neck. With the water running over her head and down her face, she could almost pretend she hadn't broken her father's cardinal rule.

Callista was a Sheridan, and Sheridans didn't cry.

* * *

"Brendan Halloran is dead."

Teague O'Malley didn't look up from the book he was reading. "And?" But he already knew where his brother was going with dropping that tidbit out of nowhere. And the death of an heir was a game changer, more so because the Sheridans had lost *their* heir less than six months ago. There was a potential power vacuum created as a result, and he had no doubt his father and brother would be racing to fill it.

Aiden dropped onto the coffee table and swatted the book from his hands. "And you know what that means."

"Shouldn't you be talking to our father about this?"

"I'm talking about it with you." His brother turned those guileless green eyes on him, a trick he'd learned from their oldest sister. It had gotten both Carrigan and Aiden out of a shit-ton of trouble while they were growing up—trouble then never failed to fall squarely into Teague's lap.

The prickling at his neck signaled that he was about to be on the receiving end of another round, and he wanted no part of it. "Go away."

"Not until you hear me out." Aiden and Teague both looked up as Carrigan came into the library and closed the door behind her. Fuck. He really was about to get into deep shit if these two were settling down to plot. Aiden must have known he was about to bolt, because he slapped a hand down on Teague's shoulder, holding him in place. "Until you hear us both out."

He wasn't going to get out of this room until he did just that. "You have five minutes."

Carrigan crossed the room, her long dress swishing around her feet, and perched on the arm of the couch.

"That's all we need." She looked particularly virginal today in the white dress with her dark hair falling loose around her face. It was a part she liked to play when it suited her—the devout Catholic good girl—and it had kept their father from pushing too hard for her to be married. Teague suspected their father thought a nun in the family would somehow magically balance the scales for all the evil shit he did, so he'd been driving her hard in that direction. After all, he had two more daughters he could use to secure a general's allegiance in marriage.

Only Teague knew she was anything but innocent when away from the watchful family protection, but he wasn't about to out her. Every one of them dealt with living in the O'Malley cage in their own ways. If her way of dealing helped her hold on to sanity, he wasn't going to judge the means. Not when he had just as many secrets.

His sister patted his foot. "With that despicable Halloran monster put out of his misery, we have an opportunity if we move fast."

Giving up the pretense of being relaxed, Teague straightened and swung his feet to the ground—and out of the reach of his sister. "The next words out of your mouth had better not be that we should take this chance to eliminate the Hallorans."

Aiden huffed. "Are you scared?"

"No, but I'm also not suicidal, either." He glared at his brother. "And that taunt stopped working on me when I was ten." It had taken months for his broken leg to heal from jumping off that bridge into the creek on their Connecticut property, and he still had the scar and fear of drowning from the result.

Carrigan laughed. "We're not suicidal."

That remained to be seen. "Then stop dicking around and tell me."

"The Sheridan daughter, the only one in the immediate family left, was set to marry Brendan Halloran. They were going to announce the engagement today." Carrigan twisted a lock of her dark hair around her finger.

That got Teague's attention. "I hadn't heard anything."

"No one did. That's the point. They brokered the deal in secret—or as secret as anything is these days. You already know the name of the game. They were consolidating power." Her tone told him her thoughts on *that*.

A deal between the Hallorans and the Sheridans would have sunk them. They held territory on either side of the O'Malleys, and he had no doubt that it wouldn't take long for them to start eating away at the edges, with the aim of crushing Teague's family and their business between them. The Boston underworld was a fat purse, but that kind of money only went so far when split three ways. Take out the largest competitor and... Yeah, he could see the reasoning behind Sheridan selling his daughter off to the Hallorans.

But, shit, everyone knew what a sadistic fuck Brendan was. His family didn't draw the same lines the other two did, and he had no problem exploiting the human trafficking they dabbled in and creating his own little harem. Word had it that when Brendan played with those girls, most of the time he broke them beyond repair.

What kind of man would knowingly sentence his daughter to that?

And why the hell were his two older siblings bringing this information to *him*? He glanced between them. "It sounds like the girl dodged a bullet."

"Most definitely." Now apparently it was Aiden's turn to talk. "She's the heir to the Sheridan fortune—and all their territory—which means she's going to be the most sought-after woman in Boston. The vultures will be circling by the end of the day."

"Which is bullshit."

Aiden glanced at Carrigan, his expression shuttered. "Which is bullshit, sure. But we'd be stupid to sit back and let someone else swoop in and snatch up this opportunity."

Teague's stomach twisted, and he couldn't shake the feeling that he was standing on the train tracks and feeling the rumble of an incoming engine. "I'm not seeing what this shit has to do with me."

"That's the thing." Aiden shifted. "If someone's going to secure an alliance with the Sheridan family, why not one of us?"

The twisting in his stomach developed teeth, but he fought to keep his voice light. "Then I suppose I should congratulate you on your impending nuptials."

"Actually, we're here to congratulate *you*." Aiden held up a hand. "Just hear me out. I can't marry her. Our father already has a couple candidates in mind for me, and any of them would expand our territory exponentially."

"Then what about Cillian? He's old enough to play husband to the Sheridan girl."

Carrigan shook her head. "That won't work and you know it. The Sheridans might forgive our passing over Aiden and offering you, but it would be insulting to go to any of our younger siblings."

Jesus Christ. Teague looked at the alcohol cabinet on the far wall. Surely it wasn't too early to start drinking?

Even as the thought crossed his mind, he pushed to his feet. It might be too early, but this wasn't a conversation he was willing to have stone-cold sober. "No."

"Don't say no. You haven't even heard us out."

He didn't have to. He knew what they would say. *It's your duty to your family. Father has given you excessive freedom to mess around with your interests. It's time to repay all those favors you tallied up.* He poured himself a splash of whiskey and then kept pouring until the glass was full. "Didn't arranged marriages go the way of the dinosaurs a couple decades ago?"

"Maybe for other families. Not for ours."

He knew that. Fuck, he wished he *didn't* know it so well. The rules of polite society were different for his family than they were for your average Joe. He'd learned a long time ago that the money and connections came with more strings than a spider's web. And walking away wasn't an option, because that same money and those connections would be ruthlessly deployed to bring any prodigal sons or daughters back into the fold—whether they wanted to come or not.

Teague took a healthy swallow of the whiskey. "You can't seriously be asking me to marry some woman I've never met from a family we were raised to hate."

"I'm not." Aiden paused, and it was like the whole room held its breath. "Father is."

Just like that, the fight went out of him. He could argue his brother and sister to a standstill and even, occasionally, come out on top. Their father? His word was law, and he had no problem ruthlessly playing upon his children's weak spots to get what he wanted. Teague had learned that the hard way when he was still young enough to believe that there was another life—another option—out there for him. "I need some time to think."

"You don't have much."

Teague didn't turn at the sound of the library door opening and closing, because he knew both siblings hadn't left. "This is bullshit and you know it."

"I know." Carrigan plucked the glass out of his hand and took a sip. It was only then that he saw her hand was shaking. "You know Father made an offhand comment last night at the dinner you conveniently missed? He thinks it's time for me to shit or get off the pot." She laughed softly at the look on his face. "He didn't say it in so many words, but the meaning was the same. My goddamn biological clock is ticking away in his ear, and the man wants heirs to bargain with."

He watched her finish the whiskey. "What are you going to do?"

"I don't know." She set the glass down with the care of someone who wanted to throw it across the room. "I'm as much in a cage as you are—as we all are—but I can't talk to anyone about it."

He knew the feeling. It all came down to the bottom line—family. It didn't matter what was good for the individual as long as the family's interests as a whole were served. "You can talk to me."

Her smile was so sad, it would have broken his heart if he had anything left to break. "No, Teague, I really can't." With that, she turned and floated out of the room, leaving him alone in his misery.

He refilled his glass and went back to his seat on the couch. It was tempting to shoot the whole thing back and chase oblivion, but he needed his wits about him if he was going to get through this in the best position possible. The idea was absurd. The best position possible? He was a drowning man with no land in sight and the sharks were circling. There was nothing to do but pick the best way to die.

Each sip, carefully controlled, gave him some much-needed distance. He mentally stepped to the side and forced himself to look at the situation without the tangled mess of emotions in his chest. There might be no way out, but he could make the best of it regardless. The Sheridans had been a thorn in the family's side for as long as there had been both Sheridans and O'Malleys in Boston. They might be looking to bolster their strength, but it wouldn't take much to weaken their position.

He took another drink. No, it wouldn't take much at all. And if he were with the Sheridans, he wouldn't be *here*, so there was something to be said for that as well. The further he got from his father's grasp, the easier it would be to slip free when the time came.

Slip free? The pipe dream of a child. He knew better by now...but that didn't stop the tiny flare of hope inside him. It was a mistake not to crush it—if he didn't now, then someone else would, and it would hurt more that way. Reality had a nasty way of intruding on pipe dreams, and the reality was that marrying into the Sheridan family wasn't likely to give him an out. It would entangle him further in the type of life he wanted to escape. They may have a different last name and territory, but the type of beast was identical to the O'Malleys.

But if there was a chance to be free—truly free—wouldn't he be a fool not to take it?

He picked up the book his brother had knocked to the

floor, and carefully marked his page before closing it. He couldn't leave Carrigan behind. Hell, he'd be a selfish prick to leave *any* of his sisters behind. And his youngest brother, Devlin, was the least suited of all of them for this life. The thought of hauling three women and Devlin into hiding with him...Teague shuddered. It was impossible. He couldn't run without them, and he couldn't run *with* them.

So what the fuck was he going to do?

He laughed, the sound harsh from his throat. He was going to do exactly what he was told, like a good little piece-of-shit son. He was going to marry the Sheridan woman.

CHAPTER TWO

Callie followed her father into the reception hall, barely keeping her questions in check. All day, he'd acted as if nothing was wrong, and now he'd dragged her here even though she *knew* she wasn't marrying Brendan any longer. She pressed a hand to her stomach, silently commanding it to stop churning. She hadn't been able to keep anything down today, and four scalding showers weren't enough to wash away what she'd done.

It wasn't supposed to be like this. She was supposed to bring the Sheridan empire, such as it was, into the future. They had enough clean money for legitimate investments now to be on the up-and-up, and she had fully intended to be the one to make the transition.

Now?

She looked at her hands, pale and clean despite the blood she was sure she could feel drenching them. Now, she was no better than her father and all the men who'd come before her.

She could almost hear Ronan in her head, as if he stood right next to her. *Jump the back fence and meet me in the park. We can be at the airport before they even know we're gone.* An old joke of theirs—all the various ways they'd slip away from their protection detail and flee for another country. He'd stopped playing when he hit eighteen and graduated high school, but she'd never stopped her side of things.

I miss you so much, big brother. If you were here, none of this would have happened. Why, oh why, didn't you call a cab that night?

She rubbed the old ache in her chest and allowed herself to really consider running for three seconds before she discarded the idea. Papa wouldn't be alive forever—not when he'd aged decades in a matter of months after her brother died. Between his blood pressure skyrocketing and the doctor's dire warnings about lifestyle choices and his heart's ability to cope, he needed her.

If she left now, she might be able to live what passed for a normal life, but it was a selfish dream. When her father passed…God, that hurt to even think about…his generals would rise up in a battle for power that would hurt the very people they were supposed to protect. Oh, they might not see it that way, but Callie did. Without her here to fight for them to become a legitimate business, things would continue to stay the same way they'd always been.

And *that* was unacceptable.

She stopped just inside the massive room where they were supposed to have the party to announce her engagement, frowning. It was full to the brim with people. She recognized enough familiar faces to know that half of them were hers, but…

Those weren't Halloran men.

Papa approached, an older man next to him. She looked into those dark eyes and her entire body went cold. Seamus O'Malley. The O'Malleys were the other third to the Irish underground, but they were barely better than street thugs. They were everything she was trying to get the Sheridans away from. He scanned her as if judging her worth.

Which was apparently exactly what he was doing, because he turned to her father. "She's as exquisite as you promised. Teague will be as pleased as I am."

Oh no. No, no, no. This couldn't possibly be happening. But, as she looked from one man to the other, she realized that it was. Brendan's death hadn't changed anything. Her father had merely switched out grooms, like they were paper dolls he'd assembled to do his bidding. *Without telling her.*

Her calming breaths weren't doing much more than making her light-headed. She felt like she'd just chewed off her leg to escape an animal trap, only to fall into a pit of sharpened stakes. "I…I need to use the ladies' room. Excuse me, please."

She spun blindly without waiting for an answer, needing to be anywhere but here. A scream worked its way up her throat, clashing against her closed teeth, demanding release. She couldn't let it out. If she started screaming, she wasn't going to stop. She pushed through the doors, moved down the hallway and through another set to the quiet of the alley.

Would this O'Malley man be any better than Brendan was? She'd met the heir, Aiden, before, and he'd been nice enough—courteous, even. Their family didn't have the same reputation the Hallorans did, but that didn't mean *this* man wasn't as much of a monster as Brendan had been.

Would he...

She pressed her hands to her mouth. *I don't think I can do it again. I'm going to have nightmares for the rest of my life about what happened to Brendan.* She leaned against the brick wall and closed her eyes, concentrating on breathing and very carefully not thinking about the fact that she'd spent several hours with her father today going over the past quarter's finances of several of the restaurants she ran for the family—and he hadn't seen fit to mention this turn of events.

It would be okay. It *had* to be okay. If this Teague was a monster, too, well she already knew she was capable of defending herself. Her stomach twisted at the thought. *Please, God, please don't make me do it again.* There had to be another way—a better way to protect her family. She was so wrapped up in her misery, she didn't realize she was no longer alone until a rough male voice cut through her spiraling thoughts. "Want a smoke?"

Callie opened her eyes to a man offering her an opened pack of cigarettes. He was attractive in a brutish sort of way, his jaw square, cheekbones to kill for, and shoulders filling out his expensive suit in a way that didn't look the least bit comfortable.

"I don't smoke."

"Now's as good a time to start as any." He shook one

out and handed it to her, and then lit the one dangling between his lips.

She started to hand hers back and then reconsidered. What was one cigarette going to hurt? It certainly couldn't make the night any worse. "Ah...thank you."

He offered the lighter, cupping the flame between his big hands, and waited for her to lean in and light it. It felt shockingly intimate, as if they were sharing a secret or other such nonsense. She looked away, inhaling sharply, and started coughing. "Oh God."

"Inhaling might not be the smartest idea." He didn't seem to have a problem with it, exhaling a stream of smoke that temporarily shielded his face from her. "I hear we're going to be married."

This was Teague O'Malley? She tensed, but he seemed content to stand in this dark alley with her and share his cigarettes. Now that she knew what to look for, she recognized the same coloring that his father and older brother had—sun-darkened skin and near-black hair. His dark eyes weren't as cold as Seamus's, but that didn't comfort her in the least. All it meant was that he was a better liar than his father was. "What do you think about that?"

He shrugged. "It doesn't really matter what either of us thinks, does it?"

Her father knew how important it was not to undermine her authority now that she was the heir, and he was usually willing to sit down and hash things out with her before making a decision that would impact their family and business on multiple levels. A decision like choosing the man she was going to marry. But he hadn't even consulted her. And she fully intended to find out why at the earliest available opportunity. It was too late to back out now. Not only would it insult the O'Malleys, who shared too much of their border to provoke into anything beyond the occasional skirmishes, but it'd further weaken a position that couldn't afford to take any more hits. "No, I suppose it doesn't."

She tried her cigarette again, and this time the smoke went down smoother. Her head spun a bit, but it wasn't an unpleasant feeling, so she did it a third time, watching him out of the corner of her eye. She wanted to know why he'd followed her out here—if there was something he'd wanted to say that couldn't be said in front of both their combined families—but he seemed content to enjoy his cigarette in silence. Maybe he'd needed the respite as much as she had?

The escape—from strategizing, from talking, from questioning—was a gift, no matter how strangely packaged. She closed her eyes, letting her thoughts drift further away with each exhale. All too soon, it'd be time to step back into the chaos and let the events neither of them could stop begin, but right now they were just two strangers, sharing a moment of silence.

Can we really be strangers if we're already engaged?

She pushed the thought away, determined to enjoy this stolen moment in time before reality set back in. By the time she finished her cigarette, her hands had almost stopped shaking. She crushed the remaining bit under the toe of her sky-high heels and turned for the door.

Only to find her way blocked by Teague.

He was taller up close, well over six feet, and broader as well. The man looked like a bruiser, which was fitting because it was exactly what he was. He stared down at her with beautiful dark eyes, and her demand that he get out of her way died in her throat. While she was debating her options, he reached up, quick as a snake, and snagged the silk scarf around her neck. She made a grab at it, but it was too late.

Teague took a step closer, and then another, backing her against the wall, his eyes narrowing at her neck. "Show me."

"Leave me alone." Was that her voice, weak and wavering? She took a shuddering breath, all her hard-won calm disappearing. "Get out of my way."

He kept going as if he hadn't heard her, stopping less than an arm's reach away. God, he seemed big this close up—bigger than Brendan, bigger than her brother had been. He cupped her chin, his grip painless but completely unmovable, and tilted her head back to bare her neck. "Who hurt you?" There was a promise of violence in every line of his body.

"No one."

"Now, I may not be the smartest man in the world, Callista, but I know what the imprint of a man's hands on a woman's neck looks like." His thumb moved, tracing the line of Brendan's fingers that she could still feel digging into her skin. Teague's touch didn't hurt, though. It felt...almost good.

She swallowed, the move pressing her throat more firmly against his thumb. "I—"

"Don't lie to me."

She shivered under that unrelenting gaze, and licked her lips, all too aware of how he tracked the movement. "It won't happen again."

"You're right. Because I'm going to kill the bastard."

He kept stroking her skin, his touch doing strange things to parts of her body that weren't anywhere near her neck. "Tell me his name."

She wouldn't, even if the man who'd hurt her wasn't already dead. Even in their messed-up world, murder was a last resort—something to be avoided at all costs—not something you did for a woman you barely knew. "No."

"Your father hasn't been keeping what's his safe." Another stroke, this one closer to her jawline. "That's his mistake—one I won't be making as well. His name, Callista."

Oh God, oh God, oh God. She had to get a handle on this now. She'd never considered herself one to crack under pressure, but this man put his hands on her and spoke in that quiet, confident way that promised violence to anyone who touched her, and she was dangerously close to losing control. *Which* kind of control was up for grabs, so she went with the least likely to reveal her secret.

She kissed him, her heels giving her enough height that she barely had to go up on her toes. Her lips brushed his, and for one interminable second she was sure neither of them took a breath.

Then his arms were around her, and he took the last step to bring their chests flush together and her back against the wall. Even knowing she should be panicking at being pinned, she slipped her arms around his neck and traced the seam of his lips with her tongue.

That was all it took.

He let go of her throat to cup the back of her head, and then she was in the middle of the single most devastating kiss of her life. His tongue stroked hers, claiming her mouth—her body—as his own. His hands stayed in place even as he continued the assault on her mouth, his touch headier than the nicotine. She arched against him, tilting her head to allow him better access, and he growled in approval.

Whatever she'd expected from this kiss, it certainly hadn't been desire. Though *desire* was too tame a word. She'd felt desire before, and this wasn't it. This was... need. All-consuming need that devoured everything in its path, leaving only destruction in its wake.

* * *

Teague couldn't get enough of her. He should back off, should let her know he recognized her kiss for the distraction ploy it was, should get back to figuring out who the fuck put their hands on her. But he couldn't think beyond the way she softened against him and how unbelievably good she tasted.

He allowed himself to skate a hand up her side and run his thumb along the underside of her breast. *Holy shit.* There was nothing between them but a thin layer of fabric. She moaned, so he moved up a little more, circling her nipple, and giving a moan of his own when her entire body quaked.

This was the woman his father demanded he marry?

Christ, if he only knew, he'd take this away from Teague just like he had every other thing of value. The thought should have been a sobering one, but he was too far gone.

Somewhere to the left of them, a male throat cleared.

He tore away from her at the same time she shoved him, but Teague had only moved to stand in front of her, putting himself between her and whoever had just entered the alley. He took in the man with a single look—tall, big-ass shoulders, and black. That suit was most definitely hiding a gun in a shoulder holster, and he probably had at least one more on his person.

Callista pushed past him, shooting him a look. "Micah."

The man—Micah—crossed his arms over his massive chest. "They're looking for you, Callie. And I guess they're looking for *you*, too."

"Then we'd best get back." Callista snatched the scarf out of Teague's hands and wrapped it around her throat once more, hiding the marks.

It was like being doused in a bucket of cold water. She'd played him, and he'd been only too happy to go for it. Teague cursed himself as they disappeared into the building. He paced the alley, his desire for the woman dwindling as memories assaulted him.

Yeah, he'd seen those marks before. He'd been young—maybe six or seven—the first and only time his father put his hands on his mother. Teague wasn't sure what the fight had even been about, but the image of Seamus's hands around his mother's neck wasn't something he'd ever been able to forget.

Or the quiet words she'd managed to squeeze out. *You put your hands on me again, and I'll kill you in your sleep.* His father had laughed it off, but he'd never touched her like that again. Even then, Teague had wanted to step in, to do something to help his mother, even if she so blatantly hadn't needed it.

It didn't matter what had happened in the past. He couldn't change it any more than he could fly to the moon. But he sure as fuck wasn't going to stand by while someone hurt his goddamn fiancée. He wasn't sure when he'd decided to accept that he was getting married—maybe it was when she'd closed her eyes and leaned against the brick wall, letting that hint of vulnerability show—but he'd gone and done it.

Besides, it was blatantly clear that Callista Sheridan couldn't protect herself, and her father wasn't interested in trying. A woman like that...He closed his eyes and gave himself a full five seconds to remember how good she'd felt in his arms, readily responding to his every touch. *Christ.* A woman like that wasn't meant to be squandered on pieces of shit like whoever had hurt her—or on Teague, for that matter. He had no illusions about being good enough for her, but he was too goddamn selfish to back off now.

Even if he'd had a choice in the matter.

"Looks like you're having a good time."

He knew that voice. Teague turned around, staring at the mouth of the alley until one shadow detached from the wall and sauntered over. "What are you doing here?"

John Finch leaned against the wall in nearly the same place where Callista had just been. "You should have called."

"I didn't think the goddamn feds would care one way or another who I got engaged to." He was lying through his teeth. They wanted to know every detail he could provide, no matter how insignificant he found it.

"We care about everything you do." Finch pinned him with those steely gray eyes. "I haven't heard from you in weeks."

Yeah, because he'd been seriously reconsidering the whole thing. It seemed like a great plan to slip information to the cops from time to time—anything to weaken his father's hold on their portion of Boston. If he ended up in jail, it would free Teague and the rest of his family.

Or so he'd thought.

After months of tips and insider information, nothing had happened. *Nothing*. He knew these investigations took time, but he'd given them more than enough to put Seamus away for years—and still they wanted more. They didn't care that his father would be only too happy to kill him if he ever found out what Teague was doing. Hell, Teague didn't particularly care about that, either. He just wanted the man to go down in flames. He shook out another cigarette and lit up.

"Those things will kill you, you know."

"There are worse ways to go."

"You've got that right." Finch laughed, but the sound died nearly before it'd begun. "We need to talk. Sooner rather than later."

He debated telling the man to fuck off, but if Finch was desperate enough to waylay him here, where anyone could catch them talking, then he was desperate enough to keep popping up. "I'll call you."

"Do that." He turned and started walking toward the street. "By the way—congratulations on your engagement."

Teague watched him walk away, wondering why the hell the fed sounded so damn pleased by this development.

* * *

James Halloran followed his younger brother, Ricky, into their father's office. His last remaining brother. The monster that had woken in his chest at the news of Brendan's death only seemed to get more vicious with each hour that passed. It didn't matter if he was inside or under the open sky—there just wasn't enough fucking air. All he wanted was some time and space to come to terms with the new order of the world. A world that didn't have his older brother in it.

He knew well enough that Brendan has his faults—more faults than virtues, though James would never say as much to anyone outside their immediate family. But to kill him like that... There was no honor in that death. He shook his head and closed the door behind him. Right. Because honor would make this hellish situation so much fucking better.

Their father sat in his great chair before a roaring fire, his gaze trained on some memory that seemed a million miles away. James stopped walking, wishing he could leave the old man alone. The news of Brendan's death was horrific enough, but what he had to report now was going to send Victor over the edge.

And he'd take what was left of their family with him.

Ricky, the idiot, had no such reservations. "We have news."

Victor shook himself and seemed to come back to them. "You've found out who's killed your brother."

"No, but—"

"Then why are you here?" He practically roared it, his voice loud enough to have come from a man twice his size.

Ricky shrank back, like a dog that'd been kicked one too many times, and it was everything James could do not to join him. For all his sins, Brendan had always stood between his younger brothers and their father, and now he was gone. Christ, every time he thought that, the claws shredding his chest seemed to grow. He stepped forward, all too aware that he was about to put himself into the warpath. "There's something else."

"Then stop standing there with your thumb up your ass, and spit it out."

Easier said than done. He took a deep breath. "The Sheridan girl—the one who was supposed to marry Brendan—is now marrying Teague O'Malley. They're announcing it tonight." Possibly right this second.

Victor's cane hit the floor with a meaty thump, and he pushed himself to his feet. "Tonight."

It wasn't a question but he answered it anyway. "Yes."

"That bastard didn't even give me the courtesy of informing me himself." He turned to the fire again, muttering under his breath. "Should have passed the girl to one of the other boys. Both worthless pieces of shit, but that's the proper way to do things."

Jesus. James didn't have to look at Ricky to know there was naked pain in his brother's eyes. They'd never measured up to Victor's standards, and in recent years he'd stopped pretending he'd ever done more than tolerate their presence. James stared at the portrait over the mantel, wondering for the millionth time what their mother had seen in this angry, bitter man. She'd loved her boys, and loved them fiercely, right up until the cancer stole her from them fifteen years ago. Maybe it was better that way—better that she'd gone the way of the angels before she'd seen the men they'd become.

Ricky shifted. "Father, we can't let this insult stand. Brendan's body isn't even cold and they're already pawning that bitch off on someone else."

James shot him a look that he pointedly ignored. He doubted the dynamics in the Sheridan family were all that much different than theirs—meaning Callista Sheridan had no say in this mess. It was her father to blame. "Don't be disrespectful."

"Your brother's right for once. Sheridan is spitting in the face of our grief, and I won't stand for it." Victor turned to them. With the fire framing his body, he looked like a devil who'd crawled his way up from hell. He turned his steely blue eyes on James. "We're going to war."

CHAPTER THREE

Everyone was taking their seats as Teague slipped through the doors and made his way to the half of the table that had been designated for the O'Malley family. He met Callista's gaze, a primal satisfaction he had no right to soaring through him at the glazed look in her eyes and the way her lips were reddened and plumped from kissing him. He stopped in front of her. "We'll be talking later."

He could see the exact moment the mask slipped into place, her desire replaced by cold disinterest. "I don't think so." That was fine. She could hide behind the mask for as long as she liked—they'd be married and sharing a home shortly, and there would be no more opportunities to dodge him then.

So he gave her a tight smile and took his place on the other side of his parents. Sitting this close to his father was enough to give him indigestion at the best of times, and tonight was hardly that, despite the silver lining of actually being attracted to Callista.

His mother leaned closer and dug her fingers into his forearm. She looked particularly put together tonight, her dress designed to show off the fact that she was still willowy and beautiful despite having brought seven children into this world. "I know you don't want this, but it's vital you keep any theatrics to yourself."

Theatrics. Like he was a spoiled little boy who was in danger of throwing a tantrum when he didn't get what he wanted. The old anger rose again, but he managed to wrangle it out of his voice. "I'll be good."

Her green eyes were sympathetic, even if her grip wasn't. "This is for the best. You'll see." It was always like this with her. In her own way, Aileen O'Malley was just as much of a hard-ass as her husband—possibly even more so.

"Whatever you say." And then there was no more time for talking, because his father and Sheridan rose. Teague tuned them out as they went through what were no doubt practiced speeches. They were just words—words about putting old arguments to rest and starting fresh with a new generation and a peace and booming business that would benefit all.

If anyone in this room thought for a second that this marriage would put an end to the backbiting and squabbling over territory, they were delusional. It was a patch, and not even a good one at that. No one spoke about the fact that, less than twenty-four hours ago, Callista had been engaged to another man.

He leaned back and watched her out of the corner of his eye. Was she broken up about Brendan's death? She seemed smart enough to be worried about marrying a man whom she didn't know, but he might have mistaken nerves for grief. It was hard to say. Teague accepted the beer Aiden handed him and took a long drink. A cigarette and a kiss weren't enough to get a good read on a person. A part of him would like to chalk the whole thing up to her being overcome with desire, but he knew better. She hadn't wanted to answer the question about her bruises, so she'd made a move on him.

Was the abuser a boyfriend? He doubted she'd chosen this path any more than he had, so it was entirely possible. Teague took another sip of his beer, waiting for the irrational jealousy to ease. Though he doubted his father had been faithful at any point in his marriage, creating an extramarital arrangement hadn't been something he'd really considered before he met her. Now? There was no fucking away.

Christ, he was a mess.

He jumped when the room broke into applause, and then Aiden elbowed him, jerking his chin to say Teague should be on his feet. Shit. He pushed out of his chair at the same time as Callista. Sheridan watched them both, but it was Seamus who roared, "Let's see a kiss from the happy couple."

Happy couple, his ass. His father was punishing him for dazing off during the speeches and, under the attention of far too many people, there wasn't a damn thing he could do except obey. He passed Seamus, earning a painful shoulder clasp, and stopped in front of Callista. She looked a little pale, and he started to say...Fuck, he didn't know. Something comforting.

But then she turned to the audience with a smile that

somehow managed to convey happiness and nerves, like a princess playing to her subjects. She went onto her toes and pressed a chaste kiss to his lips. The near-innocent contact still sent a bolt of sheer lust through him, and it was everything he could do not to drag her back against his body when she leaned away.

Teague turned to go back to his seat, but his parents had moved down while he was distracted, leaving the seat open directly next to Callista. It figured. He sank into the chair and leaned closer to her. "You will tell me his name."

Her smile didn't so much as twitch. "Not likely."

Why protect the man? Because the perpetrator was a man. The handprint was nearly as large as Teague's would have been. "Do you care about him that much?"

She shot him a look. "I don't see how it's any of your business one way or another."

"It became my business the second you agreed to marry me." Where the fuck had *that* come from? He had no business feeling possessive of this woman, future wife or not.

"You were the second choice."

The words stung far more than they should have. Of course he'd known as much, but hearing her say it with such derision? The woman had claws, and apparently she wasn't afraid to use them. He leaned closer. "And did you moan so prettily when that piece of shit Halloran had his tongue down your throat?"

She started tapping the table with her fingers. "Of course."

Liar. It was in every tense muscle in her body, and the way she wouldn't quite meet his gaze. He covered her hand with his own, his entire body perking up at the feel of her skin against his. "I don't think so."

"Could you *be* any more arrogant?"

"Probably." God help him, but he was actually *enjoying* himself. "I'll see what I can do."

She huffed out a breath. "I don't know why I'm surprised. You O'Malleys are all the same."

"Careful there, Callista." He liked the way she twitched when he said her name. "You don't know a damn thing about me."

"I know enough."

He couldn't bring himself to argue with her, mostly because she was right. His family was full of thugs, liars, and cheats—with a scattering of murderers thrown in for spice. But then, hers was, too. "Those who live in glass houses shouldn't throw stones."

She went pale, her lips parting as if she couldn't quite catch her breath. What the hell? He hadn't said anything particularly horrible. He squeezed her hand. "What's wrong?"

"Why would anything be wrong?"

Prickly thing, wasn't she? "You just went as pale as if you'd seen a ghost, and now you look about ready to lose your dinner."

"I'm not feeling well. That's all." She seemed to realize she still had her hand in his and jerked it away. "If you'd stop touching and taunting me, the nausea is sure to pass."

"Nice try." He used a single finger under her chin to force her to meet his gaze. "You have a lot of secrets, angel. I'm going to enjoy finding them out."

"Whatever helps you sleep at night."

"Tell me something."

She raised an eyebrow. "I don't think I will."

Her sass was a subtle thing. The words were delivered with a perfectly polite pitch, but she hadn't given an inch since they met. Even knowing his life would be a whole hell of a lot easier if she were a submissive little mouse, he liked that she seemed to have a spine made of steel. "How do you feel about being sold off into marriage for the sake of your family?"

"I—"

A scream cut through the low chatter of the hall, followed by sharp sounds similar to a car backfiring. Gunshots. There was a breathless pause while Teague tried to process the fact that someone was shooting, and then he *moved*, grabbing Callista and dragging her beneath the table. It wasn't an ideal position because they were on a raised stage above the other tables, but any cover was better than no cover. He shielded her body with his, while he scanned the room.

O'Malley men had done the same thing he just had with the rest of his siblings, and a good portion of the guests. There were only a handful of idiots running for the doors. He met the gaze of one of his father's men, Liam, and jerked his chin toward the exits. The scream had come from there.

They had to figure out who had pulled the trigger, and they had to figure it out now.

* * *

Callie squirmed in Teague's grip, trying not to notice how good he felt against her while she searched for her father. "Papa!"

"I'm here." He waved a hand from the other side of a wall of muscle that was John, his personal bodyguard.

Thank God. She allowed herself to relax a little. Whatever else had gone wrong, her father was okay. She glanced at Teague, taking in the intent way he searched the room. "What happened?"

"That's what we're about to find out." He let out a breath. "We can get up now."

She followed his gaze to where a man had just come back inside. One of his? It had all happened so fast, she couldn't begin to say if it had been an attack or something else altogether less sinister. But all rational responses aside, her gut said this wasn't all caused by an accident of some sort. No, this had been intentional.

It was nearly impossible to climb out from beneath a table with any level of grace, so she took Teague's offered hand and allowed him to pull her to her feet. Or that was the excuse she told herself. It certainly wasn't that she wanted to feel his skin against hers again.

Papa was already in motion, shouting orders in direct counterpoint to Teague's father. The end result was the same—a group of men rushing to the main doors to find answers.

The man who'd come back in the doors approached their table and spoke in a low voice. "A drive-by. One of the guests was winged, but the bleeding has already stopped."

A drive-by? Who would dare?

But even as the thought crossed her mind, she knew. "Halloran."

"It makes sense." Teague frowned. "Apparently he's not too keen on the idea of you switching out husbands without missing a beat."

She took a step back, removing her hand from his. For a moment there, she'd almost forgotten that he was an O'Malley and little better than an enemy. She turned away from him and stepped carefully around the fallen chairs to her father. She nodded at Micah, one of her father's long-term men. "Talk to the couple outside. Find out everything you can." She waited for him to head toward the doors to turn to her father. "Papa, I think it was the Hallorans."

"Victor Halloran might be a crazy bastard, but not even he's crazy enough to attack both our family and the O'Malleys at the same time. No, it must be someone else—some hotshot kid with a gun and more balls than sense who wants bragging rights for a skirmish with the Sheridans."

She might have believed that under different circumstances, but she'd seen firsthand how grief for Ronan had changed and warped her father, affecting both his judgment and his health. And that was *without* someone heaping humiliation on top of it like they'd effectively done with Victor Halloran.

But he wouldn't listen to reason, and now wasn't the time to argue about it. "Papa, we need to go home and regroup."

"Nonsense. The boys will take care of things."

She reined in her temper through sheer force of will. "Someone drove by and fired on innocent bystanders to prove that they could."

"Yes, and if we scurry like rats to our den, they will know they have the upper hand." He straightened, towering over her. "I've been in this game longer than you've been alive, daughter."

The same argument-ending statement he always made when he decided she was being too lippy. There would be no reasoning with him now, and if he backed down, it was a weakness he wouldn't allow himself to show. There was no option but to stay here and be a sitting duck for whatever attack the Hallorans had planned next.

Maybe they're done for the night. Wishful thinking and she knew it. Maybe they were, but it was always smarter to overestimate your enemy than to hope for the best. She tried to put herself into Victor Halloran's shoes. From everything she'd heard, he'd done wet work for a prominent empire in New York before deciding to branch out for himself and carve out a piece of Boston. He'd worked his way up the ranks and created a reputation so brutal, people here had folded for him without a fight. She'd bet everything she owned that he wasn't done for the night.

Callie motioned to John. He hesitated, looking at her father, but finally crossed over the stand next to her chair. "Yes?"

"Set up a perimeter around the building." Making a show of strength was all well and good, but they'd have to be fools not to put some extra security in place to protect the guests here. Even her father would acknowledge that—already had if the small smile he wore was any indication. He'd done that sort of thing from the time she was a child, setting up a situation and allowing her to learn how to take the lead. Once she'd basked in his approval when she made the correct decision. Now? Now, she just wanted their people taken care of.

"Will do."

Satisfied that they were as safe as they could be, she reached for her glass of champagne before realizing it had been tipped over during the scramble for cover. Just as she turned to search for another, Teague appeared by her side. "Thought you could use this to settle your nerves."

"My nerves are just fine, thank you very much." It was *anger* giving her the shakes, not fear. Mostly. But she still accepted the tumbler and eyed the amber liquid. "Scotch?"

"Whiskey."

Of course. She rarely touched the stuff, but now wasn't the time to quibble over foolish things like this. The liquid shot fire down her throat, a blaze that slowly eased and settled into comfortable warmth in her stomach. She blinked at Teague, her eyes watering a little.

He watched her like he wasn't sure if he should laugh or be worried. God, she wasn't sure which he should do, either, so she took another—smaller—sip. "My father insists that we stay and continue the party."

"That seems to be the plan." And he didn't look any more pleased with it than she was.

To keep herself from staring at him, she watched as people righted chairs and slowly settled back into whatever they'd been doing before the screaming started. Some of them looked worried, but the others cast their glances at the head table and took their cues from her and Teague's fathers. They wouldn't leave—wouldn't show dreaded weakness—until the party was over.

"It's idiocy to stay here when we know there's danger."

"It is." He shrugged those big shoulders. "But these people are scavengers. The second they smell weakness, they'll stop fearing us and it will be complete chaos."

She knew that. Truly, she did. But it was such a fine line to travel, and they were on the wrong side of it tonight. *At least there are some precautions in place now.* "There has to be a better way."

"If you figure it out, be sure to let me know."

She finished the whiskey, and decided it didn't taste half as bad as that first drink. "Things will be different when…" When her father was gone. She clamped her lips shut before the traitorous words could escape. God, what was she talking about? She loved Papa, loved him dearly. She didn't want to see him dead any more than she'd wanted to see her beloved brother, Ronan, gone. How could she possibly *think* such a thing, let alone almost say it aloud?

It had to be the whiskey. She set the tumbler onto the table with a little too much force and pushed it away from her. "I need some air."

"Of course." He started to guide her, but Seamus stepped in their way.

"One more announcement."

"Father, enough."

Just like that, the thin veil of civility on his father's face disappeared as if it'd never been. "Sit your ass in that chair before I put you there. And you, be a good girl and do the same."

Be a good girl. She started to take a step forward, but Teague dragged her back and guided her into her seat. "Now's not the time."

Callie was pretty sure it was the perfect time, but she wasn't far gone enough not to realize that was the whiskey talking. So she let Teague keep her hand and did as she was told, all while silently promising to wipe that satisfied smirk off Seamus O'Malley's face at the first available opportunity.

The man in question stood and motioned for silence. "We apologize for the confusion, but there is nothing to worry about." He smiled, once again every inch the doting father figure. "We would like to cordially invite you to the wedding in four weeks' time."

The room took a slow spin around Callie before settling into place. Four weeks. *Four weeks?* She'd known what she was signing up for, but that was so soon. From the shocked look on Teague's face, he hadn't known about the timeline, either.

As the people around her clapped, she couldn't shake the fact that she'd just tipped past the point of no return.

CHAPTER FOUR

Teague walked Callista to her town car, painfully aware of the people surrounding him. They needed a moment to just sit and have a conversation, but that wasn't happening tonight—especially with the potential war hanging over their heads. He stopped her just before she climbed into the car. "Come out with me tomorrow. Just us."

She hesitated, an expression passing over her face that might have been fear. "I don't know."

Was she afraid of him? He shook his head. Of course she was. She was a smart woman, and she'd known him only a grand total of a single night. Smart women weren't in a hurry to jaunt off with strange men—especially when they came with a reputation that attached itself to anyone in the O'Malley family. "Just dinner, angel. In public. You can meet me there."

She relaxed a little. "We do need to talk."

Without everyone and their dog standing here, watching them like predators looking for weakness. It shouldn't be that way—every single person was either family or associated with the family—but Teague stopped railing at the unfairness of the world a long time ago. "Yes, we do."

"Call me and we'll set something up." She rattled off a number, and then she was gone, sliding into the car and shutting the door firmly behind her.

He watched her drive away, before turning to his older brother. "They need an escort."

"Already taken care of." Aiden grinned. "You like her."

Yeah, he did. But he wasn't fool enough to admit it now—or ever. Instead, he headed back inside, barely making it three steps before his younger brother waylaid him. Cillian had gone all out tonight, but he'd lost his suit jacket at some point, and the dress shirt was rolled up, revealing the tattoos covering his arms. "You're a lucky bastard."

Cillian would see it that way. At twenty-five, he was still dabbling in school and finding himself or some shit. Since he was the third son and fourth child, he had been coddled and spoiled all his life. He wouldn't escape his responsibilities to the family indefinitely, but he hadn't yet started to feel the weight of it bearing down on him. Not like Teague had.

Tonight that weight might finally win and crush him on the spot.

"I saw her once last spring, out dancing down at Furies, though she was looking even better tonight." Cillian sighed. "Those moves? I bet she can ride a d—"

"You're going to stop talking now." He didn't give a fuck how well she moved on the dance floor, and he sure as hell had bigger things to worry about now than how she'd rolled her body against his earlier. But it was more than that. Before tonight, Callista was just another Sheridan. An enemy. Now that he'd seen her—talked to her—he couldn't shake the feeling that they were the only two people in a foxhole, with enemies all around them.

Cillian's eyes went wide and he backed up. "Sorry, man. I just meant that if you have to have the old ball and chain, she's not a bad one to be trapped with."

"No, she's not." He straightened as Seamus approached, flanked by his favorite muscle—Liam and Mark. "Do we have any more information?"

"Not as of yet. But we will." Seamus nodded at Liam. "Find out who's responsible."

It would have been smarter to work with Sheridan on this and combine their forces, but this marriage was more about presenting a unified front to their potential enemies than actually *being* a unified force. But at least tonight would leave no doubts—an attack on one was like an attack on both. It was enough to make Teague so damn exhausted—or it would if Callista wasn't in danger.

He never thought the day would come when he'd put himself out for someone who didn't share his blood, but the thought of her with a target painted on her chest made his hands curl into fists and his eyesight bleed to red. *It's because we're getting married. To hurt her is to hurt something that's mine.* He almost snorted. *Liar.*

Seamus focused on him. "Don't do anything to fuck this up. If it's the Hallorans, I'll take care of them."

Easier said than done. If it were so simple to dispatch them, someone would have done it years ago. "At least tell me that you're not going to strike back before you confirm that Halloran did this."

When his father didn't say anything, Teague rocked back on his heels. Christ, he wasn't going to listen to reason. He met Aiden's eyes, but there would be no help on that front. There never was. The only thing he could do was to get his sisters and Devlin home safe so at least they wouldn't be hurt by whatever bullshit plan Seamus was about to enact. No matter what his father thought, *his* priorities were the family.

He turned and headed for the exit, thinking back to Finch. Had the man known it would come to an all-out war? If he did, he could have given a goddamn warning. No one died tonight—so far. Next time, Teague doubted they would be that lucky. It might start with innocent bystanders, but it was only a matter of time before it escalated into pinpointed attacks on the people he cared most about in this world.

There had to be a way to stop this before it got to that point.

He climbed into the car that was filled with his sisters and youngest brother. They looked at him with varying degrees of trust, like they were sure that with him here, things were under control. The very idea was insane. Teague had less control over his life than they did. Or at least he had as little control.

Carrigan pulled her hair back and started twisting it into a braid, the only outward sign of her nerves. "Well?"

"They don't know anything concrete." He braced himself as the car lurched into motion. "Father wants us home until he figures out the next move." The man hadn't said as much, but he wasn't about to tell any of them that they were so far from their father's mind that he didn't leave any instructions for them before heading off.

Keira huddled next to Sloan, and it struck him that his baby sister had turned eighteen this year. They were all legally adults, and yet had less control over the direction their lives took than most minors. Keira turned green eyes so like their mother's on him. "We're going to war, aren't we?"

It was on the tip of his tongue to lie. To save them some worry. But he didn't have it in him to shield them from a truth they'd have to face before too long.

He was saved from answering by Devlin. "There's no avoiding it now."

The only question was if the war itself was started by the Hallorans, or if whatever actions Seamus took tonight would be the tipping point. It didn't really matter. They'd had skirmishes before, over territory or product, but this was another animal entirely, and no one seemed to consider that there were bound to be casualties.

For her part, Keira didn't seem that worried. "Good."

Teague frowned. "Why the fuck is that good?"

"It means Father isn't going to marry us off to one of the other two Hallorans like Callista Sheridan almost was. Do you really think no one knew about how Brendan got his rocks off? To be married to that…" She shuddered. "Whoever did us the favor of killing him probably saved her life."

"You're eighteen. What the hell would you know about it?"

Carrigan laughed, the sound as jagged as broken glass. "Please. Not everyone has the luxury of being able to take off to their apartment whenever things get rough."

Sloan finally spoke up. "We know what value our father puts on us."

Christ. This was exactly the thing he'd wanted to save them from. He looked from one face to the other. "I'd take you away with me if I could. All of you."

"We know." Sloan patted his knee. "It's not your fault, Teague."

The fact that *she* was comforting *him* about her future stuck in his throat. "I'll find a way out of this—for all of us. I promise." He'd given Finch enough information to justify witness protection or some shit. If it wasn't, he'd find a way to supply more. Because the thought of one of his sisters ending up with a man like Brendan Halloran was reputed to be...Teague would do unforgivable things to keep that from happening. He was *already* doing unforgivable things—he might as well make it worth his while.

Carrigan just shook her head like he'd said something sweet but unbelievably stupid. "There's no escape for people like us, little brother."

* * *

Callie spent the day trying to pin down Papa into telling her *something* about what he'd found out about the shooting, but he was closeted in his office all morning and then gone from the house all afternoon.

She'd done some holing up of her own with Micah. Whatever came from this conflict, she wanted to make sure the people in their territory who depended on them for protection were taken care of. Micah had grown up in this life, the same as she had, so he understood. His father had been one of *her* father's most loyal men, until he'd died in a shootout with the MacNamaras' men. As a result, Papa brought both Micah and his mother into the family home—his way of honoring his fallen man.

That loyalty wasn't something that could be picked up and put down at the Sheridans' convenience. If they couldn't keep their people safe, they didn't deserve the territory they had.

They were currently camped out on high stools, just like they used to when they were teenagers, while Micah's mother puttered around the kitchen. She'd taken to the space when she'd first moved in here and made it her own. Even Papa didn't dare cross her when it came to this room of the house. Emma Jones was a force of nature in her own right.

Micah braced his elbows on the granite counter. "You can't bring every person loyal to your family into this house, Callie. You know that."

Yes, she knew that, but it didn't make the impulse disappear. She frowned at him. "What other option do I have? Patrolling the territory won't do a damn bit of good. We don't have enough men to keep an enemy out, so it's a waste of resources."

Micah's dark eyes saw too much. "You're not solely responsible for this. Colm will have some thoughts, I'm sure."

Yes, Papa would, if she could just corner him long enough to *talk*. She'd suspect he was avoiding her if there wasn't so much else going on. Still, she didn't like being left out of the loop. Callie traced the dark-veined pattern of the countertop with a single finger. "They're our people."

"And they knew what they signed up for." He reached over and squeezed her hand. "But I'll talk to the men about getting a few extra patrols out until we figure something else out."

It wasn't enough, and they both knew it. But it was better than nothing. "Okay."

He stood. "Don't you have a date to get ready for?"

Emma chose that moment to swoop in with a plate of toast. "Eat something before you go, Miss Callie." She straightened her apron and gave Callie a stern look. "You're so nervous, you're jumping at shadows and God alone knows you won't be eating while you're out with this O'Malley boy. This will settle your stomach."

Since her stomach was currently tied up into a maze of knots, she wasn't sure she could manage even the light snack. But she'd learned a long time ago that Emma was usually right about these things, so she dutifully picked up a piece of toast and took a bite.

Emma nodded. "Good. And you—" She pointed a dark finger at her son. "You watch our Callie's back tonight. You keep her safe."

"Yes, ma'am." Micah ducked his head. "It'd be easier to do if she wasn't slipping her guard every time I turned around."

"Stop trying to get me into trouble with your mother." When he just raised his brows, she glared. "I shouldn't have even told you about going out with Teague tonight."

"If you hadn't, then I would have had to track your ass down, and gotten *my* ass reamed for letting you drive off without an escort."

"Micah! Language."

"Sorry, Mama." He nodded at the door. "Callie, go get

dressed up. Knock that O'Malley bastard's socks off—sorry again, Mama—and see what his family is up to while you're at it."

She laughed, even though her stomach did a slow turn at another go-round with Teague. "I'll be sure to get all his dirty little secrets." She grabbed the plate and stood. "I'll bring this back down when I'm done."

"Thank you, Callie." Emma's dark eyes, so similar to her son's, were sympathetic. "You try to have a good time tonight, you hear?"

"I'll do my best." As soon as she left the safe haven of the kitchen, all the fears that had been plaguing her rushed back to the forefront of her mind.

Where had Papa been all day?

She dreaded finding out what he'd been up to. Or, rather, what he'd commanded his men to get up to. This was a significant step in the wrong direction. Worse, it was all her fault. If she hadn't gone looking for Brendan, things never would have gotten so out of control, and he'd still be alive.

God, the realization that she was the cause of his death was still almost enough to have her running for the bathroom.

Would it get better over time? A small part of her almost hoped that it wouldn't, because that would mean she was different from her father and every Sheridan who'd come before her. Papa wasn't one to brag about his kills, but Ronan used to huddle down with Callie and whisper about the things he heard Papa's men talking about. The same man who'd taught her how to ride a bike was also a man who'd killed dozens of people in the name of business and revenge. She still had problems reconciling the two, even though she'd seen more glimpses of that side of him in the last few months than she had in all the twenty-five years leading up to it.

She shivered, the small hairs on the back of her neck standing at attention. Callie turned a slow circle after she shut her bedroom door, but there was no one in the room except her. "Someone just walked over my grave." She shivered again.

Nothing good would come of this—any of it.

Which was exactly why she'd agreed to go to dinner with Teague tonight. They needed to have a meeting of minds and see if they could come up with a way to get this runaway train back under control. She had a feeling that, left to their own devices, the patriarchs of the three families would be only too happy to set Boston aflame to serve their own purposes.

And she was the spark that set the whole explosion into motion.

Feeling sick all over again, she grabbed the nearest dress and pulled it on. It was a red number that did wonderful things for her cleavage, but the effect would be dimmed by the scarf required to cover her fading bruises. She wound the light fabric around her throat, wondering how Teague would react. It was imperative that she didn't give anything away. If he knew *she* was the cause of all this...

There was nothing stopping him from announcing it to the world and turning her over to the Hallorans for justice. Papa might fight for her, but even all the strength he could summon wouldn't be enough if the other two families thought her death would see justice served.

She stopped. *What if I turned myself in? Would it be*

enough to stop this? If it was, wasn't she honor bound to tell the truth? She slipped on her heels and headed for the garage. Tonight, she was driving herself. Micah would be following at a discreet distance, but at least she'd have the illusion of freedom.

Callie grabbed the first keys her hand touched, and rolled her eyes when the Cadillac chirped in response. She'd prefer something a little subtler, but in the grand scheme of things, her vehicle choice didn't matter a damn bit. Besides, with the bulletproof glass and reinforced body, this SUV was really more of a tank. If they were truly going to war with the Hallorans, she couldn't have picked anything safer.

The drive to the restaurant was blissfully uneventful, and it didn't hit her until she was walking through the front doors that she'd voluntarily agreed to meet Teague alone. Trepidation rose, but she shoved it back. She was more than capable of having a conversation with a man in public without fearing for her safety. But her body wasn't listening to reason, her skin breaking out in goose bumps and her throat closing. Despite the open floor plan of the restaurant and the low light from candles and conveniently placed lamps, the walls seemed to be inching closer, until she hunched her shoulders in response.

"Callista?"

She jumped, tripping over her heels, and would have gone down if a hand didn't grab her upper arm and haul her to her feet. She found herself looking up into Teague's dark eyes. Had she thought them cold? They were dark fire, so deep and soulful that they should belong to a poet instead of an O'Malley who may or may not be the enemy.

He gentled his grip. "Are you okay? You look spooked."

If he only knew. She'd never been a victim of panic attacks before. But then, she'd never killed anyone before, either. A hysterical laugh tried to muscle its way out of her mouth, but she clamped her teeth together until the urge passed. "I'm fine."

"If you're sure…"

"I am." She couldn't quite banish the tension from her shoulders, but she managed a half smile.

Teague looked unconvinced. "Our table is this way. I thought some privacy would be our best option."

Some, but not too much. She took a shaky breath and tried to steel herself. Panicking like this wasn't an option. Panicking *at all* wasn't an option. How was she supposed to lead her people into the future if she couldn't even hold herself together?

Because this is exactly the sort of thing I want to avoid. Murder isn't supposed to be an option.

The table he led her to was situated on the other side of a half wall, and lit by two small candles. She slid into the chair that gave her a view of most of the rest of the room, and Teague took the one directly to her right, also putting his back to the wall. They shared a humorless smile. Old habits died hard, apparently.

The waitress appeared and took their drink orders. Once Callie had her wine in hand, she shifted in her seat to look fully at him. "You have me here. What is it you plan to do with me?" The words came out low and flirty, as if inviting him to think dark thoughts. Which wasn't what she'd intended…even if she was suddenly thinking exactly those types of thoughts. It was all too easy to step back into that alley and remember the feel of his hard muscles beneath her hands and how he'd taken her mouth as if he had every right to it.

Teague leaned back, his tumbler of whiskey hanging loosely in his hand. "I could think of a few things."

Focus. You're here to figure out how to solve a problem. Not to flirt.

She couldn't quite manage to tear her gaze away from the curve of his lips. Everything else about him was so hard and rough, as if carved from stone. But those lips? They were sensual and full and promised the kind of pleasures she could only dream of. She shook her head. "I imagine so."

"Tell me something."

She tensed. He was going to ask her about the bruises again. She was sure of it. "What would you like to know?"

"Were you and Brendan together?"

Callie laughed, the sound broken. "No. I'd never met him when my father decided that we should be married."

"Hmm." He nodded, as if confirming something to himself. His face gave away nothing of his thoughts, though those dark eyes drank her in as if he couldn't make himself look away. As if he didn't want to. "Do you hope I'll go the same way?"

No. The vehemence of the thought shocked her. Really, she shouldn't care one way or another if this man lived or died—as long as it wasn't her hand holding the gun. He was nothing to her. A stranger she was about to be linked to for the rest of her life. And yet…She took a sip of her wine. "You seem like a decent man."

He laughed. "There aren't any decent men in our world, but I'm a hell of a lot better than Brendan."

She couldn't argue that. She didn't even want to. Instead, Callie looked away. "What are we going to do?"

"About the marriage? Or the fact that Victor Halloran is about to bring all sorts of fire and brimstone down on us?"

Both. But focusing on the impending marriage—just *four weeks* away—was the selfish thing to do. It was more important to head off the Halloran threat before he did any more damage. "The latter."

Something like disappointment flickered across his features, but it was gone too fast for her to be sure. "In that case, I think we should talk to James. He's not a bad sort, and he's miles better than anyone else in his family. If there's someone who can bring this thing to a grinding halt, it's him."

As long as he doesn't know I'm the one who killed his brother. Feeling sick, she set her wineglass aside. "Then we should talk to him as soon as possible." Before Papa or Seamus did something to escalate matters. Twenty-four hours since the shooting and she knew there were plans afoot, even if she didn't know the details.

"I agree." Teague pulled out his phone and started dialing.

She stared. "You have James Halloran's number in your phone?"

"We used to play poker." There was that flicker again, as if some strong emotion was trying to surface. "But that was a long time ago."

"Oh." It seemed such a strange thing, when now that their families were on the verge of trying to kill each other, that he and James used to spend time together regularly enough for Teague to have his number. She waited while Teague left a cryptic message and a request for a call back.

He hung up and pocketed the phone. "Now, we wait."

The waitress reappeared as if she'd been waiting for the opportunity, and he ordered for both of them before Callie could open her mouth. She sat back as the woman left, not sure if she was impressed by his gall or annoyed.

Teague gave her a look that was almost sheepish. "Sorry. Old habit."

There seemed to be a lot of those to go around. "I could be a vegetarian. You just ordered me a steak."

"One—you're not. The catering menu for our announcement the other night had both red meat and fish on it, so I figured it was safe to assume you had some input on that. Two—I ordered the steak and the salmon. You can have which one sounds best." He said it so calmly, as if it was perfectly normal for a man to order for a woman he barely knew.

"Whether your deductions are correct or not—and they are—doesn't matter. I make my own decisions." The words came out harsher than she intended, but there'd been too many big decisions made without consulting her lately. That wasn't Teague's fault, though. She started to apologize, but he beat her there.

"You're right. I'm being an overbearing ass. I'm sorry."

She picked up her wine to cover her smile. She liked that he was willing to admit he might have made a mistake. Most of the men she knew would have glossed over it and changed the subject. They might not have ordered for her again in the future, but they wouldn't have been so willing to apologize. "Thank you for calling James. We accomplished what I came here for."

"Maybe you did, but I'm nowhere near satisfied."

The way he said the last word warmed things low in her stomach. "Teague—"

"We have to get to know each other at some point—might as well start now."

The logic was seriously flawed, but she found herself taking another sip of wine all the same. She *had* joked with Micah about finding out all the O'Malley secrets during dinner. "What would you like to know?"

"Everything."

She froze, her glass halfway to her lips. The warmth in her stomach burned hotter. "That's a bit much for a single dinner, don't you think?"

"Where would *you* like to start?"

She had no idea. If she was smart, she'd make polite conversation through dinner and get out of here as quickly as she could. This man wasn't anything like what she'd expected, and that made him dangerous. But she found herself asking, "Do you like being an O'Malley?"

He looked away and took a long drink from his glass. "Do you always go straight for the throat? You could have eased me in with something simple like my favorite color."

It was the kind of meaningless question she should have asked. This man might be her only ally, and she should be worrying about keeping him in her corner instead of trying to figure out the way his mind worked. But she *needed* to know. So she waited, swirling her wine and watching him wrestle through her question.

Teague finally sighed. "No. I hate it. I'd burn the damn

dynasty to the ground if I thought it'd free my siblings, but that's not an option."

She went still, unable to believe he'd just told her that. It was the kind of information that someone sinister could easily use against him. If she wanted to hurt the O'Malleys, cozying up to a son who hated them was a good way to go about it. "Ah."

"You wanted to go in with the big guns, you get big answers." He gave a humorless smile. "And it's not new information. All you'd have to do is ask around to realize that my father and I see things differently."

"You hate it that much?" She could barely wrap her mind around it. Callie didn't like some of the things that being a Sheridan necessitated, but she *loved* other aspects of it. To her thought process, you dealt with the bad in order to do the most good. Their world was all about balance.

"Look at us, angel. We're little more than strangers and we're going to be married inside of four weeks. And that's the least of my problems—no offense."

"None taken." Didn't she feel exactly the same way? He seemed like a decent enough man, but he was still one that she'd known for a grand total of a single day. The difference between them was that she'd willingly do this and worse to tip the Sheridans onto the right side of the law. "I just can't imagine hating my family." As soon as the words were out, she wanted to take them back. It was too personal, too *much*, to admit to this man.

"I don't. Not really." He stared into his whiskey. "I just hate the things they do in the name of power."

"I see." And, strangely enough, she did. "There's always good and bad, all mixed together."

"Exactly." He finally looked at her, pinning her in place with his gaze. "Though I'll admit there's more good to this situation than I would have expected."

Desire rose up in a tidal wave that had shivers working their way through her body. *Good lord*, the man knew how to turn a conversation into something else entirely with a single look. She reached for her wine again, only to find the glass empty. *Keep it together, Callie. You know how to flirt.*

Yes, she did. But this wasn't harmless flirting. Nothing about Teague was harmless. He saw too much. He was an O'Malley. And, perhaps most importantly, he was going to be her husband in a very short time.

He seemed to realize her mind was going a million miles a second, because he sat back, breaking the moment. "Now I have a question for you."

"Yes?" She put as much nonchalance into her tone as she possibly could. The candlelight played along his cheekbones and jaw, the shadows dancing over his skin, following a path her fingers itched to trace. What was wrong with her? She should be focusing on what their next move was, not on how intimate it was to sit this close to him.

"Would you have actually married Brendan if someone hadn't done you the favor of offing him?"

She looked into his dark eyes and couldn't lie. "No." That man was a monster. She might regret the events that had brought her to that horrible strip club and put a gun into her hands, but once she knew the truth about him, she never could have signed her life away to him. And if it took her all of a week to find out what kind of man he was, Papa should have known a long time ago. She shifted, the realization sitting like a block of concrete in her stomach. Had he known and gone forward with the engagement anyway?

He must have. There was no other explanation.

"Which begs the question—are you planning on marrying *me*?"

It shouldn't be different—Teague was just as much a stranger as Brendan had been. But it *was* different. Even knowing him such a short time, she couldn't shake the belief that he'd never raise a hand against her. That didn't mean she could trust him, though, unexpectedly revealing information or not. He was loyal to his family first and foremost, the same way she was.

She wanted Teague, and a part of her that didn't have a lick of sense thought she could trust him. That, more than anything else, made him a potential threat in a way that Brendan never could have been.

"That's quite the proposal, Teague O'Malley."

He grinned, completely unrepentant. "I plan on making up for the lack of originality in other ways."

It was all too easy to imagine exactly the sort of thing his tone suggested. It took her back to that alley, to that kiss, to her desire for more. Callie reached across the table and snagged his whiskey, lifting it to her lips with a shaking hand. "Yes, Teague. I'll marry you."

CHAPTER FIVE

Teague couldn't decide if he was the luckiest son of a bitch in existence, or if fate was dangling Callista in front of him, waiting to kick him in the teeth as soon as he relaxed. Judging from his history, it was far more likely to be the latter, but he couldn't help reaching over and tucking a strand of her hair behind her ear. "If you could see the way you're looking at me right now."

She immediately dropped her eyes, but only for a heartbeat. "How am I looking at you?"

The waiter appeared to replace her empty wineglass, buying Teague some time to think better of his answer. It didn't make a damn bit of difference, though. As soon as they were alone again, he answered her. "Like there are a thousand thoughts rushing behind those beautiful blue eyes and every single one of them involves us, naked and sweaty." It was bold to say, probably too bold, but there was something about this woman that had him speaking freely—something he'd thought twenty-seven years in the O'Malley home had cured him of. He leaned forward, until their shoulders brushed and it would have been the most natural thing in the world to close the minuscule distance between them and kiss her. He wanted to. Christ almighty, he wanted to.

"We should be focusing on other things." Then she touched him. It was just the brushing of her fingers over his knuckles, innocent as such things went, but he felt it like a bolt of lightning.

"Most definitely." His gaze fell to the lightweight black scarf around her neck, and the reminder of the violence done to her was enough to have him sitting back. "Callista—"

"Not tonight. Please." She picked up her glass of wine, and he'd have to be blind not to notice the way her hands shook. He stayed silent, watching her put herself together. He'd seen his older sister do it enough to recognize the signs—the deep breath, the slow sip of wine, the way she closed her eyes for a three-count before opening them and turning back to him, her armor firmly in place. It was a survival skill, one he hated that Carrigan had been forced to learn. He found he hated it all the more in Callista. She set the glass back on the table. "And, please, call me Callie."

"Callie." He liked the way it sounded on his lips.

She must have, too, because her gaze fastened onto his mouth, like she wanted a repeat of their kiss as much as he did. Before he could do something stupid like lean in, though, she glanced away. "What do you do for fun?"

"Fun?"

"Yes." A small smile pulled at the edges of her lips. "You have to have some sort of free time."

He did. And even when he wasn't supposed to, he found ways to slip free for a few hours, if only to get his head on straight. Those little escapes had been doing less and less for him in recent years, though. He always had to come back to reality too soon, and he was starting to suspect that it would *always* be too soon to come back. He craved freedom the way a caged bird craved the sky.

It wasn't in the cards for him—it never had been— and he knew better than most that wanting something so desperately was as good as handing over the most effective tool to hurt him to an enemy. His father was a genius when it came to applying just the right amount of hurt to a pressure point to get his children to do what he wanted without ever raising his hand. All he had to do was make an offhand comment about his wayward son's apartment in the city—paid for with O'Malley money—or the night classes he'd been slowly wading through over the years, and Teague folded. As bad as it was being under his father's thumb, it would be a million times worse if he lost his own space.

And losing the normalcy of being able to sit in class and know he was working toward an MBA. He couldn't let it go.

He blinked, coming back to himself to find Callie watching him with curiosity. She'd asked a question, hadn't she? He sat back. "I play poker."

"Just not with James Halloran anymore."

"No, not with James anymore." He missed that big bastard, but there had been no fighting the pressure from everyone around them. O'Malleys did not associate with

Hallorans unless there was business to be done—and they sure as fuck didn't become *friends*. God forbid. Worse, he couldn't shake the feeling that if James still numbered as one of his friends, there might have been some way to avoid the current situation.

It was too late to worry about it now, though.

"Are you any good?" She moved closer, her perfume teasing him, something light and feminine that he couldn't place.

He shrugged. "I win more than I lose." Though he hadn't touched cards in months. The thrill of playing, of manipulating the other people at the table until he walked away with everything they had, had dulled. Hell, everything around him had dulled. He was living a half-life and he damn well knew it. Even the classes he'd fought so hard to be able to take weren't enough to have him more than going through the motions. Last night was the first time in far too long that he'd been *awake*.

And the woman next to him was at least partially responsible.

"Do you play?"

Her smile widened, becoming something less politely interested and more real. "On occasion."

He tried to picture it, and the image came to him all too easily. He'd seen Callie play the part of mob princess at the dinner, even though he knew for a fact she was as displeased about the whole three-ring circus as he was. It wasn't too far a leap to see her at a table, wearing something like the red number she had on now, smiling sweetly and taking the men around her for everything they had. "I bet they don't even know what hit them."

She laughed softly. "Well, I do win more than I lose."

"We should play sometime." The words were out before he had a chance to reconsider them. "Though not for anything as mundane as money."

Her blue eyes lit with interest that had nothing to do with cards. Christ, did she know the effect she had? It was everything he could do not to reach for her, to see if her skin was as soft as he remembered, if her mouth was as yielding.

If he could get her to make another of those sweet whimpers.

He looked away, trying to get control of himself. "Any other untoward habits I should know about in my future wife?" Future wife. Fuck if he didn't love the sound of that, especially when it meant that four short weeks from now, Callie would be *his*. It was a savage thought, but he couldn't shake it. Or deny exactly how much he wanted it.

"I love old movies." That brought his attention back around to her, a moth to her flame. She twisted a lock of her blond hair around her finger. "If it has Marilyn Monroe, Jane Russell, or Audrey Hepburn in it, then I own it and have watched it entirely too many times to admit in public."

He could see that. There was something about Callie that brought to mind the glamour and grace of actresses from that time period. He took a drink of his whiskey, enjoying the ease of their conversation. It didn't matter that he'd convinced her to come out tonight in order to stop a war he was beginning to get the feeling there was no way to stop. Hell, he liked *her*. "I'd like us to be clear on something."

"Yes?"

"This"—he motioned between them—"is a date."

She gave him a look like she wasn't sure if he was joking or not. "Okay..."

"Which means that we're going to eat, and after that, I'm going to walk you to your car." He leaned forward, crowding her a little. "Then I'm going to kiss you."

Her eyes went wide. "And if I don't want you to?"

He didn't so much as twitch, because she looked like she was torn between bolting and actually liking the idea. He wanted to point out that, reasons for initiating it aside, she'd sure as fuck enjoyed their kiss in the alley. Not to mention the fact that they were getting married in a month, but that wasn't a threat he was willing to utter. Neither of them had chosen this pairing, no matter how well they seemed to get along right now, and he couldn't go into this expecting a certain outcome. But he could hope—and he could stack the deck in his favor as much as possible. "Do you?"

"I..." Her mouth opened and then closed, as if reconsidering whatever her knee-jerk reaction had been. "Yes."

His breath left him in a whoosh. He'd thought she was just as interested as he was, but there was always the risk of miscommunication. No longer. Now he knew exactly where Callie stood. She wanted him, whether she was comfortable with the feeling or not. He took her hand and lifted it to his lips, pressing a kiss to the back of her knuckles. "In that case, I hope you're hungry, because here comes our food."

* * *

Callie had no idea what she ate. It could have been the most magnificent meal ever put in front of her or something served out the back of a truck, and she never would have known. Not when all she could focus on was Teague. He didn't touch her again, but she was painfully aware of every move he made. How hadn't she noticed his hands last night? They were wide and strong, and there was a scattering of tattoos across his knuckles. She'd seen them before, of course, but most of the men she knew had tattoos of one sort or another so it hadn't really registered until now.

God, she wanted his hands on her.

The strength of the desire was enough to have her feeling skittish and uncertain, to the point that if he'd pushed any harder, she would have made some excuse and gotten out of there. It was a distraction, and not one she could afford. She hadn't forgotten the fact that he wanted to know who caused the bruises on her neck—it was only a matter of time before he asked about it again. She didn't know him nearly well enough to put her life and the safety of everyone under Sheridan protection in his hands.

Which meant she had to start finding out more information—the sooner, the better. "What are your thoughts on human trafficking?"

Teague raised his brows. "You leave something to be desired when it comes to light dinner conversation."

"Would you rather I ask for your favorite color?"

"It's gray." He speared a piece of his salmon. "And I think human trafficking is one of the most despicable things people do to each other. I was under the impression that the Sheridans shared the sentiment."

They did, but that didn't mean she could take anything for granted. "We do."

"Thought so." He watched her for a long moment.

"Any deep, dark secrets that I should know about before I slip the ring onto your finger?"

It took everything she had not to choke on her steak. Callie chewed mechanically, staring at her plate. He didn't know. He was just teasing. She hoped. She swallowed. "Of course not. All my secrets are right out in the open."

Teague snorted. "I doubt that."

Because he wasn't stupid. Even normal people had secrets that they kept close to their chest and never shared, even with the ones they loved most. For someone in their lifestyle, it was a given. She sipped her wine. "And you? Do you have skeletons in your closet that will pop up at the first available opportunity?"

"Not a single one."

He was lying the same way she was, but she couldn't call him on it without giving him the opportunity of doing the same. She hadn't really thought it would be that easy, had she? She gave a reluctant smile. "Then it seems we're more fortunate than most engaged couples."

"Most definitely." The curve of his lips was tempered with the considering look in his eyes, and she had to remind herself for the millionth time not to underestimate him.

She sat back. "Good."

"Wonderful."

"Perfect." She paused, and then laughed. A real one this time. "We're quite the pair."

"I couldn't agree more."

The waiter appeared with the check. She started to reach for it, but froze when Teague shot her a sharp look. He plucked the book from the man's hands. "Don't insult me by suggesting we split the check."

Since she'd been about to do just that, she kept her mouth shut and watched as he pulled out his wallet and left a stack of bills on the table. He pushed to his feet and moved behind her chair to pull it out for her. It was such an old-world gentlemanly thing to do, she found herself letting down her guard a little as she stood. Teague offered her his arm, and she wasted no time resting her hand on his forearm, acutely aware of the strength she felt beneath the thin fabric of his dress shirt.

They drew stares as they made their way to the entrance, but she kept her eyes forward. Most people had heard the names of their families in passing—one was hard pressed to live in Boston and *not* know such things—but she'd always made an effort to stay out of the news. Being known as a Mafia princess was enough to put a bad taste in her mouth, and that was before Ronan had died. Now? Now, she had bigger things to worry about.

The chill in the night did nothing to cool her heated skin, not when she knew where this was headed. He'd been explicitly clear when it came to his intentions, something she still wasn't sure if she was grateful for or not. It took the uncertainty out of how this would end, but it left her unable to think of anything other than how it would feel to have his mouth on hers again.

Normally, she made an effort to be aware of her surroundings, protection in place or not, but the Saint Paddy's parade could have been marching down the street and she still would have had her eyes glued to his face. The shadows of the parking garage seemed to deepen as they walked past, reaching out to flicker across his jaw, as if unable to resist touching him.

He stopped walking, turning to her with a raised brow. "What did you drive here?"

Of course. He was waiting for her to chime in with the information and she was too busy mooning over him to realize it. She gave herself a mental shake. "Ah, the Escalade." She dug the keys out of her purse and hit the unlock button, making the SUV chirp a few spots away. Behind them. A flush spread across her cheeks as he grinned, the expression of a man who knew he had a heady effect on her.

They walked over to the vehicle, her heels clicking in the silence. She barely had time to wonder if she should open the door when he pulled her into his arms. "I'm not going to lie—I've been waiting for this moment all damn night."

She had, too.

Teague ran his hands up her back, pressing her more firmly against him, and threaded them into her hair. He used his hold to tilt her head back so she met his eyes. They were dark and stormy and full of too many things to name. She recognized the presiding emotion, though.

Desire.

He kissed her, the slightest brushing of his lips against hers. When she would have deepened it, he tightened his grip on her hair, holding her in place. He kissed each corner of her mouth and then trailed down her jaw. She barely had a second to realize his intention and tense, but he already had her scarf off. Callie braced herself for another interrogation, but he just reached around her to open the passenger door and toss the discarded item into the vehicle. Then his mouth was on her neck. She didn't have to see the path he took to know he was tracing the map of bruises, his lips so incredibly gentle that she whimpered.

"Am I hurting you?" His voice was rough against her skin.

"No." Not in the way he meant. But his tender way of touching her was affecting her more than she could have anticipated. Her throat burned, trying to close as he continued his path, working from right to left. He was taking something ugly and shameful and turning it into something else altogether. How was she supposed to keep her head about her when this man kept surprising her?

She didn't know if she could.

He lifted his head. "Just because we're not talking about this now, don't think the discussion is closed." Then his mouth was on hers. Where the first kiss had been so sweet it made her heart ache, this one was exactly the opposite. She opened for him the moment he made contact, and he wasted no time in reacquainting himself. His tongue stroked hers, sending a bolt of heat straight to her core. She slid her hands up his chest and then around his neck, needing as much contact as possible. She felt like she'd been starved and hadn't realized it until the moment he touched her.

One of his hands left her hair, trailing down her spine to line up their bodies. She gasped at the feel of him. Her hips rolled against him so wantonly, she would have been embarrassed if he hadn't groaned. "Fuck, angel. I'm trying to do this right, but if you keep doing that…"

She did it again. She couldn't help it. She wanted him to follow through on the promise in his mouth, his body, his hands. It had been so incredibly long since she'd felt safe enough to get this close to a man. If she was smart, she wouldn't feel safe with *this* man. He might be her fiancé, but he was still the enemy.

Except he didn't feel like the enemy with his arms around her, his forehead resting against hers, his breath coming just as fast as hers was. His fingers dug into her ass, urging her on. He was so incredibly hard, and the feel of him through the fabric of their clothes was almost unbearably good. She moaned against his mouth, and he took that as an invitation to angle her head back and take the kiss deeper yet. He kissed her like he'd never get enough, with a heat that she felt to her very toes.

He cursed. "Angel—"

Emboldened by the need in his voice, she tangled her fingers in his hair and rolled her hips again, unable to keep in her breathy moan at the feeling of him. She was close to coming and they'd barely done anything. It would be pathetic if it weren't so hot. "Teague, please." She wasn't even sure what she was begging for, but only he could give it to her.

He lifted his head and looked around, his gaze narrowing when he took in the running car that was farther down the aisle. She didn't have to glance over to know it was someone's protection—though whether it was hers or his was up for debate. His dark eyes pinned her in place. "In the SUV?"

She was already nodding. It was like the last of his control broke in that moment. He lifted her into the back and guided her into the captain's seat on the far side. Then he followed her in and shut the door. It had been dim in the parking garage, but it was nothing compared to inside the Escalade with its darkly tinted windows. She had half a second to wonder if she'd just made a mistake, but then

Teague was kneeling in the space between the seats, his big body between her thighs.

The position hiked up her dress as he moved closer, until it was around her hips. He ran his hands up her bare legs, making a deep sound of appreciation. "You are so goddamn beautiful." And then his mouth was on hers, kissing her like his next breath could be found in her lungs. She wrapped her legs around his waist, moaning. His hands continued their upward movement, cupping her ass and lifting her so he could thrust against her. He kissed his way over to the sensitive spot behind her ear. "I could finish you like this, but I'm dying to taste you."

Taste her.

There was no mistaking his meaning, not when his fingers were playing with the edges of her panties. She held her breath several heartbeats, trying to focus. She wanted this man like she'd never wanted another in longer than she cared to remember, but that didn't mean she wanted to have sex with him after a first date in the back of her family's SUV while their protection duty sat less than twenty feet away.

He must have felt her tense, because he moved so he could meet her gaze. The heat there stole her breath. He smoothed his thumb across her temple and down over her cheekbone. "Let me take care of you, angel. Just that. Nothing else." She started to speak, but he beat her there. "When I finally sink between your thighs—and at this point it's a matter of *when* and not *if*—it's going to be in a bed with a locked door between us and the rest of the world." His thumb kept up its gentle stroking, a strange counterpoint to the rest of their bodies. "I might not deserve you, but I'm sure as fuck going to do right by you."

Maybe she was a fool and a half for finding his words comforting, but she cupped his jaw and kissed him. "Yes."

"Yes?"

"Yes, you can...taste me." Saying the words out loud felt strange, but the look on his face was more than worth it.

He hooked his thumbs into her panties and dragged them down her legs. His grin was a flash of white in the darkness. "Find something to hang on to."

She almost laughed, but then he nipped her thigh, licking his way up to the center of her thighs. He groaned at his first contact, almost as if he wanted this just as much as she suddenly did. He kissed her there with the same intensity he seemed to bring to every interaction. She reached blindly over her head to grasp the handle at the top of the door, half fearing she'd float away on a sea of almost painfully good sensation if she wasn't careful.

Teague gripped her thighs, parting them even further as he drew his tongue down her center. It was as if he was determined to explore every inch of her, his rough hands holding her in place so she couldn't have moved even if she wanted to. He circled her clit once, twice, a third time, drawing sounds from her throat that she hadn't been aware she was capable of making. Helpless whimpers and sharp cries, and through it all, a demand for *more*.

She hadn't realized she said the word aloud until he chuckled against her heated flesh. "Not yet, angel. First you've got to come for me."

He sucked her clit into his mouth, rolling the sensitive bundle of nerves between his lips and tongue. It was too much. Her body went tight, unbelievable pleasure spiking through her again and again, drawn out by his mouth. It was only when her cries quieted and her body's reaction had dimmed to a mere shake here and there that he gave her one last kiss and raised his head. "Damn, angel. Just…damn." He lifted her, shifting until he was beneath her and she was curled in his lap. She could feel his cock against her ass, but he made no move to do anything about it. He smoothed her hair down and pressed his lips to her forehead. "Do you want me to drive you home?"

Yes. Stay.

She didn't let the words free. No matter what she thought of this man—and she was beginning to think quite a few things—if she showed up at her house with him in the driver's seat, there would be hell to pay from her father. Pending marriage or not, if he knew what they'd just done…Her skin broke out in goose bumps.

What had she been thinking? The sky was falling in so many ways, and one kiss from Teague and she'd been nearly willing to have sex with him in the backseat of her SUV. It was so incredibly selfish that it threatened to make her sick.

"Whatever you're thinking, stop."

She blinked and tilted her head back to see his face. "What?"

"It was a reprieve, angel. Even heirs to the Sheridan empire get reprieves." His lips brushed hers. "We'll figure this out, just hang in there. Deal?"

She fought back some of the irrational guilt and nodded. "Deal."

CHAPTER SIX

James listened to the message Teague had left him a second time and then deleted it. If it had been anyone else from that fucking family, he would have suspected some kind of trap, but Teague was as close to the up-and-up as an O'Malley could be. In another life, they might have actually been able to realize the friendship that they'd started over a poker game. But that relationship had been sacrificed at the altar of family—just like everything else he'd cared about.

He shook his head and pocketed his phone. Now wasn't the time for melancholy thoughts. The message had confirmed exactly what he'd suspected—Teague was as much as victim in this mess as Callista was.

And both of them were a whole hell of a lot closer to innocent than Brendan had been.

If his father or brother heard him say as much, they'd call him a traitor or worse, but it was the goddamn truth. James loved his brother in the way you had to love family, despite their flaws. But that didn't mean he was blind. Brendan was the one who had brought their business transactions into a realm even James wasn't comfortable with. Shipping in girls from God alone knew where? That was human fucking trafficking. It didn't matter if the girls had volunteered—they were all desperate enough to do or say anything to get into the States. They didn't know what the hell they were signing up for.

He'd fought it as hard as he dared, and when he couldn't fight, he slipped money to the girls who had the most spirit, and gave them a window where they could run. Some did. Some stayed. The shit curdled his stomach every time he thought about it, and it was worse because Brendan had never shied away from using those girls in every way a man could use a woman.

Some things were unforgivable, even when it was family doing them.

Knowing that—accepting that—didn't mean he wanted his brother dead, but he was the only one who seemed to wonder if maybe Brendan hadn't brought his death upon himself. James knew what else was found in the room with his brother—that there was evidence of another girl. A girl who'd most likely been the one to pull the trigger.

He made his way down the hall to his father's office, and knocked. "Father?"

"Get your ass in here and report."

He stepped into the room and closed the door behind him. The fire was once again built high and hot, so much that the room had to be damn near ninety degrees. James shifted, his T-shirt already starting to stick to his back. "The grounds are secured. No one will get through."

"Good, good. We need to plan our next attack."

Now was the time to speak up. If he stayed silent and someone ended up killed, he'd never forgive himself. "We should reconsider this."

His old man turned rheumy eyes in his direction. "Your brother is dead, and you want to let his killer go free?"

"Of course not." Even though he'd been considering doing just that if it turned out one of the girls really had been the one to kill Brendan. But he couldn't say that to his father, not when the man had praised his oldest son's initiative in some of his more creative ways of bringing in money. "But the O'Malleys and Sheridans didn't kill him."

"How can you be sure of that? Those bastards have been plotting against us from the very beginning. I'll see them all hang even if I have to sacrifice everything I busted my ass for to do it."

The truth hit him, leaving him so cold, it was a wonder his breath didn't ghost the air in front of him. His old man was willing to get them all killed to fulfill some paranoid agenda he'd been nursing for fucking ages. James clasped his hands behind his back, wishing he could will them not to shake. There had to be some way to do damage control, though hell if he could find it right now. He *had* to, though.

The alternative was too horrible to even consider.

* * *

Callie pulled into the giant garage and waited for the door to shut behind her before she climbed out of the Escalade. It was unlikely someone would try to hurt her here, but old habits died hard. She hoped Teague's call to James would work, but she couldn't dismiss the Halloran threat until there was an official truce called. If James was anything like his older brother...

She shuddered. Best not to think about that, because if he was, then this whole thing was a lost cause. As things stood, she still wasn't sure she trusted Teague. It was entirely possible he was playing her—probable, even. She certainly hadn't told him everything over dinner, and she'd be a fool to think he hadn't kept back more than he'd divulged. Only time would tell if she could trust him.

And time was the one thing she didn't have.

Movement beside the car made her jump, but she took a deep breath when she recognized John. He'd been with her father since she was too young to remember otherwise and, as a result, she recognized the tightness of his jaw and the disapproval written across his face. He opened the door. "Miss Sheridan, your father is worried." He gave her a significant look. "He expected you home an hour ago."

Which she would have been if she'd come straight here after walking out of the restaurant with Teague. Apparently Micah hadn't seen fit to report back exactly how long she and her fiancé had been in the backseat of the SUV. *That* shouldn't matter, though. What mattered was that John was treating her as if she were still sixteen and he'd caught her sneaking out with her high school friends to meet some boys. Callie lifted her chin. "I had something to take care of."

Something that her body was *still* humming with. That tangle of emotions was too messy to deal with right now, so she pushed it aside in favor of focusing on the problem at hand. "Is something happening?"

Instead of answering, he stepped back and let her pass. "If you'll come with me."

It was always like this with the old-timers who'd watched her grow up. The younger guys were mostly willing to follow whichever Sheridan was in charge, as long as they proved they were willing to do what it took to keep the family in power. They, at least, were willing to sit back and hold off judgment until Callie either sank or swam.

But the men who'd known her long enough to watch her play dolls and run crying to her father whenever Ronan's playing got too rough and she ended up hurt? They couldn't seem to acknowledge the fact that she was no longer ten, and was more than capable of leading if they'd just give her the chance.

She was the one who'd taken Moira's, a floundering restaurant they used as a way to import some of the more sensitive illegal materials, and turned it into a raging success in its own right. At first Papa hadn't been thrilled with the increase in clientele, but even he had to admit that the more people they had coming and going, the easier it was to cover up *their* people coming and going. Even better, with the expansion, it was now bringing in a good amount of clean money.

Riding high on that success, Callie had just turned her attention to another restaurant they owned when Ronan had died and she'd been thrust into the darker side of what being a Sheridan meant. She didn't particularly like dealing with everything that it entailed, but she was more than qualified to do it.

The familiar frustration rose, but she refused to let it show on her face as she followed John through the hallway connecting the garage to the house and to her father's office. He and another of his men, Lee, were talking intently, but broke off when she walked through the door. Her father rose, straightening to his full six feet. "Where have you been?"

She stopped short. "What's going on?"

"We have a strike against the Hallorans tonight, but it was on hold until you got home—which you should have been over an hour ago." He nodded at Lee, and both he and John left the room, closing the door behind them.

She turned to look, the sinking feeling in her chest telling her everything she needed to know about what kind of violence was planned tonight. "Papa, you have to call them off."

"I have to do no such thing."

"Victor Halloran is striking out because he just lost his son. Surely you can understand that and *talk* to him instead of escalating the issue?" With each strike and counterstrike, it was becoming more and more likely that this war couldn't be stopped, no matter what Callie and Teague did.

My fault. She tried to brush the thought away, but it grew teeth and burrowed into her mind. If she'd gone along with her father's plans to have her marry Brendan, then they wouldn't be facing war and the deaths of people she knew and cared about. "Please, Papa."

"You dare to compare Brendan to your brother?" His fists clenched, and her stomach dropped before she forcibly reminded herself that her father had never raised a hand to her in twenty-five years. It was unlikely he'd start now. She hoped. Papa glared at her like he knew this was truly her fault. "You must hold your brother in low esteem."

Ronan had been *nothing* like Brendan. He'd hardly been perfect, but he wasn't a monster by any definition. How could Papa think she really felt that way? Her heart beat so quickly, she half feared it'd beat itself right out of her chest. It was tempting to back down and slink away to her room to take her fourth shower of the day, but there was more at stake than her pride. She took a deep breath and tried to keep her voice temperate. "I'm not saying that at all. I'm just saying our resources would be better spent doing anything except going to war."

He waved that away as if it weren't a completely legitimate argument. "You're too soft, my girl. Oh, you can be ruthless when you're backed into a corner, but you always hesitate to take preemptive attacks. Halloran struck at us during a moment of celebration. If I allow it to pass without retribution, all the little weasels and cockroaches will come calling, and no one will be safe. You value your safety, don't you? Our people's safety?"

Of course she did. That's why she'd worked with Micah to get safeguards in place in case the Hallorans attempted a strike closer to home. But she hated the fact that they were potentially escalating the violence in the name of safety. It seemed so backward no matter which way she looked at it. "There has to be another way."

"There's not. Now, go get some sleep." His gaze coasted over her, settling on her neck. "You look like you need it."

Her hand flew to her throat. She'd been so distracted

with thoughts of Teague that she'd completely forgotten to put her scarf back on. "I—"

"Did I ask for an explanation?"

She froze, searching his face. There was a heavy knowledge in his eyes. "Papa…" She forced herself to stop talking and *think*. He'd been in this line of work far too long not to recognize what the bruises on her throat meant. He might not know who put them there, but he must suspect something or he would be grilling her for more information the same way Teague had.

Does he know?

Papa moved around his desk and set his hands on her shoulders. "I failed you once, Callie. Let me make it right." He pressed a kiss to her forehead, and then he walked away, leaving her staring at the empty chair behind his desk.

He knows.

She reached blindly for a chair and stumbled over to sink into it. Her father knew she was the one who killed Brendan—had probably known from the second the news got out. She'd done her best to slip her tail, but someone had seen something. Callie touched her still-tender neck, guilt making her want to curl into a ball and sob.

Papa was doing this for *her*.

There was no other explanation that made sense. He wasn't the type to let a skirmish escalate into a war, not if there was any other option. The fact that he was doing it now made her think he was waving the red flag in front of the bull that was Victor Halloran to keep their people distracted from their investigation.

Her father was taking the Sheridans to war in order to protect her.

* * *

Teague carefully shut the door to his suite, even though all he wanted to do was slam it. He should have known better than to try to reason with his father, but he'd been flying high after things going so well with Callie that he'd decided to try. *Idiot.* If he'd stopped to think about it, he would have known that there was a better way to approach his father, rather than directly head-on. He should've gone through Aiden. His oldest brother was excellent at the tightrope act of getting their father to agree to anything required. Teague had never had the patience for that shit, and it showed in the fact that his father barely took him seriously on the best of days.

Today sure as hell wasn't that.

His phone rang, distracting him from his anger. He saw the familiar number, and tried to get his shit under control. There was only the slightest thread of discontent in his voice when he answered, "Hey, James."

"Long time."

"Yeah. Too long." The years stretched out between them, too many to ever make shit right. That was assuming James even missed the weekly poker games and bullshitting. He shook his head. He was acting like a little bitch about this. Their friendship was over and done with, but he hoped that old affection would be enough to accomplish what he needed to accomplish. "You got my message?"

"Yeah." James sighed. "Look, man, I'd love to stop this shit as much as you would, but there's not much I can do."

The last bit of hope he'd been holding out that they

could circumvent the upcoming war disappeared in a puff of smoke. He didn't give the man grief—he knew how little control an heir really had, especially when someone like Victor had the reins tightly in his grip. That man wouldn't be handing over any more power than he had to until he was on his deathbed. He scrubbed his hand over his face. "I had to try."

"I know you did. I'll do what I can to keep things from truly blowing up, but I've gotta be honest—it's not looking good. My old man is out for blood."

He'd expected as much. "I appreciate it. I'm working this end as hard as I can right now, but I've got even less influence than you do."

"What's that brother of yours have to say about this?"

That was the question, wasn't it? Aiden's insistence that he marry Callie was part of the reason they were in this shit storm to begin with. Teague sure as hell hoped his brother had thought about the potential consequences before he pulled the trigger on their plans. Though, if he had, he should have seen that this war was possible— even likely. So either he didn't, or he'd been okay with the cost. "I'll be sure to ask him."

"You do that." James hesitated. "Hey, Teague?"

"Yeah?"

"If we're not both dead by the end of this, you want to grab a beer sometime?"

He laughed. "Yeah, for sure."

"Good luck." Then he was gone, leaving Teague alone with his thoughts.

It wasn't a pretty place to be. He'd never once thought that his brother would hang him out to dry as a means to justify the end, but now he couldn't shake the feeling that

Aiden had done just that. He typed out a quick text. *Need to talk, STAT.*

Five seconds later he got his reply. *Library. Ten minutes.*

Enough time for him to jump in the shower. It felt a little like a betrayal to wash off the memory of Callie as soon as he walked through the damn door, but he needed his head on straight for confronting Aiden. He toweled off and dragged on a pair of jeans. Since his brother still hadn't shown, he texted her. *Sleep sweet, angel. I'll call you tomorrow.* He set his phone on the nightstand and ran his hands over his face. Maybe he should have waited to do this shit until morning when he was fresh, but he wasn't going to be able to get a damn bit of sleep until he knew the truth.

Exactly ten minutes after he'd texted, Aiden walked into the library and closed the door. His brother was nothing if not punctual. Teague barely waited for him to drop onto the leather couch before he spoke, "Tell me that you didn't pawn me off on Callista Sheridan to provoke a war with the Hallorans."

"We didn't fire the first shot. That was all Victor and his men."

That wasn't an answer, and Aiden damn well knew it. Teague crossed his arms over his chest. "I want the truth. If you and our father are using me in a grab for territory, I damn well deserve to know."

"I do what's best for our family. That's all any of us do." His brother's face showed nothing. It was like looking at a stranger instead of his old partner in crime. He'd known Aiden was changing in recent years, but he'd been so wrapped up in his own misery that he hadn't paid as close attention as he should have. A mistake, Teague realized now. He'd been sure his brother would support him over his father.

Now he couldn't shake the feeling that belief was wrong.

"What happened to you?"

"I grew the fuck up." Aiden paced from one side of the room to the other, agitation in every move. "And you know what I saw, Teague? Our father isn't as cracked as we thought he was."

His brother had to be insane to think that. Seamus O'Malley would have been perfectly at home a few centuries ago, ruling some kingdom and answering to no one. But he'd never moved into the future, and how he conducted the family now was damn near unforgivable. "He moves us around like pawns on his own personal chessboard."

"He's doing what it takes to keep our family safe. That calls for hard decisions, which you'd see if you pulled your head out of your ass long enough to look around and think about anyone but yourself. Times are changing, and we can't afford to be on the wrong side of it."

The words could have come straight from his father. Teague had ever been the disappointment—the son who wouldn't fall in line, who questioned everything, who wasn't cold enough to believe the end justified the means. Apparently Aiden didn't have that problem. "I see things clearly enough." Enough to know if he wanted to stop this shit, he was going to have to do it himself.

A small voice chose that moment to pipe up and demand to know what the fuck he thought he could do to stop it, but he ignored it. He'd find a way. He'd promised his sisters that he'd keep them safe, and now there was Callie to consider as well. Anything his family did to aggravate the issue painted a target on her back the same as it did his. Unacceptable.

Aiden made it all the way to his door before a thought occurred to him. "Brendan Halloran."

His brother stopped. "What?"

"You responsible for that?"

He turned back. "You've got some goddamn nerve asking me that question with a straight face."

Normally it never would have crossed his mind, but it was becoming increasingly clear that he'd been a hell of a lot more checked out than he'd realized. The ground had shifted beneath his feet, and he had no idea what the terrain would look like once things settled into place—or if he'd still consider Aiden on the side of angels.

Not that any of them could claim that. Not anymore.

And his brother still hadn't given a direct answer. "Yes or no. I need to hear you say it."

Aiden glared. "No." Before Teague could relax, he went on, "Though I'd love to know who pulled the trigger so I can send them a fucking gift basket. Father was thinking about pushing Carrigan in his direction—until I looked into him."

What the hell had Brendan been into that would give their father pause? The man really must have been a monster. Only something dire would make their father take him off the list for potential son-in-laws, given how advantageous it would be to merge their territory with the bordering Hallorans'.

And Callie had almost married him.

He shared a look with his brother, a moment of perfect understanding that was gone nearly as quickly as it'd come. Then Aiden was gone, too, closing the door softly behind him.

"Goddamn it." Teague paced from one side of the room to the other, the movement doing nothing to calm him down. He was in the middle of a fight where he had no resources and not a single ally in his corner. How the fuck was he supposed to keep his younger siblings and Callie safe if he couldn't even make his older brother listen to reason?

He dug his phone out of his pocket and dialed from memory. It would have been safer to grab a burner phone like he had every other time he'd called Finch, but he wasn't in the mood to jump through those hoops. The man had some shit to answer for, and now was as good a time as any. It barely rang twice before Finch answered, "You shouldn't be calling me from this phone."

Teague didn't ask how his private cell number was public information. It was the least of things they should know. "You know what's going on with the Hallorans."

It wasn't a question but he answered anyway. "We're aware of it."

"Then why haven't you done something?" For one of the most feared government agencies in the States, all they seemed to do was sit around with their thumbs up their collective asses.

"There are steps that have to be taken. You know that as well as I do."

All he knew was that it was the same excuse they'd been feeding him for six months. It didn't sit any better now than it had every other time he'd heard it. "If you're not going to arrest someone—fine. But you need to get my sisters and Devlin out of here and into witness protection or some shit." He'd ship off Callie if he thought for a second that she'd go, but at least if his sisters were safe he could focus his efforts on his fiancée. And Devlin...Of them all, Devlin alone had the ability to have a better life if someone just gave him the chance to get the hell away from the rest of the family.

"Now, son, I'll see what I can do, but that kind of thing takes time."

Another excuse. He resisted the urge to throw his phone across the room. "Make it take less time." Teague hung up, adrenaline making him shake. He hated this shit, being helpless and relying on others to make things right. Hadn't he learned a long time ago that the only way to get something done was to do it himself?

So the question remained—what would it take to bring this whole fucking mess to a standstill?

He poured himself a glass of whiskey, thinking hard. Victor Halloran might be one scary motherfucker, but he hadn't crawled to the top of the food chain without having smarts to go with it—and war wasn't smart no matter which way you looked at it. If he hadn't just lost his son, he'd be more willing to let go of the insult of Callie marrying an O'Malley. The man had to want vengeance before anything else. Teague just had to position himself in a place where he could hand the old man his justice on a silver platter.

That meant he had to find Brendan Halloran's killer.

CHAPTER SEVEN

Carrigan O'Malley waited for her brother to stalk past where she stood in the little nook outside the library, bathed in shadow. Teague didn't see her there, just like Aiden hadn't before him. She'd learned at a very young age that if she wanted to find out the unfiltered truth, she had to eavesdrop. She'd gotten pretty good at it since then, which led to all sorts of interesting—and terrifying—discoveries.

Like the fact that Teague had someone with the FBI on speed dial.

She shook her head. He'd always been an idealist, even when they were kids. To him, everything was black and white, good or bad. Life didn't work that way, especially *their* lives, but she already knew what had spurred him to take the leap from minor rebellion straight into being a true traitor.

His sisters.

Growing up, he'd always been the protector, the one who stood between them and the rest of the world. It was something he'd have been wise to grow out of—no one could save them, not really—but he hadn't.

Why the feds, Teague? They aren't going to help us unless they benefit, which means everything we love is going up in flames.

She wouldn't rat him out, though. They all had their secrets, from Aiden right down to Keira—the little parts of themselves they kept close and quiet, and refused to share. His might be more damaging than most, but hers were right up there in the running. If her father ever found out what she did on the nights she slipped her protection duty, he'd ship her off faster than she could say *fucked*.

And that was if she was lucky.

She stepped into the hall and headed in the direction of her room. Things were quiet at this time of night, the old house echoing strangely enough that when she was ten, she'd been sure there were at least a few resident ghosts. Now she knew better. The only one who haunted these halls was Carrigan, floating from one room to the next, never free enough to actually leave, never restful enough to just go along with the path her father had set out for her.

Marriage.

That was the only future for her and both her sisters. They would be married to an appropriate man—meaning, one who would serve the family business—and then go on to extend the empire with as many children as possible. The only chance she had of avoiding that fate was joining a convent—her father would be willing to give up a breeder for a nun.

She just wasn't sure *she* was.

It was far too tempting to dwell on the choice that was bearing down on her, closing a cage around her ribs until each breath burned. She didn't have much time left, the clock in her head ticking down in time with her biological clock, the buzzer ready to go off at any moment. More and more, her father kept making comments about her advancing age and how there wasn't much time left at all if she was going to be good marriage material.

Easier to focus on her little brother's problems than her own. She'd have to talk to him soon, to let him know she knew the sacrifice he was trying to make for them. He was selling his soul in the process—once the feds got their claws into you, you were never truly free—and that was the best-case scenario. If their father found out...

He'd kill Teague.

The realization settled in her chest, an added weight to the anvil she currently carried. Father might say family before all, but what Teague was doing was a betrayal no matter which way they spun it. He was a rat, and Father was famous for saying "Thou shall not suffer a rat to live." He wouldn't suddenly develop a forgiving streak just because it was his own flesh and blood slipping secrets to the enemy.

She closed her bedroom door behind her and sank to the floor. "God, Teague, what are you doing to us?"

* * *

Callie pushed the button on the treadmill to bring her speed up, desperate to outrun the thoughts and worries plaguing her. She would have preferred to run outside, but her father had forbidden it, given the situation with the Hallorans. Three days in this house and she was on the verge of going mad. Every time she turned around, there was some sort of furtive movement or quiet conversation—all of which stopped the second she walked into the room. She knew her father was trying to protect her. But she should be right there in the middle of all the planning instead of relegated to hurried updates from Micah between his running her father's errands.

Papa told her to use this time to plan her wedding. As if picking out the perfect flowers and catering options were somehow more important than—or even equally important to—dealing with the Halloran threat.

She ran faster, until her breath sawed through her chest, and her legs felt like they couldn't manage another step without toppling her onto her face. Only then did she hit the button to stop. She needed to get out of here, even if only for a few hours. If she didn't, she was liable to start screaming and never stop—not the actions of a leader.

God, she was so incredibly tired. Tired of wearing the mask and pretending she was okay. Tired of fighting a losing battle with her father. Tired of acting like she wasn't waking up every hour on the hour, sweat-soaked, with a cry just inside her lips, the memory of Brendan's hands around her throat imprinted on her waking mind.

Her body shook as she climbed the stairs to her room, and she comforted herself by blaming it on the workout. But she couldn't lie to herself as well as she seemed to be able to lie to those around her. Her once steady hands had become as jittery as an old woman's. Once upon a time, Callie had thought herself a woman with nerves of steel.

Now she knew better.

She stripped and stepped into her shower, turning the heat up until it nearly scalded her skin. She ducked her head beneath the spray, her mind going to the single bright point in the last week. Teague. They'd texted here and there over the last few days, enough that she knew he was thinking of her, even though he was busy. She envied that ability to keep occupied, but he never failed to make her smile and help her forget her frustrations, if only for a little while.

Though continuing to talk to him only made *other* frustrations more apparent.

She closed her eyes and pictured his face, painting those wonderful cheekbones and that strong jaw with her mind, moving over his sensual mouth and to those soulful dark eyes. Eyes that had looked at her as if he wanted her more than he wanted his next breath. And his hands, wide palms and long fingers, knuckles decorated with tattoos that she fully intended to explore at the first available opportunity. Those hands had felt deliriously good on her skin, but they were nothing compared to his mouth between her legs.

Her hand coasted down her body as she took a step back into the memory. God, the way he'd touched her, a strange combination of tenderness and animal need, stoking a fire inside her that burned hotter than she could have dreamed. Callie slipped her hand between her legs, letting the water beat against her back as she stroked herself. It was all too easy to imagine it was *his* fingers on her, dipping inside her and then back out to play over her clit. She hissed out a breath, and did it again. Pressure built low in her stomach, deep and demanding, and she was only too happy to give in to the release bearing down on her. She moaned as she came, her lips forming his name. "Teague."

The water had started to run lukewarm by the time she opened her eyes. She hadn't told anyone about how their date had ended, but she'd given in to these little fantasy sessions every day since then. She shook her head and finished washing off. Her time with Teague was the only few hours in the last week where she hadn't felt totally and completely out of control.

A reprieve, he'd called it, and he'd been right.

She wanted another reprieve.

Desperately.

She dried off and reached for her phone, not bothering to dress yet. His number was already programmed in as a contact and she pushed the button to call him. The phone rang and rang, and she was on the verge of hanging up when he answered, out of breath as if he'd been running. "Callie?"

"I want to see you." Touch him, kiss him, cling to him until the ugly realities of her life faded into the background.

He paused and, when he spoke again, he was more composed. "What are you doing tonight? I have an apartment up near Boston University where we can talk without having to worry about...things." He meant eavesdropping ears—or maybe he meant that they weren't in danger of a drive-by there. She shuddered at the thought.

"That sounds wonderful. What time?" The sooner the better. She couldn't imagine Papa protesting to her leaving the house to see her fiancé. If worse came to worst, she could always tell him it was part of the wedding planning.

"I have some information I'm trying to run down at the moment, but I can be there at seven." He laughed. "It would also give me the opportunity to pick up some food. The only thing in the fridge is beer and a bottle of ketchup."

"The important food groups." It didn't sound like he spent much time there, but maybe he didn't cook. When it came to Teague, she had more questions than answers. She knew he could drive her out of her mind with a touch, but she had no idea what his relationship with his many siblings was, or what he would have chosen to do with his life if he weren't an O'Malley.

A part of her, simple and selfish, wasn't sure she even wanted to know. He made her feel good, and that was enough for now. The more they talked, the greater the chance was that she'd find something completely unforgivable—and vice versa. What if he thought her goals to bring the Sheridans onto the legal side of business were laughable? The idea turned her stomach. No, it was better that they kept things physical, where at least they knew they matched up.

"Callie?"

She blinked. From the tone of his voice, he'd said her name more than once. "I'm sorry, I missed that last part."

"I could tell. I asked you what you wanted for dinner."

Her answer sprang from her lips before she had a chance to call it back. "You."

* * *

Teague moved through the market, Callie's last word ringing in his ears the same way it had been all afternoon.

You. There was no mistaking her meaning, and he still hadn't decided what he was going to do about it. His first instinct was to take her up on the implied offer. But then common sense was quick to jump in and say that rushing things with the woman he was supposed to spend the rest of his life with wasn't building the foundation in the most effective way possible. Sex was all well and good, but he wanted this shit between them to be about more than that.

He had to talk to her, to figure out where she was coming from. If she thought she could use her body to manipulate him... well, part of him was more than happy to go along with it. He wanted her like he hadn't wanted another woman in living memory, and it was more than her tight body and the sweet sounds she made when she came. She was strong in an understated way that he was drawn to despite himself, and there were still the bruises on her throat to consider. He was nowhere close to willing to walk away from finding out who had laid a hand on her.

He paid for the groceries and walked back to his apartment, keeping an eye on his surroundings. This neighborhood wasn't anything like some of the ones he was forced to frequent on family business, but danger could reach out and touch him anywhere in Boston. It paid to be aware of his surroundings. It was only because he was watching that he saw Callie walk up. She frowned, looking around as if she wasn't sure she was in the right place. "Hey, angel."

She jumped. "I didn't see you there."

"That's less my being stealthy than your being distracted." He nodded at the doorway behind her. "This is me." As he led her up the narrow stairs to his door, he wondered what she'd think of the place. It was a far cry from the opulence of his family home—or the Sheridan residence. He'd never gotten close to either the Sheridan home or the Halloran one, but he knew enough to know both buildings were as large as the O'Malley residence, and surrounded by a similar-sized property. Compared to his little apartment, they might as well be on the moon.

But she smiled as she stepped inside. He set the groceries on the counter of the kitchen and put them away while she wandered around, pausing in front of the bookshelf filled with movies and video games. She picked up the photo on the top of it, and he didn't need to look over her shoulder to know it was the one of him and his six siblings that his mother had insisted upon a few years ago. She spoke without looking up, "You all look so happy."

It was one of the rare moments when they had been. It was in the time firmly planted *before*. Before Carrigan started shrinking under the pressure of a future she didn't want. Before the shadows appeared in Sloan's eyes and she stopped talking almost completely. Before Cillian's attitude got so out of control that he was damn near unbearable.

Before Aiden turned into Seamus O'Malley 2.0.

He pushed the beer aside and set the various vegetables in the fridge. "We were." Past tense. Always past tense.

"Sometimes I wish…" She set the picture back onto the bookshelf and squared her shoulders, seeming to force herself to finish the thought. "Sometimes I wish I had more siblings. Ronan and I weren't as close in recent years as we were growing up, but his loss was still earth-shattering."

And now she was alone. He shut the fridge and tried to picture life without his siblings. Over the years he'd loved them and damn near hated them to varying degrees, but he'd always had the comfort of their being *there*. He couldn't imagine how deep the loss would go if something ever happened to any of them.

Yet another reason to put a stop to this war.

"I'm sorry about your brother." He crossed over to her and did what he'd wanted to do ever since he saw her standing there on the sidewalk. He pulled her into his arms, something settling in his chest as he rested his chin on the top of her head.

"Sometimes I'm so *angry* at him. How could he be so stupid to drink and drive when we have half a dozen men ready and waiting to take us where we need to go if the situation calls for it?" A shudder worked its way through her body. "That makes me sound like a horrible person, doesn't it?"

"No." He smoothed his hand over her hair. "Death is bad enough when it's unavoidable. It's hard not to resent someone for bringing it to your door."

"Yeah." She sounded strange, choked up and rigid, but he kept holding her until she relaxed against him. "I'm sorry. It's been a trying few days."

"For me, too. It doesn't seem to matter what I do, or what arguments I come up with—everyone is hell-bent on moving this war forward." Which had only solidified his determination to use the identity of Brendan's killer to leverage the Hallorans to back off. If they did, then the O'Malleys and Sheridans would be forced to do the same since things hadn't escalated to a point where they couldn't take it back. He just had to pin James down for a meeting and convince him that vengeance would have to be enough to make his father happy.

"Teague..." His name sounded so damn sweet coming from her lips, somewhere halfway between a sigh and a plea. Her hands coasted up his back on either side of his spine.

"Yeah?"

"I don't want to talk about this anymore. Kiss me instead?"

His body responded even as his mind hesitated. That first night, she'd kissed him to distract him from questioning her about the bruises on her neck. On the surface, it didn't seem like she was doing the same thing now, but he couldn't shake the feeling that that was exactly what was happening. He kept his arms tense so she couldn't wiggle out of them—not that she seemed to want distance between them, not when she kept up those distracting circles on his back, lightly dragging her nails over the thin fabric of his shirt. "Our problems aren't going to go away just because we stop talking about them."

"I know." It was little more than a whisper. She tilted her head and pressed a kiss to his neck. "But I'm in danger of breaking under this stress if I can't check out for a little while. Please, Teague, please help me check out." She had to know what her saying his name did to him. There was no way she didn't.

But still he resisted. "Angel, you're making it fucking hard to do right by you."

She laughed against his skin. "You don't have a bed in this place?"

Fuck. He closed his eyes, but that only made it worse, his entire world narrowing down to the feel of her in his arms, warm and more than willing. She wanted him. He should be thrilled to figure that shit out. But she didn't want him because she was so overwhelmed with feeling or desire or…anything except the need to "check out." He'd had sex for a variety of reasons in the past—and some of those were pretty flimsy—but this was the first time it'd stung to be used for his cock.

He'd wanted more with Callie.

He tangled his fingers in her hair and used that hold to move her back so he could meet those baby blues. "I'll help you stop thinking for a while, angel, but we're doing it on *my* terms." She opened her mouth, but he talked right over whatever argument she had ready. "I'll give you everything you need and more—but we're not fucking tonight." It felt wrong to term it that way, but if he gave in tonight that's exactly what it would be. Fucking. He'd barely known this woman a week, and he already knew that he wasn't going to be happy with just sex.

No, he wanted it all.

If they survived this conflict with the Hallorans, he might even get it. But only if he played his cards right.

So he waited for her to work through it, and saw the moment she decided not to fight him on this. She frowned. "You don't want to have sex with me."

"On the contrary, I want it a whole hell of a lot. But not like this."

"You're a very strange man, Teague O'Malley." Her frown cleared. "But I'll agree—on one condition."

She'd agreed far too easily. He braced himself and asked, "What's your one condition?"

"You let me take care of you tonight, too." Her smile had a wicked edge that promised all sorts of pleasure.

"I think we can work something out." He framed her face with his hands and kissed her, the smallest taste to herald a night he planned to make unforgettable. "Stay with me tonight. I want you in my bed when I wake up."

She smiled against his lips. "Okay."

It was a start. He couldn't ask for more.

CHAPTER EIGHT

Callie didn't know what to make of this man. For all intents and purposes, she'd come over here ready to strip naked and have her wicked way with him. And he'd... turned her down. No, that wasn't completely correct. Teague wanted her. The way he was staring at her said as much, those soulful eyes filled with a dark desire that called to her on a level she wasn't prepared to deal with. She was starting to fear he wanted more than she could ever give.

Everything.

He kissed her again before the thought could take root and truly terrify her, his tongue coaxing her mouth open and delving inside. They stood in his living room, fully clothed and with a breath of distance between them, and it was one of the single most seductive moments of her life. Because the man made love to her mouth, taking his time and seeming to savor every second, in no rush to move on until he'd had his fill. She sank into the kiss, letting it sweep her away as nothing else had in the last three days. This. *This* was why she was here. She'd never let herself go like this with another man—though she was hardly a virgin—but she and Teague were in this together, for better or worse.

He nipped her bottom lip, the shock slamming her back into the present. "You're thinking too much, angel."

"I don't know how to stop."

He lifted his head and grinned down at her, the wolfish expression threatening to curl her toes. "I can think of a few ways."

Yes, yes, yes. This was what she'd come here wanting. Needing. She licked her lips. "I like the sound of that."

"I thought you might." He stepped back and drank her entire body in with a single glance. She resisted the urge to smooth her hand down the dress she'd picked out with seduction in mind—the hem hitting halfway down her thighs and the neckline offering up her breasts for temptation. The perfect little black dress. With the way his gaze lingered on her chest and legs, she was suddenly glad she'd chosen it.

Teague stroked a hand up her side, stopping at her ribs and running his thumb along the underside of her breast. "It kills me that every time I've seen you, you're never wearing a bra."

Normally she did, but the memory of his strangled curse that first night when he found her without one was enough to drive her to leave that part of her wardrobe out when she knew she was going to see him. "I'm sorry."

"I'm not." He dragged the straps of her dress over her shoulders and down, baring her from the waist up. "Fuck,

I'm not even a little bit sorry when this is all it takes to be able to see you."

Heat built under her skin as he cupped her breasts, his big hands playing over them with surprising gentleness. She held her breath, trying to keep in the moan building in her chest. Teague touched her like she was breakable and utterly priceless. It was a far cry from the way he'd driven her out of her mind in the back of her SUV, and the contrast only made her hotter. Because this man had both sides in him—the feral beast and the poet.

How was she supposed to keep her emotional distance when she never knew which one would come to the fore?

He went to his knees and dragged her dress the rest of the way off, leaving her in only a pair of red panties. Teague's harsh exhale was music to her ears. He helped her step out of the dress and then tossed it to the side, sitting back on his heels. He was tall enough that it put his line of sight directly with her panties, and he didn't seem interested in moving.

Callie shifted, trying not to clench her thighs together. She'd never had a man look at her like that—it was foreplay all on its own. Her hands fell to the sides of her panties, ready to shove them down her legs to join her dress, but he stopped her. "Not yet."

He waited for her to move her hands to use his grip on her hips to bring her a step closer. "I've been thinking about that night a lot."

She didn't have to ask what night he was talking about, because she'd been thinking about it, too. "Me too."

His breath ghosted the skin directly below her belly button. "Have you touched yourself while thinking about me, angel?"

It was a question she never would have dreamed of answering under normal circumstances—except these were hardly normal. So she ran her fingers through his hair and nodded. "Yes."

"Fuck, I love hearing that." His eyes slid shut and he hummed in pleasure. "And while you were touching yourself, what were you fantasizing about?"

The apartment seemed to heat ten degrees while she fought against her instinctive response to beg off. If she told him what she'd fantasized about, would he do it to her? The desire for that was far stronger than any embarrassment she might have felt saying the forbidden words aloud. "You. Your mouth on me." She hissed out a breath when he kissed the sensitive skin just below her belly button. "Your...hands." His tongue dipped beneath the band. It wasn't nearly close enough to where she wanted it, but her body still practically sizzled for him. "Your cock."

"Mmm. And when you take my cock, how do you picture it?"

Oh God. She couldn't believe he wanted details, but she found herself answering—anything to keep him kissing his way closer to the apex of her thighs. "Me on top, riding you. You, taking me from behind." His thumbs moved, inching her panties down her hips. She gave a desperate laugh. "God, all different ways and places. The shower, your bed, the SUV again."

"You've spent a lot of time thinking about my cock inside you."

"Yes."

Her panties hit the floor. He looked up at her, his slow grin doing a number on her heart rate. "I've said it before, and I'll say it again—you're the most beautiful woman I've ever seen. I don't think I'll ever get tired of looking at you."

She had the insane urge to argue with him, but she kept her lips sealed to prevent it from escaping and ruining the moment. Teague thought she was beautiful, and who was she to tell him he was wrong? Instead, she ran her fingers through his hair, enjoying the feel of it—the feel of *him*. He'd promised that she'd get her turn to do some exploring of her own, and she fully intended to take him up on it. So she tugged on his hair. "My turn."

For a second, she thought he may argue, but he pushed to his feet. She wasted no time in slipping her hands beneath the hem of his old, faded T-shirt. It was soft with countless washings and obviously well loved. She paused in the middle of pushing it up and read the text across his chest. "The Pogues?"

"They're one of my favorite bands."

She made a mental note to look them up when she had the chance. That was the least of her concerns right now, though. He lifted his arms so she could drag the shirt over his head and drop it on the ground next to them. Then she stepped back so she could see him.

Good lord. He was magnificent, his muscles drawing her attention across his chest and down his stomach to where a trail of hair disappeared beneath the waistband of his jeans. She ran her hand up his stomach, silently delighting in the way his skin jumped at the contact, and stopped at the scar stretching diagonally across his left pectoral and over his shoulder. "What happened?"

Teague captured her hand and pressed a kiss to her knuckles. "I don't want to talk about it."

"Okay." Another time, they would. But even as she continued her path over his shoulder and down his arm, she knew she couldn't ask without risking him pushing *her*. Turnabout was fair play, after all, so she couldn't open that conversation unless she planned on being honest with him.

Yearning rose inside her, strong enough to steal her breath, a need to tell *someone* the truth. Maybe it would lighten her burden to do so, to the point where she might actually get more than forty-five minutes of sleep at a time. If only she was sure she could trust Teague totally and completely, she could risk it.

But she couldn't.

She wanted, him—desperately—but desire and trust weren't even in the same stratosphere. So she pressed a kiss to the scar instead. That brought her to the medallion hanging around his neck. It was familiar—she had a similar one at home, though with a different saint. "Saint Jude."

"Patron saint of lost and forgotten causes."

She knew that. What she didn't know what why he'd chosen that particular saint to wear so close to his heart. It said something about the man, something that seemed to indicate scars that ran deeper than the ones on his skin. She had the ridiculous urge to bundle him close and hold him until all that hurt him disappeared.

That wasn't why Callie was here. She was here so *she* could forget. Needing to get back on track, she went for the button of his jeans.

* * *

Teague did his damnedest to focus on Callie, instead of the memories the scar across his chest evoked. He'd had it since he was twelve, the badge of a mouthy kid who hadn't yet learned that sometimes it was better to keep his head down instead of trying to speak up over every injustice he saw. His father had made sure the lesson was one he'd never forgotten.

Her hands at his pants startled him back to the present. He held perfectly still as she unbuttoned the jeans and carefully dragged the zipper down. Her knuckles brushed his cock, and it took every ounce of control he possessed not to reach for her then and there. It had been hard enough to restrain himself when he'd been fully clothed and she still had her dress on. With them both naked, he didn't like his chances of sticking to his guns.

No, damn it. He wanted to do right by her, and he fucking would. He'd decided he wanted this thing with Callie to work, really work. He liked her, wanted her, even respected her. But he didn't trust her...yet. So right now it was all or nothing.

Easier said than done, though.

Especially as Callie worked his jeans down his legs, and he helped her out by stepping out of them. Her hands traveled over his skin as she rose, pausing over this scar and that—he had a few—until she was standing before him again. He raised his eyebrows. "Do I meet your inspection?"

"You'll do." Her smile warmed him in ways he wasn't prepared for, because this serious woman was teasing him. It was a side of her he'd only gotten hints of up to this point, and he found himself wanting more.

"Are you sure? I think I have an upgraded model stashed in a closet around here somewhere."

She laughed, the sound light and free, and went up on her tiptoes to kiss him. The move had the entire front of her body pressed against his, the first time with absolutely nothing between them. He ran his hands over her, marveling at how perfect she was, soft and full and seemingly made for him. Before he could get carried away, he dipped down, swooping her into his arms with a move that had another of her infectious laughs slipping free.

He decided that he could spend his life trying to tease that sound from her.

He hadn't forgotten that she came here specifically for what he could offer her physically, but he was willing to work with whatever he had to in order to keep her coming back for more. If he pushed too hard elsewhere, she might shut him out, and that was unforgivable.

So he'd bide his time and help her forget for a while whatever demons dogged her heels.

Eventually she'd open up to him. Maybe he'd go so far as to return the favor—though he doubted she really wanted to hear him bitch about his shitty father.

He used his foot to nudge open the door into his bedroom. It wasn't anything particularly fancy, though the sheets were a high thread count and clean. The king-sized bed took up most of the space, barely leaving room for a single nightstand and a closet that was pathetically empty. A signal that he didn't spend nearly as much time here as he'd like to—most of his valued possessions were in his room in the family home.

He laid Callie out on the bed, suddenly as desperate to stop thinking as she seemed to be. There were worse solutions than getting lost in the arms of a beautiful woman whom he was going to marry. He kissed her as he settled next to her, propping himself up on his elbow. The position gave him the freedom to touch her again, and he wasted no time cupping first one breast and then the other, lightly pinching her nipples until she writhed for him. Only then did he slide down her stomach to cup her between her legs. She was wet and ready for him, and he groaned against her mouth as he pushed a single finger into her. He pumped gently, gauging her reaction.

She dug her fingers into his hair and kissed him harder, her tongue thrusting into his mouth as she moaned. *Like that, do you? I'm just getting started, angel*. He spread her wetness around, circling her clit a few times like he'd learned she liked it, and then pushed two fingers into her. While he worked her with his fingers, he kissed down her jawline to her neck and then claimed one nipple.

"Oh God." Her grip on his hair was damn near painful, but he relished the feeling of her losing control around him. For a woman would seemed to be buttoned up in day-to-day life, she was so fucking responsive and unfettered once he got his hands on her. It was enough to make him want to never let her go.

"Tell me what you want, angel." He'd loved hearing that she'd been touching herself and thinking of him the last few days. Teague could get addicted to filthy words coming from that prim mouth of hers.

She arched her back and spread her legs wider. "Make me come, Teague. Please."

Fuck. All the dirty words in the world didn't compare to her saying his name in that tone of voice. "Tell me how you want it."

"Your mouth." Her hands stayed in his hair as he moved down her body to settle between her thighs. He started to slip his fingers out of her, but her grip tightened. "And your hands. I want both."

"Greedy girl." It struck him that he'd give this woman the world if she asked it of him in that breathless voice. A shudder worked through him, but he pushed the thought away. Right now he had something else to focus on. He pumped his fingers in and out of her, adjusting to just the right angle that had her upper body nearly coming off the mattress. *There it is*. He pressed an openmouthed kiss to her clit while he kept up that motion, giving himself a few seconds to just enjoy the taste and feel of her before he zeroed in on the little flicks that had gotten her off last time.

She went wild beneath him, until he had to use his free hand to pin her hips. Her entire body tightened, her pussy milking his fingers. She cried out, his name on her lips as she came. "*Teague*."

He gave his fingers a few more pumps, drawing her orgasm out as much as possible. Only when she was limp and flushed did he give her clit one last thorough kiss and then move up to lie next to her. He was so fucking hard, it was a wonder he didn't lose it while he'd been going down on her. It was far too tempting to sink into all that welcoming wet heat.

Not yet. Not tonight.

Callie stretched, her arms over her head, her body one long line that had his mouth watering, and then she moved, pushing his shoulder and shoving him onto his back. She came with him, ending up straddling his waist. Her grin was back, and he drank in the sight of it like a starving man. She shifted, her pussy sliding along his cock, teasing him. "You make me so hot."

He grabbed her hips, but then froze, not sure if he wanted to make her stop that mind-blowing movement or if he wanted to lift her, adjust their angle, and then sheath himself to the hilt. She took the choice away from him, sliding down his body to take his cock in hand. "I've thought about doing this, too."

"I'm sure as fuck not going to stop you." He reached down, gathering her hair in his fist and drawing it to the side so he could see everything. She stroked him, somewhere between teasing and exploration, before finally dipping her head and taking him between her lips. His eyes damn nearly rolled back in his head as she sucked him down until he bumped the back of her throat. "Holy shit."

She hummed a little as she licked and sucked and drove him out of his godforsaken mind. Watching his cock disappear between those sinful lips was almost as good as the feel of her around him. Almost. He closed his eyes, trying to hold on, to keep control, but she reached between his legs and cupped his balls, squeezing just hard enough that he was lost. "Angel, I'm—"

She didn't stop. Fuck, she picked up her pace, driving him crazy, building the pleasure until he couldn't hang on a second more. He came, thrusting into her mouth as she sucked him down. When she finally lifted her head, he was well and truly spent. "You're fucking amazing."

"I do what I can." She kissed his hip bone and let him drag her up his body to tuck against his side.

"Stay the night."

"I already said I would."

"I know." He kissed her forehead. "Still thinking too much?"

She laughed. "It's safe to say you drove every single thought right out of my mind."

And she'd more than returned the favor. All in all, he considered the night a tally in the win column. His time with Callie was a little oasis in the shit storm of their current circumstances, but he was willing to fight tooth and nail to keep it. Apparently he'd needed the break nearly as much as she had. He pulled her closer, something settling in his chest when her arms slid around his waist. "Good."

Tomorrow would be a new day. At least they had tonight.

CHAPTER NINE

Callie woke up wrapped in Teague's arms. She blinked at the faint morning light steaming through the windows, the disorientation of not being in her own bed making her frown before the events of the night before came rushing back. She relaxed, inhaling the spicy male scent that seemed to permeate the space around her. It was tempting to close her eyes and move closer to the man now nuzzling the back of her neck, but she'd already been gone from home too long.

The responsibility settling around her shoulders seemed to get heavier each time she picked it up. Instead of this reprieve lightening the load, it had actually added to her worries.

Because she *liked* Teague.

He wasn't like any man she'd known before—something that was becoming clearer and clearer the more time she spent with him. He treated her like a woman of worth, which shouldn't be so startling. But it was. She slipped out of his arms, holding her breath until she was sure he hadn't woken. She dressed quickly, her gaze darting back to the man sprawled across the bed. The features that had seemed so harsh and unforgiving when she first met him turned into something else entirely when relaxed in sleep. He was almost… beautiful.

Or perhaps she was becoming biased because her body came alive when he touched her.

Callie slipped out the door, pausing to make sure it was locked behind her, and hurried to her car. The entire drive home, her mind kept helpfully replaying everything they'd done last night. The man held her like he actually cared, which was preposterous considering how short of a time they'd known each other.

It dawned on her that maybe she wasn't the only one with growing emotional attachment.

No. I can't afford to lose focus—especially right now. The words did nothing to reassure her. Because she'd barely been out of his presence for twenty minutes and she was already craving him again. The insane impulse to turn around and drive back to his place rose so intensely, she actually reached for her blinker before she stopped herself. The real world wouldn't wait, and the longer she hid, the worse it would be when she came home.

And if she never came home?

She shut the thought down before it could take root. She couldn't walk away from the Sheridan empire, even if she were so inclined—and she wasn't. She was the heir, which meant she was responsible for ensuring the safety of her people and the ongoing lucrative income of their various businesses. *She* was the one who would bring them into the legal side of things and remove as much danger as possible from their lives. If she could get all of their front businesses running as well as Moira's, they wouldn't need the money generated by the illegal side of things.

If she disappeared, things would fall apart when her father died. The generals would fight among themselves, and the clawing and battling for power would destroy what was left of their people.

She couldn't let that happen.

No, her fantasies about holing up with Teague until this nightmare passed were just that—fantasy. She'd already been too lax in letting Papa keep her out of things, no matter if he wanted to protect her or if he had other reasons altogether. Whatever his thinking, it had to stop.

She parked the car in the garage and strode into the house. Her footsteps echoed on the tile, the click of her heels standing out in the silence. At this hour there should be people around. It was Friday, which meant the cleaning ladies, at least; should be here for their weekly tidy up. Callie headed for her father's office—the one place there was guaranteed to be some sort of activity—and knocked.

"Come in."

A part of her that she hadn't even realized was tense relaxed at the sound of Papa's voice. Nothing was wrong. There hadn't been an attack of some sort on the house. They were safe. For now.

She slipped into the office and shut the door. She took a deep breath, deciding it'd be best to get straight to the point. "Papa, no more shutting me out. If you expect me to stand as heir, you need to let me be part of making the decisions." He had to know the days of trying to protect her had passed. It was time for her to step up and deal with the consequences, one way or another, and take an active role in this mess.

It was her fault, after all.

A throat clearing brought her up short. She turned around to find that her father wasn't the only one in the room. It wouldn't have been so bad if it were Micah, or even John, but she didn't immediately recognize the two women standing by the bookshelves that lined the wall on either side of the door. She attempted a smile. "I apologize. I didn't realize you had company."

"I don't. You do." He motioned at the older of the two, a woman who could have been anywhere between thirty-five and fifty-five, though the self-assured way she carried herself made Callie think she fell somewhere on the older end of the spectrum. Her long dark hair didn't have so much as a hint of gray, but there were faint crow's-feet fanning out from her green eyes when she smiled.

"Callista, it's wonderful to see you again."

Again?

Things fell into place, and the reason the woman looked so familiar became clear. "Mrs. O'Malley." Teague's mother.

Which made the other woman—a younger version of her mother, right down to the green eyes—one of Teague's sisters.

"Oh, no, please call me Aileen. We're about to be family." She sailed over and enveloped Callie in a cloud of Chanel No. 5. Her warmth would be significantly more convincing if her daughter didn't look so shocked by it before she wiped the expression off her face.

Good to know.

She pasted a bright smile on her face. "Of course." But why were they here? It was poor timing, to say the least, especially with Papa looking like he wanting nothing more than to boot the entire lot of them out of his office.

Aileen must have caught her look. "Carrigan and I are here to help with wedding planning."

She blinked, the words forming and reforming in her mind as she tried to make sense of them. Wedding planning. They were on the brink of war and these women wanted to drag her off for *wedding planning*? She shot a look in her father's direction. "Are you sure that's wise?"

"Of course. Your wedding is less than four weeks away." Aileen's sharp look at Papa was enough to tell everyone in the room what she thought of the accelerated timeline. "I'd be a poor mother if I didn't ensure that the first of my brood to marry had the wedding of his dreams."

Considering she knew Teague hadn't chosen this wedding any more than she had—and they were on the verge of all-out war—the statement bordered on preposterous. "Perhaps we can reschedule? I have a meeting with my father—"

"Your father has assured me that you have no plans for the day. Carrigan, why don't you help Callista pick out something a bit more appropriate to wear while I discuss the budget with Colm?"

Which was how Callie found herself being escorted out of her father's office and getting the door slammed in her face. She glared at the heavy wood for a long moment before remembering that she wasn't alone in the hall. "Is your mother always so . . . ?"

"She gets what she wants, when she wants it. Even our father doesn't cross her." Carrigan shrugged. "You can try to get out of what she has planned today, but I wouldn't bet against her."

Frustration threatened to choke her. There were so many more important things to be worried about right now. War. Threats from the Hallorans. The future of the Sheridans with her at the helm. The wedding didn't even place top ten. She closed her eyes and took a deep breath, holding for it a few seconds and then releasing it. The frustration didn't disappear, but it was manageable now. She knew better than to fight battles she wouldn't win, and she definitely didn't want to cause any tension with the O'Malleys. It was more than potentially alienating a future mother-in-law. They were allies against the Hallorans and any other threat that arose—allies that, frankly, Callie's people needed.

Which meant she had to spend today doing mindless errands like picking out flowers and deciding on catering.

She opened her eyes to find Carrigan watching her closely. The woman was as beautiful as her mother— possibly even more so. She had the kind of flawless bone structure that would last through the years, her softness burning away to leave only steel in its wake. Callie recognized it because *her* mother had had the same thing. She'd like to think she did as well, but she was hardly unbiased. "I need twenty minutes." It would be cutting it close, but she refused to leave the house without at least a shower.

Especially since she swore she could smell Teague on her skin.

"I'll stall her, but you should hurry."

She hurried.

Twenty-two minutes later, she was back downstairs, showered and dressed in a pair of slacks and a silk shirt. Aileen swept a quick look over her. "You'll do."

Callie tamped down on her irritation. She'd dealt with women like Aileen O'Malley before, though most of them didn't actually have the power they seemed to think they possessed. Aileen actually did.

So she smiled and followed the woman out to the limo parked in front of the house. Five minutes in her future mother-in-law's presence, and she was already exhausted. The woman might smile and fawn when it suited her, but it had to be a mask. Callie had met Seamus O'Malley, and he was the kind of person who chewed up everyone around him and left them bleeding in his wake if they weren't strong enough to endure.

Aileen was anything but broken.

In some ways, that made her even scarier than her husband.

* * *

After his night with Callie, Teague was only more determined to put a stop to this bullshit war. He spent the morning trying to get a hold of James, and finally pinned the man into agreeing to drinks tonight. It was at Mickey's, which was right in the middle of Halloran territory, but beggars couldn't be choosers. It had the slight bonus that no one connected with the O'Malleys would see him talking to James. He doubted his father or Aiden would support it—not when it was growing clearer every day that they weren't particularly torn up about the impending war.

Impending. He didn't even know if he could call it that anymore. It was here, whether he liked it or not.

He walked into Mickey's, stopping just inside the door to take in the room. On the surface, it looked just like a hundred other Irish pubs scattered around Boston—a little dark, a little dingy, and mostly empty. Or it did until he saw the crest above the bar—a shield, half-white and half-red, with a white horse on the bottom half—marking it as owned by the Hallorans. His family had something similar in the places they patronized regularly.

He'd suggested meeting somewhere in neutral territory, but James had shot him down immediately. For whatever reason, he wanted the home court advantage. Unfortunately, Teague wasn't in a position to tell him no. So here he was, hoping like hell he wasn't walking into a trap.

The bartender stopped wiping down the bar and looked at him, the man's thick, bushy brows lowering until they practically covered his eyes. "Help you?" His tone said the only thing he was helping Teague with was to get his ass out the door.

"He's with me, Tommy." James walked through the door leading into the back—most likely to a private room—and stopped. "Been a long time."

"Yeah." He took in the man's changes the same way he suspected James was surveying him. He'd grown in the years since they'd last laid eyes on each other, his blond hair now hitting his shoulders and a close-cropped beard covering his jaw. James looked closer to a biker than a businessman, but then his father had never put the emphasis on poise and surface manners the way Teague's had.

"Nice suit."

He looked down at the Armani clothing and shrugged. "It works."

"Sit your ass down and let's talk."

He followed James to a booth tucked in the back of the bar and slid in. "I—"

"Hold on." He raised his voice. "Tommy?" A few seconds later, the bartender set two beers down and lumbered away. James picked his up, his eyes never leaving Teague's face. "Didn't your piece-of-shit old man teach you any manners? First you make small talk. Then you go in with your pitch."

Teague grabbed his own beer, and grinned despite the clock ticking away in the back of his mind. As much as he'd like to spend time with the man under different circumstances, keeping the people he cared about safe was his only priority right now.

And James was one of the few people who could help make that happen.

But the man was right—there was a way to do these things, even if the custom annoyed the shit out of him. He sat back and motioned with his bottle. "How about them Red Sox?"

James grinned. "Hell of a year they're having."

"Think they have any chance at the play-offs?" With all the shit going on, he'd missed the game last week— and would probably be missing more in the future. The thought was too damn depressing.

"Who knows? I sure as fuck hope so." He glanced away. "It'd be a nice distraction."

Wasn't that the truth? Anything that was a distraction from the shit show they were currently running was welcome. Sadly, it would be months before the play-offs, and he had a feeling this thing would be done and over with by then—or they'd be so busy killing each other that they wouldn't have time for baseball.

Teague sat back. "How the hell are you?"

"My brother's dead and my old man's gone and lost his goddamn mind." James shrugged. "I'm doing exactly how you'd expect."

A fair point. None of them was doing great these days, but James certainly had the shit end of the stick. He took a long pull of his beer. "I thought we were making small talk."

"I got nothing after the Sox."

"Um, a scorcher of a summer we're having." He laughed when James shot him a look. Needling the man shouldn't be so damn delightful, but he'd take his silver lining where he could find it. It was all harmless—or as close to harmless as possible.

"Heard you're getting married. Never thought you'd be one to play the dancing monkey for your old man."

He hadn't, either. James was one of the few people he'd talked to about his pipe dreams—to get out of this life and put as much distance between himself and the O'Malley legacy as he could. He examined the rough wood grain of the table, and then forced himself to look up and meet his former friend's gaze. "Life never quite works out like we want it to."

"Isn't that the damn truth?"

The world had seemed different when they first met, when their respective responsibilities hadn't been so suffocating. They'd had countless conversations about what they'd be doing if they weren't part of families like theirs. That time of hope had passed right along with their friendship.

The silence stretched out between them as they drank, filled with all the broken dreams of the past. They were dead and gone, buried beneath a cold reality neither of them could avoid.

They weren't the same men they'd been years ago. James was now heir to the Halloran family. And, Teague... Well, Teague was marrying Callie at his father's command. It might not be the end of the world like he'd originally thought, but it didn't change the fact that Seamus had told him to jump and he'd asked how high.

He noted the circles under James's eyes—just one of the indications of how exhausted he had to be. "How are you doing, though? Seriously."

"Christ, what do you expect me to say? We're not friends anymore. I'm not going to cry on your shoulder about how shitty my life is, and I'm sure as fuck not down for a sleepover where we tell secrets and braid each other's hair."

"Good, because that'd be some one-sided shit."

"Glad we're on the same page." James downed half his beer. "Look, my brother wasn't a saint and we both know it. But he was still family so, yeah, I'm not exactly bursting with happiness right now."

That was about what he expected. "What if I can find out who killed him?"

He frowned. "What?"

This was it—where he'd either garner support or alienate the man completely. Teague took a deep breath, praying it was the former. "I don't want this war. Neither does Callie."

"No one wants this war, except maybe our fathers." He smirked. "And Callie, huh? Sounds like you're getting plenty cozy with that fiancée of yours."

"I like her. I didn't expect to."

"Then you're goddamn lucky."

"I know." He let out the breath he was holding. He'd been sure James didn't want to go to war, but six years could change a person. They'd changed Aiden. Taking another drink, he steered clear of that thought. "If I can find out who killed Brendan, will your father call off his dogs?"

"You know something?" He zeroed in like a hunting dog catching a scent.

It was almost a shame Teague didn't have concrete information yet. "I had some men who were there that night, up in one of the private rooms on the same floor. I've talked to them, and word is that it's a woman. One of the strippers."

James's shoulders slumped and he scrubbed a hand over his face. "Fuck. I'd hoped it wasn't."

"Why?" The question was out before he could think better of it.

The man's expression was bleak. "Do you know the types of girls my brother staffed that place with?" He went on before Teague could answer. "Runaways. Girls—and I do mean girls, not women—who came stateside on the promise of a dream. Most of them wouldn't have chosen that for themselves."

It was all too easy to imagine his sisters there, helpless and doing their damnedest to survive. How long before one of them broke and lashed back? Sloan might take it until it killed her. She was the type to keep her head down until she was in danger of breaking. Keira…How long until the fire inside her that he loved so much was doused? And Carrigan…

He set his beer down carefully. Carrigan would stick a broken bottle in someone the first chance she got. He studied James, trying to figure out where he was going with this. "What are you saying?"

"If one of those girls killed my brother, she's long gone by now." He looked away, his voice so low, Teague almost convinced himself he was imagining the next words. "And maybe Brendan got what he deserved."

As much as he understood the sentiment—he would have killed Brendan himself if he tried to lay a hand on Teague's sisters—knowing that didn't solve the current issue. He cleared his throat. "If I can find the person who did it, will your father pull back?"

James sighed. "I don't know. Maybe. I can't guarantee anything, but being able to get his vengeance might be enough to make him hold off punishing the insult of your marriage."

He tapped the table. "I get that you have mixed feelings about this, but I'll do damn near anything to stop this war from escalating before someone does something they can't take back."

"Even if it means some poor girl who might have just been defending herself is going to die?"

Teague stared at the wall, trying to come up with an answer that wasn't cold and heartless and completely self-serving. If he were a better man, he'd let this search go. His father's men were better equipped to deal with the inevitable violence of war than some runaway who'd gotten in over her head. But war never came without collateral damage, and it was the thought of one of his younger siblings or, worse in some ways, Callie, being hurt that had him turning back to James. "Yes."

He was a bastard and a half for sacrificing a woman who was likely already a victim for the sake of those he loved, but he'd own that.

"Cold." James finished his beer. "I can't make promises and I don't particularly support this, but there's a chance it would be enough for my old man. A *chance*, Teague. I can't guarantee anything."

It wasn't the firm agreement he'd wanted, but a chance was better than being turned down flat. There wasn't much he could bring to the table as leverage, so he had to work with what he had. "I have to do whatever it takes to put a stop to this."

"Yeah, I know." He didn't look too happy about it.

Teague drained his beer and set it back on the table. "It was good seeing you—though I wish it were under better circumstances."

James's smile was brief and more than a little bitter. "Haven't you figured it out yet? There are no better circumstances."

He nodded, because the man was right. This was their lot in life. At least it had perks from time to time, though he would have given them up in a heartbeat for some office job that he was able to leave behind when he came home and a family whose biggest drama was his parents not liking one of his sister's boyfriends. But that was a pipe dream that would never be realized.

He had to deal with facts, and right now that meant

minimizing the damage Victor Halloran was inclined to do. "I'll be in touch."

"Wish I could say I look forward to it."

Teague turned and walked through the bar. There were more men than there had been when he came in, and every single one of them followed his movements over the rim of their drinks. The small hairs on the back of his neck rose, and he had to make an effort to keep his pace measured and slow. If they knew he was worried, it would be like sharks scenting blood. Normally, he wouldn't be too concerned—he was more than capable of handling himself—but he was on enemy territory and alone. The disadvantages of his current position were legion.

He pushed through the door and onto the street, the warm night air doing nothing to combat the chill running up his spine. He waited for the door to click shut behind him—and then for someone to follow him out—but a second passed and then another, until it became clear no one was coming. He'd hoped James wouldn't send someone after him.

But he wouldn't bet his life on it.

He adjusted his jacket and started down the street to where he'd parked. He'd done what he'd come here to do. It might not be enough—at this point there was no telling if *anything* he did would be enough—but it was something. James hadn't shot him down, even if he'd opened the door to dark thoughts Teague didn't like considering. He'd never thought of himself as anything like his father, but the call he'd made tonight was something Seamus O'Malley would be proud of.

Family first. Everyone else dead last.

The thought made him sick to his stomach.

A scrape of a shoe against concrete had him turning to look behind him. He got a glimpse of three dark figures as he caught a fist in the gut. He grunted, doubling over, and was already moving to return the blow before the pain crippled him. He struck, hitting a man in the jaw, and turned for the second attacker.

Before he could swing, something crashed into the back of his head and everything went black.

CHAPTER TEN

Callie blew out a sigh of relief when she was finally able to shut the front door on the back of the two O'Malley women. If she never saw another floral arrangement or tasted another bite of tester cake, it would be too soon. Aileen had seemed determined to fit six months of wedding plans into a single day, and she'd made a damn good job of it.

Worse, she promised to circle around next week sometime for dress shopping.

Callie hadn't spent significant time fantasizing about what her wedding would be like as a young girl, and once she graduated from college, took over Moira's, and began supervising the assortment of other businesses the Sheridans owned, she simply hadn't had the time to really consider what a marriage—even a political marriage—would mean as far as planning went.

The whole thing was just *wrong*. She would have liked

a small private event, not the circus the O'Malleys seemed determined to throw together. She understood the reasoning—the wedding had become a physical representation of their refusing to be cowed by their enemy—but the whole process was as pleasurable as walking over a bed of nails.

There were so many other things she needed to be doing. She hadn't been down to Moira's in nearly a week. It had been running just fine under the manager, Janey, before Callie graduated, and it would continue running just fine once she was forced to focus most of her energy on the other Sheridan assets, but she still liked the hands-on approach.

She'd been dropping balls left and right since that night at the strip club, and this wedding planning business threatened to be just another distraction. She didn't *care* about the flowers or the venue or the guest list, and Aileen damn well knew it. So did Papa. But because she was the feminine half of this partnership, she was expected to pretty herself up and be delighted by the colossal waste of time.

If she had a normal life, she would have been enjoying every second of this, towing friends behind her to the various appointments, looking forward to the moment when the love of her life slipped a ring on her finger.

But she didn't have a normal life—she was a goddamn Sheridan—and she hadn't even been allowed to choose her groom. Thoughts of Teague brought a tired smile to her face. He was the sole high point, but thoughts of him too quickly turned to whom she'd been *supposed* to marry.

Brendan.

She rubbed a hand over her chest, the massive house suddenly feeling altogether too small. She needed to talk to Papa, to get this all out into the open once and for all. Maybe if she could tell *someone* about what she'd done, the awful weight on her chest would become bearable. She peeked into his office, and found him huddled down with John, talking strategy. He spoke with his hands, and though his expression was grim, he was more alive than she'd seen him in the months since the cops showed up to tell them her big brother had died.

I wish you were here, Ronan. Things would be so much simpler.

She'd had the thought more times than she could count, but it never brought him back. His loss was no longer an aching open wound in her chest, but it still smarted on days like this, when she was embroiled in the midst of things that never would have happened if she wasn't the heir.

But she was.

So it was up to her to deal with it.

She moved past her father's office and headed up to her room to change into running clothes. She had too much pent-up frustration after today. The feeling of being swept along with a current she couldn't fight was stronger now than it had ever been, and what she needed more than anything was to regain some small bit of control. Running didn't give her much—not in comparison—but it calmed her mind, and that was better than nothing.

The treadmill just wouldn't do today, though. She felt like she'd been cooped up in this house for weeks on end, even though it'd been less than a week since everything went to hell in a hand basket. Micah looked up as she approached the front door. "Callie?"

"I'm going running." She forced her voice calm. She was informing him of her intentions so he could best protect her—not asking permission. The whole respect thing wasn't usually an issue with Micah, but he still answered to her father, and it was Papa who'd basically put her under house arrest. She didn't like forcing him to choose between them, but the only alternative was losing her sanity by staying in this house for another minute.

"That's a bad idea. Your father—"

"Micah, while I respect your opinion, I'm not asking for it." She made a point of glancing at his Italian loafers. "I'd change your shoes if you're coming along. It's going to be a few miles at least."

He sighed, looking like he still wanted to argue. She waited, letting him work through it. Papa might be angry, but Micah and she had spent enough time together that he had to know she'd go running with or without his permission. The only way he could stop her was by physically restraining her, and that was out of the question. She watched the thoughts flash across his face before settling into resignation. "Give me five minutes."

"Happily." She pulled her hair back into a ponytail and cued up her running playlist. By the time she'd warmed up a bit and stretched, Micah was back, now wearing a pair of basketball shorts and tennis shoes. He didn't look any happier now than when he left, but he was here. She opened the door. "Let's go."

Before her world had blown up in her face, she had

several routes around the neighborhood that she liked to take, depending on her mood. Today, she wanted to go through Cambridge Common. It never failed to lift her spirits, even if there was always a small tinge of jealousy since the people she saw there were from a completely different world than she was.

Micah easily kept pace, staying a few feet back where he could survey the threats to her before they got too close. They'd run together before, though not recently, so it was easy to fall back into the sound of his footsteps echoing hers. She pushed play on her phone and let the first strains of "Chasing Twisters" by Delta Rae roll over her as she wound through the streets. The heat of the day had given way to a slightly cooler evening, but the humidity made her clothes cling to her skin before she was through with her first mile.

She crossed the street to the common, slowing down so she could drink in the view. It was a strange comfort to know that her life might be falling apart in many ways, but the world kept on spinning. The huge, grassy field was broken up by a handful of trees and a scattering of summer students. It was nowhere near as busy as it'd be in the fall, but the normalcy she craved could always be found here.

She picked up her pace again, circling the block before heading back. It was good five miles, and the paths through the trees settled her in a way that little else was able to.

Teague could.

He'd done an excellent job of it last night. It was more than the orgasms—although those had been outstanding. When he held her in his arms, she could almost believe that she was truly safe and that, together, they could vanquish any enemy who rose against them. It was a foolish romantic notion, but even now she craved his mouth on hers and his skin sliding against her own. Maybe she'd call him when she got home. There were still half a million worries plaguing her mind, but it wouldn't hurt to have another *reprieve* again.

Selfish? Most definitely. But she was so terribly alone in her guilt of Brendan's murder. She wanted Teague to tell her everything would be okay, even if she couldn't be completely honest with him.

She turned for home, her pacing slowing as her muscles cataloged their exhaustion. She didn't see the car approaching, but a strong hand around her stomach yanked her away from the street as the SUV screeched to a halt in front of them. Micah turned, putting his body between her and the threat, but she saw the rear door fly open when she peered around his arm. Callie flinched, but no attack came.

Instead, a body fell to the pavement with a dull thud and the door slammed shut as the vehicle peeled out, its tires smoking as it fled down the street. *Not a drive-by.* She ducked around Micah. "The plates. Memorize the plates." She didn't pause to make sure he obeyed, because she'd reached the man.

She turned him over carefully, and went cold when she caught sight of his face. "Teague. Oh my God." His face was swollen and there was blood…everywhere. She felt for a pulse even as she raised her voice slightly. "Micah, I need you." His chest rose and fell slightly, and she nearly cried out with relief. "We have to get him back to the house."

Micah crouched on the other side of Teague. "It's that little O'Malley shit. I say we leave him."

She froze, barely holding in the impulse to scream in his face. Instead, her tone came out icy and low. "That is my fiancé you're speaking of, so I suggest you watch your tone."

His jaw hardened. "Yes, ma'am." He only ever called her that when he was pissed, but she couldn't bring herself to care right now. She'd deal with Micah's hurt feelings when she was sure Teague would be okay.

She hadn't wanted Brendan. If he had been the one dumped, she barely would have spared the step it required to move over his body. Perhaps that made her a monster, but she couldn't change the way she felt. But this wasn't Brendan—this was *Teague*. The man who'd helped her forget, at least for a little while, who'd held her in his arms and made her feel safe so she could actually sleep through the night. She'd no more leave him here than she would one of her people.

Hers.

The thought was almost enough to make her laugh. She wasn't sure when he'd slipped beneath her defenses, but she already cared about him more than was safe. She waited for Micah to heft him off the ground. The man wasn't a weakling by any means, but Teague was a large man in his own right. Thank God they weren't far from the house.

As they hurried the last few blocks, she dialed Dr. Harris. Ever since Papa had extracted justice for the harm done to the good doctor's son all those years ago, he'd been loyal to a fault. They'd required his help less in the last few years, but he was willing to make house calls and was discreet.

She had a feeling she'd be seeing a lot more of him before this thing ended.

Callie gave him the information and he promised to leave immediately. She hung up as they hit the property, and glanced over. Teague looked even worse under the glaring floodlights that lit up as they approached—beneath the blood, his skin was too pale. In the quiet of the night, she could hear the rasp of his breathing, which was as comforting as it was worrisome.

Please be okay. Please. I can't lose you, too.

Panic rose, fluttering in her chest like a trapped bird, but she wouldn't give in to the scream building inside her. She opened the door, pretending she didn't see Micah's hesitation to bring him inside, and led the way up to her room. It wasn't proper, but she could give a rat's ass about proper right now. Her father had decreed she'd marry Teague, so he could deal with the man in his house until they figured out what had happened. Micah laid him down on the bed, none too gently.

She didn't comment on it, though good lord, she wanted to. "Run the plates. Find out who did this."

"I will, Callie." He managed to actually sound respectful this time, but she had bigger worries right now.

"And when Dr. Harris gets here, send him up." She sat on the edge of the bed, not sure where to start. Should she take off his shirt? They probably shouldn't have moved him at all because he could have some sort of spine injury, but leaving him on the side of the road wasn't an option. She took a calming breath that did little to calm her.

What-if questions would do no good here. She had to deal in facts—facts she wouldn't know until the doctor showed up.

Since there wasn't much she could do, she called downstairs to have someone bring a bowl so she could start cleaning him up.

The door opened a few minutes later to reveal Emma. She shut it carefully behind her and crossed to the bed, every move efficient. She'd always been like this, to the point where being in the same room with her calmed Callie down because Emma always seemed perfectly in control of her environment, even when she wasn't in her kitchen domain. "Micah says this fiancé of yours is in a bad way. I brought ice."

Ice. Of course. She should have thought of that herself. "Thank you, Emma."

"No need to thank me. Let's get this boy cleaned up." She didn't show an ounce of fear or worry as she looked Teague over with a critical eye, but no doubt she'd seen worse. When her father's men were injured and brought back here, someone had to be capable and in control while they waited for the doctor to show up. Nine times out of ten, that task fell to Emma.

Callie filled the bowl with water and returned to the bed to find Emma scooping the ice into a cloth and folding it up. She glanced up. "Let's get the blood off his face and then I'll hold the ice while you do the rest."

The woman's no-nonsense tone calmed Callie's racing thoughts. She could do this. One thing at a time. She dipped a washcloth into the water and started cleaning away the blood on Teague's face. The swelling was alarming, and she hoped to God that nothing was broken. He groaned a little with each contact, but didn't wake.

Emma placed the ice over the left side of his face. "Just keep breathing, Miss Callie." She hesitated. "We appreciate what you're doing—the sacrifice you're making." She took Callie's hand and set it over the ice, and then stood. "I'll go make sure the boys don't give that doctor any hassle."

Callie watched Emma go, her heart in her throat. If she'd needed the reminder of why she was doing this, it was embodied in Micah's mother and the other people like her. People who depended on the Sheridans to keep them safe.

She took a deep breath and went back to cleaning Teague up, working her way down his throat and over the parts of his skin not covered by clothes. By the time the door opened to reveal Dr. Harris, she had most of the blood gone.

Dr. Harris was a wizened little man who looked like a goblin from Harry Potter, a comparison she'd come up with when she was younger and never been able to shake. He closed the door softly behind him, and got right down to business. "What can you tell me about how this happened?"

"I don't know." No, that wasn't strictly the truth. She took a deep breath, trying to still her frantic thoughts. It was hard, harder than she could have dreamed, because all she could focus on was the fact that Teague was hurt and they needed to do *something*. "He was dumped intentionally in front of me. He's been beaten, but I don't think he's been tortured." She'd just seen him this morning, and...Her heart clenched. It didn't take long to torture someone. It was something that could be drawn out, certainly, but there were rough and dirty methods that didn't require too much time.

She really wished she didn't know that.

Harris moved to the other side of the bed and rolled up his sleeves, every inch the calm professional. "You've gotten him cleaned up and started with the ice. Good. It makes it easier to see the damage, and will help with the swelling." He disappeared into the bathroom and she heard him washing his hands. Callie made an effort to keep breathing, which was difficult with dread trying to choke her. He reappeared and went to work, prodding Teague's face in a way that made her wince.

He looked up. "If this is too difficult…"

"No, it's fine." She trusted the doctor with her life, but she wouldn't leave him alone with Teague. Micah's words still echoed in her head, threatening to make her jump at shadows. It was one thing to know that some of the men didn't approve, and completely another to hear him saying they should leave Teague to his fate. She wasn't about to admit to them that Ronan's death had altered the landscape so much that her marriage was vitally important in keeping the lot of them safe. There were more sharks in this ocean than just the Hallorans and O'Malleys—better to go with the devil she knew than the one she didn't. At least the older men recognized the threat, which was why there'd only been a minimum of mumbling discontent from them.

The younger ones, like Micah? She suspected they'd hoped she'd pick one of them to marry, bringing them up in the ranks and avoiding the need to invite in an outsider. It was a shortsighted goal, but since none of them had openly spoke against her marriage, she hadn't been forced to address it directly. Thank God. She didn't have enough time or energy to deal with yet another mess.

Harris pulled out a pair of scissors and carefully cut

away Teague's shirt and pants. He paused, but left his underwear. She could have told him it wasn't necessary, but she couldn't force the words out, not when all she could focus on was the mass of bruises darkening the skin she'd just spent hours worshipping. "Oh, Teague."

The doctor continued his careful poking and prodding, and part of her was grateful Teague wasn't awake for it since there was no way it *didn't* hurt. From his little suitcase, he pulled out what looked like an ultrasound machine and went to work on Teague's stomach, where the majority of the bruises were concentrated, watching the screen with a small frown on his face. He finally sat back with a sigh. "I won't know for sure without a few more tests, but it looks like he came off relatively lucky."

Lucky? "How bad is it?"

"Lots of bruises and swelling, and I suspect a few bruised ribs, but nothing seems to be broken and there isn't any internal bleeding. I'll need to see him in about a week, though don't hesitate to call if it looks like he's getting worse."

She waited, but it didn't look like there was more forthcoming. "That's it?"

He smiled, reaching out to pat her hand. "As long as he takes it easy, he should make a full recovery."

She let out a breath she hadn't realized she was holding. "Thank you, Dr. Harris. I really appreciate you rushing over here."

"Of course, Callista." He frowned. "Are you getting enough sleep? You look exhausted."

She tried for a smile. "It's nothing. I'm just a bit stressed."

His frown deepened. "Stress can do a significant

amount of harm. Whatever's going on can wait—you have to take care of yourself first."

Easier said than done. She wished it was as easy as jaunting off on a vacation and recharging, but that wasn't an option. Her father and her people needed her. Hell, right now, *Teague* needed her. She smoothed back the matted hair on his head. "I'll do what I can."

"Would you like me to prescribe you some sleeping aids? It's not a long-term solution, but it may help you get to the other side of whatever you're dealing with."

She started to demur before she noticed the stubborn look on his face. He wasn't going to leave before he had some sort of assurance that she'd take his advice. Callie sighed. "I'd like that very much." She wouldn't use the pills, though. She didn't deserve the peaceful slumber of someone with a clean conscience. More than that—as if that wasn't reason enough—she couldn't risk some threat arising while she was knocked out and her being unable to deal with it.

He scribbled out the prescription on a pad of paper he pulled from his pocket and handed it over. "Get it filled, Callista. And eat a full meal or two." His kind smile took some of the sting out of his words.

"Thank you, Dr. Harris."

"Remember, I'm only a phone call away." He repacked his bag and walked out of the room, closing the door softly behind him. She sagged, fighting against the burning in her throat and eyes. It was okay. Teague was okay.

But it could have been so much worse.

She lifted his hand into her lap, careful to not jar him, and stroked her fingers over the broken skin on his knuckles, tracing the tattoos there. *He's okay. Just keep breathing, because he's going to be fine.* It helped, but not nearly enough. Her gaze kept going back to his bruised face, to that moment when she thought she might never see those soulful dark eyes look at her with hunger again. She could have lost him today, and she'd barely gotten used to the idea of having him.

Someone had done this to him.

It didn't matter to whoever hurt him—and she had some ideas about that—that he didn't ask for this, or that *he* wasn't remotely responsible for Brendan's death, even by proxy. All they'd seen was an insult that had to be avenged.

A goddamn *insult*.

Rationally, she knew wars had been started over less, but the anger unfolding in her chest didn't care. They'd hurt him. They could have even killed him, and there was nothing she could do to stop it. She'd been helpless, just as she'd been helpless when Brendan wrapped his meaty hands around her throat, her death in his eyes.

Her body shook, her stomach trying to revolt, but she closed her eyes and rode it out. That nightmare was over, but this one was just getting started. She might be responsible for Brendan's death, but she hadn't gone into that strip club looking to hurt him. All she'd wanted was answers. To *talk*. To get a feel for the man she was supposed to marry.

He was the one who'd brought them to violence, to a life-or-death struggle that only she had walked away from—just like *his* kin had been responsible for hurting Teague. It didn't matter if they were the ones to actually deliver the blows. Her men didn't move on an enemy without her father's okay, and she seriously doubted that

Victor Halloran went about things any differently. If anything, he was even more controlling that Papa.

No, the attack on Teague was because a Halloran had ordered it.

She'd find out who and then she'd...What? Kill him like she killed Brendan?

This time, when her stomach lurched, she couldn't fight it back down. She barely made it to the bathroom in time to lose every last bit of cake she'd eaten today. Callie threw up until she couldn't throw up any more, and then she washed her face and brushed her teeth, her mind reeling and her body shaking. No matter how angry she was, she couldn't make that call. They hadn't killed Teague. They hadn't even injured him critically, for all that it looked horrible. She couldn't call for a death as a result. She stopped in the doorway and watched his chest rise and fall, reassuring herself that he was still breathing.

But if they'd killed him...Her heart tried to beat itself out of her chest, but she forced herself to finish the thought. If they'd killed him, there wasn't a single spot in Boston where they could hide that she wouldn't find them and make them pay.

CHAPTER ELEVEN

James nursed his second whiskey as time ticked by. There were things to do and calls to make, but he hadn't moved from this spot since Teague left hours ago. He respected the man's willingness to put the safety of his family before anything else—even a relative innocent. Because whatever the family—O'Malley, Halloran, or Sheridan—none of *them* were truly innocents.

It just went to shine the light on *his* willingness to let the girl who may or may not have murdered his older brother get away. If his old man knew, he'd lose his shit. The skin between James's shoulder blades twitched, as if expecting the lash. His father wouldn't go so far as to kill him—probably—but he had no problem exacting his punishments in blood.

James had the scars to prove it.

He downed half his whiskey, the burn in his throat doing nothing to calm his mind. He didn't want this shit any more than Teague seemed to, but at least the other man was taking steps to put it to a stop. He sighed. The time for indecision was over.

They had to find the girl.

The door to the pub opened and a group of men streamed through, Ricky in the center of them. Their voices cut through the relative quiet of the room, their laughter too loud and too sharp. Ricky lifted his hand. "Tommy, we're celebrating! First round's on the house."

What. The. Fuck?

There was nothing to celebrate. He straightened, his fingers tightening around the glass. They were acting suspiciously like they were coming off a successful hit, but he knew for a fact he hadn't ordered one. He finished his whiskey and got up, moving slowly to the bar to set the glass down, leaning there while he listened to the men at Ricky's table.

"Fuck, that guy hit hard."

Ricky laughed. "Not for long. Did you see the look on that bitch's face when we dropped him? I think she pissed her tiny little running shorts." More laughter all around.

James turned, waiting for them to realize he was there. He could rush over and start demanding answers, but one of the few useful things he'd learned from his old man was that how you entered a situation determined whether you'd come out on top or bottom. These were *his* men and *his* brother, and as great as it'd be to pretend that this was a perfect world where the men would always respect him, that wasn't how things worked. Love and fear were the only two emotions that forged loyalty, and he knew better than to aim for the former.

The man facing the bar noticed him first, his left eye

swollen nearly shut. James couldn't place his name—
any of their names aside from his brother—but the man
knew him. He went silent. The guy next to him turned to
see what he was looking at, and paled. It went like that
around the table, until Ricky was the only one still laughing and bragging.

His littler brother finally looked over and his grin
widened. "Here to celebrate, James?"

Another tumbler of whiskey showed up at his elbow,
courtesy of Tommy. He picked it up, fighting to keep relaxed. He knew from dealing with Brendan and their old
man that there was nothing scarier than the eerie calm that
preceded an explosion of violence. He hoped like hell that
he wouldn't have to go there tonight, but Ricky was obliv-
ious to the men exchanging leery glances around him.
"What are we celebrating?"

"We whooped that O'Malley douche's ass." Ricky
laughed, too loud in the now-silent room. "You should
have seen his face. That pussy went down and didn't get
back up again."

Motherfucker. He watched any chance of peace slide
down the drain, along with his ability to walk away from
his brother tonight. He had to make an example of him.
God*damn* it. James pushed off the bar. "You beat Teague
O'Malley."

Ricky's smile melted off his face, as if he was just now
realizing there was danger. "He insulted our family."

The idiot never stopped to consider why an O'Malley
would be walking away from one of *their* pubs without
a scratch on him. His younger brother didn't have the
vicious streak that had made Brendan a force of nature,
but he was shaping up to be just as stupid when it came

to thinking things through. James met each of the men's gazes at the table in turn. "Get the fuck out." He raised his voice slightly. "*Everyone* get the fuck out. Now."

No one questioned the order, and they scattered faster than he would have credited. Then there was only him and Ricky. He wasted no time grabbing the front of his brother's shirt and hauling him out of his chair. "What the fuck is wrong with you?"

"Get your hands off me."

Instead, he shook Ricky. "Answer the goddamn question."

"He was on our turf!"

Disgusted, James shoved him back into the chair hard enough that it almost toppled over backward. "And you never stopped to think that maybe there was a reason for that, did you? He was here to meet with me so we could attempt to resolve this shit peacefully."

"Peacefully." Ricky's lip curled. "Those fuckers spit in our face. They deserve to pay."

"You sound like our old man."

"Maybe because he's got some balls. Brendan did, too." He made a show of looking James up and down. "The old man is right—you're as much a pussy as the O'Malleys and Sheridans. Even more so, because at least they're willing to fight."

The decision played out before James, lightning fast. He could yell at his fool brother and hope to God it was enough to make him see reason. Or he could make damn sure Ricky never crossed him again. *He* was the heir now. He couldn't afford to spend the rest of his life cleaning up his brother's messes, or worse, constantly looking over his shoulder.

Fear or love.

It was painfully obvious that love wouldn't do it—hadn't done it despite the fact that they'd always been close. The only way to stop this shit in its tracks was to cut it off at the source. He hauled Ricky out of his seat again and dragged the struggling man toward the back room. His brother realized their destination and fought harder. "What the hell? Jesus, James, I was just screwing with you. Stop. Holy shit, *stop*."

James shoved him through the door and followed him inside, kicking it shut behind him, feeling like he tore off a ragged chunk of his soul in the process. He took a deep breath, the scent of old blood and fear almost enough to make him gag. "I don't give a fuck if you hate every damn decision I'm making, you don't move without my permission. Hell, you don't even *breathe* unless I give the okay. You got it?"

"Yeah, James. I get it. I swear I do." His brother nodded frantically, his hands still outstretched as if that would really save either of them from what was coming.

James rolled his shoulders. "You know the drill, Ricky. Canes or the whip?"

* * *

Teague woke up in waves of pain. He felt like a train had hit him—maybe two. It hurt to breathe, and he had no illusions about the fun times ahead when he actually moved. He cracked open his eyes, finding himself in a dim room that he'd never seen before. He looked around as much as possible without moving his head, taking in the feminine four-poster bed and white canopy that wouldn't look out of place in a fairy tale. Everything was white—the dresser, the vanity, the walls.

"You're awake."

He gritted his teeth and turned his head to see Callie standing in the doorway that seemed to lead into a bathroom. Fuck, that hurt. "I thought I might be in heaven, but now I'm sure."

She gave a tired smile. "At least you still have your charm."

"I have more than that. Come here and—" He winced at the sharp pain that shot through him when he lifted his arm. "On second thought, maybe I'll just lie here."

"Smart." She crossed to carefully sit on the edge of the bed. "How are you feeling?"

"That's a stupid question."

She rolled her eyes. "I know you're in pain, but do you feel like you're going to be sick? Or dizzy?"

Signs of a concussion. He took careful stock, because while being manly and tough was great for impressing the people around him, it wouldn't do him any good if he passed out the second he sat up. "No. My face feels like someone took a two-by-four to it, and I'm pretty sure those assholes kicked me once I was down, but nothing more serious than that."

"That's plenty serious."

He'd dealt with worse, albeit not often. Teague looked around the room again. "Not that I'm complaining, exactly, how but did I get here?"

"You don't remember?"

He didn't remember *anything* after that coward hit him in the back of the head. From the state of his body, they must have kept beating him for a while, and then transported him somewhere. There was no other reason for him being in what he figured what must be Callie's room. "I suspect I was unconscious at the time."

She looked away, twisting at the edge of the comforter. "You were dumped in front of me by an SUV registered to Ricky Halloran."

"Fuck." He closed his eyes, trying to get a hold of his anger. That little shit had always been a troublemaker, even if he was nowhere near as dangerous as Brendan. Or he hadn't been. It looked like he was gunning for the rep, and he wasn't smart enough to pull it off without getting himself killed. Jumping Teague in Halloran territory right after he met with James? Dumping Teague's unconscious body from his own goddamn SUV?

He was an idiot.

But just because he was stupid didn't mean he wasn't dangerous. Teague could anticipate what James would do in most situations—or at least he'd like to think he could. He stopped, thinking hard. Was it possible James had been the one to order the beating? His mind immediately rebelled at the thought, but he forced himself to reason through it. James had met him in good faith. The man might have changed in the years since they were close, but he was smart. He would know that attacking Teague would only escalate things. Even if it was part of his plan, he'd still wait for a time when they hadn't just had a damn meeting. It was too obvious. Too clumsy. It wasn't James's style at all, even if he was willing to betray Teague.

But Ricky? Ricky was a loose goddamn cannon.

Teague cursed long and hard. "Every time I think this situation can't get worse, the universe decides to go and prove me wrong."

"At least you're alive." He opened his eyes to find Callie closer, an unreadable expression on her face. "I thought you were dead for a moment."

And it had obviously scared the shit out of her. He ignored the protest of his ribs and raised his hand. "Come here, angel." She crawled across the bed to settle next to him, leaving a few scant inches between them as if she was afraid of hurting him further. He smoothed back her hair, taking in her tank top and faded sweatpants. If asked before, he would have guessed that she slept in some sort of slinky teddy or something equally feminine.

Apparently he would have been wrong.

He met her gaze. "I'm okay." Mostly okay.

Obviously her thoughts had gone down the same path. "This time. What about next time?"

There were no guarantees in life. But he couldn't say that with her so blatantly looking to him for reassurance. Sometimes life was about the comforting little white lies you told to make the people around you feel better, at least for a little while. "We'll figure it out before it gets to that point."

Her expression said she didn't believe that any more than he did. She traced his face with her gaze, and he could almost hear her cataloging every bruise and cut. "The doctor said you've got to take it easy for a bit, but you should make a full recovery."

It was strange having someone worried about him. He was used to being on the other side of things—of constantly being concerned about the future and his siblings. Her scrutiny made his skin feel too tight. Uncomfortable. Because he couldn't say the words she needed to hear in order to feel better. They didn't exist. She was obviously too smart to fall for that kind of lie, too.

He took her hand. "I'll take care of myself. I promise."

"Liar." But she smiled a little. "You're going to go rushing into danger at the first opportunity, and we both know it."

Maybe. Probably. He stroked her knuckles with his thumb. "What if I promise to be as careful as I can be?"

"It's better than nothing, I suppose." She stared at their joined hands. "I don't like the idea of losing you, Teague."

He understood. The thought of something happening to her had crippling panic flaring inside him. He'd move heaven and earth to keep her safe. He should be doing his damnedest to keep his list of people he wanted to keep safe from growing, but for better or worse, Callie's name was on it now. He took a breath, ignoring the pain in his chest. "I plan on making it to our wedding."

She didn't look like that comforted her, but it was the best he could do right now. Once he found Brendan's killer, he'd put them both into a safer position. He rolled onto his side with a grunt and caught sight of the clock. "Shit, I've got to get moving."

"What? To where?"

"Mass."

Her disbelief might have been funnier under different circumstances. "You need to stay in bed."

He didn't expect her to understand. The Sheridans may be Irish-Catholic, but they weren't anywhere near the insane level as his family. Somewhere along the line, his father had decided that going every Sunday, regardless of whatever crisis they were currently in the middle of, somehow balanced the scales of all the bad shit he brought into the world.

The only excuse for missing Mass was if Teague was in a coffin. He could argue that he was a grown-ass adult and not subject to the approval of his parents, but it was a relatively small price to pay to keep them off his back.

Plus, he hadn't seen his siblings—aside from that delightful run-in with Aiden—in almost a week. It might be foolish to think that he could keep them safe, but at least if he laid eyes on them all in the same place he'd get a little reassurance. He sat up and waited impatiently for the room to stop spinning. "I'll get back in bed after Mass."

"You're joking." She stared, and he held her gaze. "You're not joking."

"Nope." He pushed to his feet. "I don't suppose you have any clothes that would come close to fitting me?"

She huffed out a breath. "You're not going to be reasonable about this, are you?" When he didn't answer, she threw up her hands. "Fine. I think I can scrounge up something. Try not to fall on your face while I'm gone."

He waited until the door shut behind her to shuffle to the bathroom and turn on the shower. As tempting as it was to ask for her help to wash off, he had too much pride for that shit. He couldn't follow through on any sort of desire right now, and it would be a damn shame to waste the opportunity if he got Callie in the shower. Not to mention he had the feeling that she'd jump on any chance to get his ass back to bed, rather than standing by while he left the house. No, he'd have to do this himself—and quickly.

Luckily, he was already mostly naked. He shucked off his underwear and carefully stepped beneath the hot water, gritting his teeth when it hit the cuts on his face. He scrubbed himself down, taking the extra time to make sure all the dried blood was gone, and shut the water off. The sound of Callie's pacing reached him as he dried off, and he wrapped the towel around his waist before opening the door.

She turned, her hands on her hips. "You have a death wish."

"More like a wish to be clean." He caught sight of the clothes she'd dumped on the bed. Slacks and a button-down—fitting attire for Mass. "Thanks."

"Do you need help getting dressed?"

Even if he did, he wouldn't admit it. Pride was foolish thing, but he couldn't shake it. "I'm fine."

"Of course you are." She turned, her spine rigid. "Hurry up, then."

He managed not to make a sound as he dressed— though twice he had to pause and wait for the black spots dancing across his vision to retreat—and he turned to the mirror when he was done, surprised that the clothes actually fit. He started to ask where they'd come from, and decided maybe it was better he didn't know. If he was wearing her dead brother's clothes... Yeah, he sure as fuck didn't need that information.

"They aren't Ronan's."

He froze, not sure when she'd turned around. "I—"

"You had a look on your face like you thought you might be wearing a dead man's clothes." Her smile was mirthless. "You're not. Even if they'd fit—which they wouldn't—I donated them months ago. It was too hard... Never mind."

He sighed, feeling like the world's biggest ass. She'd picked his unconscious body off the street, hauled him back here safely, obviously had a doctor see to him, and wasn't standing in his way of leaving even though she didn't approve. He forced himself to stop and take a breath. If her being worried about him made him uncomfortable, it was his damn problem. Not hers. "I'm sorry."

"Don't be. This isn't exactly the easiest of situations. You're doing the best you can—we all are." She motioned to the door, her face a perfect mask of politeness. "There's a car waiting downstairs. You should go if you're not going to be late."

She was right, but he was loath to leave things like they were. He'd hurt her, whether he intended to or not. Teague stopped in front of her. "Thank you, angel. Last night you went above and beyond the call of duty. I wouldn't have blamed you for leaving my ass where they dropped me."

Her eyes flashed, the blue extra vivid in her anger. "That's a downright stupid thing to say, and you damn well know it. I might not have been the one to choose you, but you're mine, Teague O'Malley, for better or worse."

He kissed her, the barest brushing of lips, and then he walked out the door, a stupid grin pulling his lips up. Even the throbbing of the left side of his face wasn't enough to dim the strange joy her words had brought. Because she'd as much as declared her intentions for him. It shouldn't have been surprising—they were getting married in three short weeks, after all, but there was a world of difference between going through the motions and declaring him *hers*.

Callie had done the latter.

The entire ride to Our Lady of Victories, he let himself soak that in. She wanted him. He'd known she wanted him physically, but now he knew she *wanted* him. That was so much easier to focus on than her worry. He relished that snap of anger, the possessiveness of her words.

But when they pulled to a stop, he forced himself to put that small happiness aside. There was business to attend to, and he couldn't afford to be off his game because he was mooning over his fiancée.

He stepped onto the sidewalk and merged with the small crowd making their way inside. A murmur went up in the people around him, and they stepped back as he climbed the stairs. He was used to getting more than his fair share of attention—most of the parish knew what his family did for money—but his face must have appeared worse than he'd thought.

His youngest brother, Devlin, stood at the top of the stone steps, brows raised. "You look like you had an eventful night."

Trust Devlin to understate things without rushing down to ask if he was okay. "You could call it that."

"Father isn't pleased."

Of that he had no doubt. "Is he ever?"

Devlin fell into step with him as they walked into church. Despite how bittersweet he found attending Mass, Our Lady of Victories was a sort of second home to Teague with its old-world architecture and feel—like stepping into the past. They stopped in the second pew, the one that was designated for the family despite their never officially being assigned seats. But, every Sunday, it was empty and waiting.

Sloan looked up as he slid in next to her, and gasped quietly. Sometimes it seemed like she did everything quietly—a mouse who did her best to stay out of the spotlight of their parents' attention. She put her hand on his forearm, her voice barely above a whisper. "Are you okay?"

"Right as rain."

"Liar."

He met her dark eyes, so similar to his own. "I'll be okay. Promise."

"You can't promise that, and you know it." She sat back and stared forward, her eyes shining in a way he was all too familiar with. He wanted to say or do something to comfort her, but she was right—he couldn't promise shit.

It seemed like he was destined to piss off and upset every woman he cared about that he came in contact with today.

He sighed, grateful when the priest began speaking. With the ease of long practice, he intoned the words and fell into the old familiar motions. Sloan had always been the most sensitive of his siblings, and he hated causing her any kind of pain, but he was stuck. Fuck, he was up to his neck and sinking fast. He wasn't even aware that Devlin was moving until he slipped behind Teague and nudged him to the end of the aisle. He wrapped his arm around their sister, leaning down to murmur something in her ear.

Devlin was the best of them all.

He'd thought it before, but it only became clearer as time went on. His youngest brother always knew what to say or do to defuse a situation or comfort someone who was upset. Teague should have thought that maybe Sloan needed a shoulder to lean on, even if he couldn't say the words that would make everything okay. But he hadn't. It hadn't even crossed his mind.

Just another way he'd failed his siblings.

He was still embroiled in his internal torment when the sermon wound to an end. Ignoring his family, he stood and walked out of the church, needing fresh air. No, he needed a whole hell of a lot more than fresh air. But taking a second to breathe was all he could accomplish in this moment, so that was what he did.

Knowing someone would come looking for him before too long, he circled around the corner and stopped beneath the nearest tree. *Shit.* As much as he'd like to blame his current pounding headache on the beating last night, it wasn't the truth.

"Smoke?"

He looked up, already knowing who he'd see. "What are you doing here?"

Finch shrugged and passed over a cigarette. "Maybe I'm praying for my immortal soul."

"Sure." He snorted and lit up. It had been a while since his last cigarette, and he closed his eyes for a second to savor his first inhalation.

"Who tuned up your face?"

Teague flashed him a look. "Why? Are you going to get off your ass and arrest them?"

"I think I'm detecting some bitterness." Finch laughed softly, not looking the least bit sorry. "You know we value you."

Maybe. Maybe not. But the one thing he did know was that they valued their asses more. There was some deeper game being played by the feds right now, but hell if he knew what it was. Teague inhaled again. "I'd hate to think you're sitting back and waiting for shit to hit the fan so you can mop the whole lot of us up."

Finch froze. He recovered almost instantly, but it was too late. Teague knew. He huffed out a laugh, and once he started, he couldn't stop. "Oh God, you are. That's the funniest shit I've heard all day." Even though he'd suspected he wouldn't get any help from them, it was something else altogether to know it for sure. He laughed again and shook his head. "You really are a bastard, Finch."

"See you around." He moved off, slipping into a doorway of a business further down the block mere seconds before someone called Teague's name. He crushed the cigarette beneath his shoe and turned. As shitty as it was to realize he couldn't count on the feds to help him out, it was better to know now rather than later—when he might actually be relying on them. Or that's what he told himself, even though part of him threatened to wallow in despair.

He was well and truly on his own.

CHAPTER TWELVE

Four days later, Teague stumbled up to his room, so damn exhausted, it was like he'd been running a marathon all day instead of making phone calls. But nothing had come to fruition, and his frustration was high.

James wasn't returning his calls. The men he'd sent out to canvass the area around Tit for Tat had been run off by Halloran men. Neither his father nor Aiden would talk to him about the plans they had in the works.

And, to top it off, his younger sisters had taken it as their own personal mission to make sure he made a full recovery. Every time he turned around, Sloan was pushing him into the nearest chair and offering a blanket, or Keira was shoving hot tea into his hands.

They meant well, but he was losing his goddamn mind.

He locked his bedroom door and sat gingerly on the edge of his bed. His ribs still smarted like nobody's business, but the family doctor had assured him that nothing was broken or seriously injured. He'd be back in fighting shape in no time.

Teague sighed and stripped, moving carefully. A quick glance at the clock told him it was late—later than he'd wanted to be out and about. His promise to Callie lingered in the back of his mind. It was the only reason he allowed his sisters to run rampant over him. At least that way he had something to tell her when he called her at night to reassure her that he was taking care of himself.

His shower was quick and miserable, the hot water doing nothing to pound the tension from his muscles. He needed a week on a beach somewhere and daily massages to work the stress out, but it was more likely that a unicorn would burst through his door.

The fight was here. Callie was here. His family was here.

Which meant he was where he needed to be.

He shut off the water and grabbed a towel. Lying down on his bed was a slice of sheer heaven, but he didn't close his eyes. There was one last thing to do before he could give over to sleep. He smiled and reached for his phone.

A few seconds later, Callie answered. "Late night."

"Yeah." He adjusted his pillows. "My mother cornered me to ask about tux choices. She sat me down for an hour to go over pictures. An *hour*." And when he'd told her to just pick whatever she thought was best, she'd ripped him a new one without ever once raising her voice or letting the smile slip off her face.

Callie made a sympathetic noise. "She called me three times today. I'm not particularly proud to admit I dodged every single one of them."

"I don't blame you." He laughed. "I'd be doing the same thing, but the woman knows where I sleep."

"So what did you decide on?"

"Hell if I know. I chose three options before she was finally satisfied."

"Poor baby." She moved, the sound of fabric sliding coming through the phone. He closed his eyes, picturing her lying out on her bed the same way he currently was on his, wearing a pair of sweats and a tank top. He liked that she went for comfort instead of sexiness for sleeping. It was such a contrast from how she carried herself during the daytime—perfectly put together in every way.

"I wish you were here." He wasn't sure where the words came from, but they were the stark truth.

"I wish I was there, too. I don't trust that you're taking care of yourself." She paused. "And I miss you. I know it's only been a few days, but—"

He cut in before she could tag some qualifier on there to take away from the statement. "I miss you, too. Do you want to go get lunch tomorrow?" Or breakfast. Or dinner. Or, hell, he'd settle for coffee. Anything that got them into the same room and settled the uncomfortable feeling he hadn't been able to shake after the way they left things the other day. They might have talked every night they'd been apart, but it wasn't close to the same thing.

"I wish I could." The regret in her voice was real. "Papa and I have a meeting that I can't reschedule."

It was on the tip of his tongue to ask what the meeting concerned. He knew for a fact his father was coordinating things on his own without talking to Colm about them, so it only stood to reason that Colm was doing the same thing. But bringing business up meant taking away from the comfort and intimacy that came from just having a conversation with Callie. Business could wait, at least until tomorrow.

Instead, he said, "Soon, Callie. I want to see you soon."

She shifted again, maybe rolling over on her bed. "Let me see how the meeting goes, and then I'll have a better idea of when I'm free. I want to see you, too."

"Deal." It wasn't an exact date, but the intent was clear. She wanted to see him as much as he wanted to see her. He yawned, a wave of exhaustion rolling over him.

"Go to sleep, Teague. You need it."

"You too." She wasn't getting enough. He didn't have to sleep next to her every night to know that. Every time he talked to her, she sounded more run-down and tired. Last night she hadn't been able to remember the last time she ate when he asked. It was added motivation to get some alone time with her—at least then he could make sure she got a full meal and maybe a nap. "Good night, angel."

* * *

"I will say, Callie, I'm surprised by what you're proposing."

Callie kept her nerves off her face through sheer force of will. In the days since Teague's attack, she'd been petitioning hard for her father to let her in. It was only today that he finally relented and promised to hear her out. The admiration on his face almost made the fight worthwhile.

Almost.

She took a deep breath. Every time she brought up Brendan, Papa changed the subject, making it abundantly clear that he didn't want to hear her confession, no matter what he might think happened. With that avenue closed to her, she'd focused on the war itself. "They'll be expecting a full-frontal attack, which means they'll be prepared for it. This will cripple a significant portion of their income." And destroying the factory where the Hallorans stored their illicit goods dealt them a blow that was unlikely to result in casualties. It wasn't a perfect plan as such things went, but it was better than what John was suggesting— work their way through Halloran territory, taking out every hub they used on the way. The loss of life would be devastating on both sides—she refused to sit back and allow it to happen.

Thank God Papa seemed intrigued by her plan.

He sat back, tapping his steepled fingers against his lips. "They'll use more than one location—they're too smart to store everything valuable in one place."

"Even so, taking out one will hurt them with less chance of loss on our side." She met her father's gaze, her hands folded demurely in her lap. "When we go for their throat, I want it to be in a way that doesn't put any more of our men at risk than necessary." *Please, God, let this end before we have to take such measures.*

It was becoming increasingly clear to Callie that she was capable of doing just that if they backed her into a corner. She hated knowing that about herself, but there wasn't time for her to wrestle with her bruised conscience. Brendan had been one thing. Even though she knew differently in her darkest soul of souls, she could still argue with herself that it had been solely self-defense. This was something else altogether.

But seeing Teague hurt and helpless had driven the stakes home in a way she couldn't ignore. If left unchecked, the Hallorans wouldn't hesitate to kill every last one of them. By holding herself back, she might be putting the people she cared about at risk. Teague. Micah. Emma. All of them. When she weighed her conscience against those lives, it was no contest. She'd do what needed to be done to keep her people safe, no matter how unpalatable she found it.

Especially since she was the one who struck the match that blew a tense treaty sky-high.

He nodded to John. "Make it happen." Papa waited until the door shut behind his man to pin her with a look. "Enough about business. How are the wedding plans going?"

It was on the tip of her tongue to remark that the wedding was just as much business as the strike against the Hallorans, but she wrestled the words back at the last moment and forced a smile instead. "My future mother-in-law is a force of nature."

Papa shook his head. "Yes, that's one way to describe Aileen. Be careful, Callie. That woman is ruthless to the core—she'd smile sweetly while she gutted you if she thought the situation called for it."

She'd suspected as much, but it was enough to make her wonder what the woman had done to make even Colm Sheridan feel it necessary to dole out a warning. There seemed to be so many things she could no longer talk to her father about, but this was safe enough. "What did she do?"

"Nothing in the way that you mean." He laughed softly. "But any woman who could survive thirty-five years of marriage to Seamus O'Malley—and bear him seven children—is not one I'm inclined to take lightly."

There was something beneath the words, but she couldn't put her finger on what it was. "Perhaps Seamus isn't as bad at home as he is with his enemies."

Papa raised his eyebrows. "Do you really believe that?"

She thought over how even being within touching distance of the man was enough to raise the small hairs on the back of her neck, and the way Teague spoke of him. Her father could be ruthless when the situation called for it, but she'd never once doubted that he loved her and her brother with everything he had. And, when push came to shove, he was willing to let her make the decisions that ultimately impacted her life. Like agreeing to marry a stranger. All Seamus cared about was his children's compliance. Their happiness didn't even come into the equation.

Callie sat back. "I think that any woman who would go to bed with that man—and keep doing it—is someone I'm not inclined to underestimate."

He nodded like she'd given the right answer on a test. "All the same, try to enjoy the preparations. I know you didn't choose this, and after Brendan…"

She reached across the desk and covered his hand with her own. She might want to air her confession to make herself feel better, but her father obviously didn't want to hear it. She wouldn't burden him with her sins just to lighten the weight she carried. "It will be okay, Papa. Though I can think of a thousand things more important than wedding planning."

"Unfortunately it's necessary. The wedding itself is as much a statement as the marriage."

"I know." Which was why she'd gritted her teeth and

kept her complaints to herself. She squeezed his hand again. "We'll figure out a way out of this."

"Sometimes the only way out is through, Callie. You know that." His smile was tired. "But we'll get through it. We always do."

Guilt rose, threatening to choke her. She used to wish she could consider things as coldly and calculatingly as her father seemed to be able to when push came to shove, but now that she realized the ability was within her, all she wanted was to go back to how things were. Before she'd agreed to her engagement to Brendan. Before she'd let frustration and fear get the best of her. Before her entire world had come crashing down around her.

It would have happened sooner or later.

She *knew* that, but the knowing didn't make the guilt easier to bear. She pushed to her feet. "I'm going out tonight."

"To see that boy of yours again."

She didn't comment on his knowing that she'd been at Teague's. It went without saying that Micah would have reported back to Papa. The fact that he chose not to bring it up until now was surprising. She hesitated just inside the door. "I...I think I like him."

"I'm glad." The naked relief in his voice made her feel both better and worse.

"Good night, Papa." She walked out of his office and closed the door softly behind her. Once she was alone, the worry that had been plaguing her every waking moment since Teague left her sight rose up with a vengeance. They'd shared short phone calls every night, but that did little to reassure her that he was taking care of himself.

He sounded as tired as she felt, which wasn't comforting in the least. She dialed him before she could talk herself out of it.

"Hey, angel."

"Hello." She walked into the kitchen and opened the fridge, closing it almost before she registered its contents. The quiet sound of his breathing soothed her, but not nearly as much as the feel of his arms around her did. She needed that—desperately. Words rose before she could think better of them. "I wrapped things up earlier than anticipated. Can I see you tonight?"

"How soon can you be to my place?"

Relief made her knees a little shaky. "An hour."

"I'll meet you there."

"See you then." She hung up, the giddy feeling rising through her enough to make her wonder why she hadn't suggested this before. In the insanity of their lives, how safe she felt in Teague's presence was a glowing constant. It didn't seem to matter how briefly she'd known him, because he looked at her with those dark eyes and she felt like nothing bad in the world could touch her.

That feeling was dangerous, to be frank, but she couldn't resist hurrying to her room and throwing some choice clothing into an overnight bag. She paused, considering her closet. Tonight, they would escape from the real world for a while. Her hands hovered over the lingerie she'd bought the other day with him in mind, but she reluctantly put it back into the drawer. As much as she wanted the reprieve that came from their physical relationship, they both needed something else right now. Comfort. She'd stop on the way over and pick up some food and a few movies. Tonight was as close to an escape as they were allowed, and she intended to make the most of it.

The real world would have to wait until morning.

* * *

Teague wasn't prepared for what the sight of Callie would do to him. He opened the door to find her standing there, her cheeks rosy from the brisk breeze, her hair wind-blown, and her eyes drinking him in the same way he couldn't help but drink her in. "I missed you."

Her smile was like the sun peeking out from behind the clouds. "I missed you, too."

He kissed her, because going another moment without doing so was unacceptable. She melted against him at the first brushing of lips, her arms sliding around his neck. He nipped her bottom lip, and then soothed the spot with his tongue, the taste of her going straight to his head. "You'd better come in before we do something to scandalize the neighbors."

"God forbid."

He led her into the apartment, pausing only to lock the door. "You look good." And she did, wearing a white sundress with red flowers on it. Her blond hair had an artful curl to it, but there were still faint circles under her eyes that were a mirror to his. She held a bulging bag over each shoulder, and when he tried to take them from her, she slipped past him down the hallway.

"You're lying, but thank you." She set one of the bags down on the floor near the wall and put the other one on the kitchen counter. Then she turned back to face him, her blue eyes narrowing. Her fingers hovered an inch from his face, tracing the pattern of his bruise. It had faded to a truly impressive yellow-green tint that made his mother shake her head every time she looked at him. Callie motioned to his torso. "How are your ribs? I suppose it's too much to hope that you've followed the doctor's orders to take things slowly."

There was comfort in starting this night with a conversation similar to the ones they'd had the last few nights. "It depends on your definition of slowly." He laughed when she scowled. "Ah, angel, I'm mostly joking. I've managed to go a whole five days without fighting or doing anything else that would injure me further." Mostly because Carrigan had threatened his life if he left the house, and Sloan and Keira basically pounced on him if he got within ten feet of the front door. He'd had to conduct his investigation to find Brendan's killer via Devlin and Liam. The former he would have liked to avoid including despite the work being low-risk, but his youngest brother had insisted.

They hadn't found much conclusive, but three of the strippers who worked at Tit for Tat were sure they saw a woman who wasn't an employee leaving through the back door with blood on her. On one hand, it would no doubt reassure both James's and Teague's conscience that it didn't seem to be a case of self-defense that came about from some runaway. On the other hand, it made it a hell of a lot harder to track the woman down. Two of the three strippers said she was wearing a bright red wig, and he couldn't exactly search Boston for a woman with "a body to kill for."

No, he was temporarily stalled out, at least until a few

of the feelers he put out came back. He paused in the kitchen. "Beer or wine?"

"Wine, please."

He poured her a glass and then grabbed a bottle of beer for himself. If he was stuck for the time being in his search for the truth, there wasn't anyone else he'd rather be stuck with. "Have I mentioned that I missed you?"

"It might have come up." She smiled and moved to peer into his cupboards. "Sit down before you fall down."

He'd half expected her to show up ready to seduce him—especially considering how the last time had gone when they were in this apartment. The fact that she so obviously had other priorities stung his pride a little. He stepped up to wrap himself around her from behind. "What's the hurry, angel?"

"None of that." She slapped his wandering hands away and turned in his arms to face him. "It's been a rough week, Teague. Let me take care of you for a little while." She pressed a light kiss to his throat. "It'll make us both feel better."

There was no rush. He'd wanted to prove to her that this meant more to him than hot sex, and dragging her off to his bedroom to show how much better he was suddenly feeling wasn't going to do that. They had all night. Teague kissed her forehead and let her turn back around. "What's for dinner?"

"Pizza." She glanced at him over her shoulder. "Our cook, Emma, has tried to teach me the finer points of putting together a meal, but I'm a lost cause. I can do the simple things, but that's about it."

It didn't matter if she was making mac and cheese.

Callie was here, cooking for him, making sure he took care of himself. "How can I help?"

"Sit down and drink your beer. You might be feeling better, but you still look like you're about to keel over." She pulled out two jars of pizza sauce and started laying the various toppings out on the counter.

He sat. "You sure know how to make a man feel ten feet tall."

"I just—"

"It's okay. I understand." She'd been worried about him—was *still* worried about him. He'd had the last five days to get used to the idea of another person being that close to him—someone who wasn't family.

She offered him a small smile. "That's good, because I'm still wrapping my mind around it." She started the oven preheating and rifled through the lower drawers until she found two cookie sheets he hadn't known he owned. "How was your day?"

"Better than yesterday because there was no wedding planning involved."

She laughed. "You were dodging your mother."

"Unashamedly. I saw her coming up the stairs and looking determined, and I ducked into my brother's room and hid." The look on Devlin's face when he rushed in had been priceless.

"I'd make fun, but Aileen is very...formidable." She greased the cookie sheets and rolled the pizza dough onto them. "And I did my own bit of dodging yesterday."

"It's easier with phone calls." He sipped his beer.

Callie checked the oven and then popped the cookie sheets in. "For now. It's only a matter of time before she shows up on my doorstep again."

It was on the tip of his tongue to suggest they make a run for it, but Teague bit the words back. She wouldn't leave her family behind any more than he would. That loyalty was something that he'd previously considered a weakness. Now, he wasn't so sure. It seemed like family got them into as many problems as it got them out of, but he couldn't imagine his life without his siblings. And Callie obviously loved her father dearly. "You could always tell her no."

She raised her eyebrows and propped her elbows on the counter. "Have you met your mother?"

"Good point." He laughed. This was...nice. He'd known he enjoyed Callie's company, but he hadn't gotten to experience it on this level. Even with the world falling to pieces around them, he could see a glimpse of what the future might look like. A future where they had quiet nights like this. Where there'd be laughter and conversation and a home that was a bastion against the outside world. A sanctuary. "Do you want kids?"

The oven beeped and she busied herself taking the cookie sheets out and setting them on the stovetop. Then she turned back to him. "Eventually, yes. Maybe not seven." She smiled. "But, once things calm down, yes, I'd like a few children. Do you?"

"Yes." He answered in a rush, and cleared his throat. "My siblings are one of the most important parts of my life."

"That's how I felt about Ronan. He was always in my corner, even when we were growing up and fighting like cats and dogs." A shadow passed over her face. "I miss him."

"I'm sorry, angel. I didn't mean to bring up bad thoughts."

"No, it's okay. He's gone no matter if we talk about it or not, and not talking about it might make me feel better in the short term, but I'm partially afraid I'll start to forget him."

"Come here." He waited for her to walk around to him and then wrapped his arms around her. The physical touch wouldn't drive away all the bad things in the world, but it was all he knew how to offer. "You can talk about your brother to me whenever you want. I'll always be here to listen."

"Thank you." Her voice was partially muffled by his shirt. She clung to him, her fingers digging into his back. "I'm glad you're okay, Teague."

He stroked his hands up her back to tangle in her hair and tip her head so he could see her eyes. "I'm here, angel." He kissed one corner of her mouth and then the other. "I'm right here." His next kiss took her mouth, slow and sweet, and he went rock hard at the little whimper she made when his tongue brushed hers.

Callie jerked back, but she didn't leave the circle of his arms. "You're trying to seduce me."

"Trying? I thought I was doing a pretty damn good job of it."

"You are—were." She shivered. "But that's not why I'm here."

Maybe not, but he didn't think he could let tonight end without tasting her again and feeling her come apart in his arms. "What did you have planned for tonight?" Because she obviously had plans in place, or she wouldn't be digging in her heels so spectacularly.

"Dinner." She slipped away from him and grabbed the jars of pizza sauce. "Movies. A full night of sleep."

It struck him all over again that she wanted to take care of him. "I'm willing to negotiate."

"Negotiate all you want." She finished spreading the sauce and started on the cheese. "You need to take it easy."

No, what he needed to take was *her*.

Teague finished his beer and pushed to his feet. He crossed the kitchen to her and caught her hips when she turned around. "Teague!"

"Here's a newsflash, angel." He pulled her closer, lining up their hips so she could feel exactly how turned on he was. "I'd have to be in a goddamn coffin not to want you."

"Don't say things like that." Her hands came up to fist in the front of his shirt, but she didn't push him away.

"It's the truth." He kissed her, taking her mouth like he'd wanted to since she walked through the door. She melted against him, and he backed her up to the counter, taking the kiss deeper yet. He knew he should back off, should let them go back to the domestic scene he'd been enjoying so much, but his head was full of too many things he couldn't say. Not yet. Not without potentially scaring the shit out of Callie.

But he could show her.

"Do you think the pizza can wait awhile?"

"I think we can work something out." She unbuttoned his shirt with quick movements, and slid it off his shoulders. Then she froze. "Oh, Teague."

He didn't have to look down to know what she saw— a rainbow of bruises up his side that were a match for the one on his face. "It looks worse than it is."

"Don't lie to me." She traced a finger over the edge

of the one covering his ribs, still an ugly purple. "This is why I wanted to wait. I couldn't stand it if I hurt you."

His heart gave a painful lurch, and he covered her hand with his own. "I'm not broken—just a little banged up."

"Still—"

He kissed her again to stop her words. She didn't want to hurt him. Well, he'd make damn sure she didn't get the chance to worry about it. "Hands on the counter." She obeyed with a little hiss of relief, the positioning leaving her body open for him, an opportunity he had no intention of wasting. He cupped her breasts, playing with her nipples through the thin fabric, and then slipped a hand up her skirt, and groaned. "No panties, angel?"

"You already know the answer to that." Her lips brushed his with every word.

"The thought of you walking around Boston with only this sad excuse for a dress in between you and the rest of the world makes me crazy." He pushed a finger into her, finding her wetter than he could have dreamed.

She spread her legs a bit wider. "My dress is cute."

"Cute doesn't begin to cover it." He used his free hand to tug the strap off first one shoulder and then the other. It fell to her waist, leaving her breasts bare for him. He kept fucking her with his finger, and added a second. "But if we'd met outside this apartment, I would have been sorely tempted to do exactly what I'm doing right now, and to hell with the consequences. Keep your hands there."

Her knuckles went white as she gripped the edge of the counter, even as her hips rolled to take him deeper. "You'd touch me like this out in public?"

"Angel, I'd drag you to the nearest private spot and

bury myself inside you the first chance I got." He circled her clit with his thumb, twisting his wrist to flick his fingertips over that sensitive spot he'd found inside her.

Her eyes went wide. "Teague, I—"

"I know. Let go. I've got you." He kissed her as she came apart around him, her moans the sweetest thing he'd ever heard. He held her through the aftershocks, gentling his strokes until her knees buckled. Teague caught her easily, ignoring the twinge of his bruises as he lifted her into his arms.

"Put me down. You're going to hurt yourself."

"You're going to give me a complex." He walked down the hall to his bedroom and carefully set her on the bed. Her smile was a balm to his soul, and the fact that she lay back without trying to cover herself only made him hotter. She was damn near perfect, and she knew it.

He sat on the edge of the bed and had to fight back a wince. He thought he'd hid it in time, but she saw. "Your ribs?"

"They're still tender." He wasn't about to tell her that they hurt like a fucking bitch more often than not. Not with what he had in mind for tonight.

For a second she looked like she might protest again, but Callie sat up. "Well, then, I suppose we'll have to go about this another way." She kissed him gently and then gave his shoulders a push. "I promise not to jar them too much."

Teague laughed. "So I should just lie back and think of England."

"I think that's for the best." Her grin was downright impish. "We all do what we have to do."

He lay down, pulling her on top of him. She settled

over his hips, sliding against his cock in a move that made him curse. He leaned up to kiss her, ribs be damned. "Do your worst."

"With pleasure." She moved over him, tantalizingly close, but the angle was wrong for him to slide home. Christ, he wanted that more than he wanted his next breath. Which was exactly why he needed to put on the brakes, at least temporarily.

"Angel, if you don't get a condom right fucking now, I'm going to take you like this."

"I thought I was the one doing the taking." But she rose and moved to where he pointed—the nightstand drawer—and came back with a condom. Callie ripped it open with a wicked grin and took his cock in her hand. She stroked him once, squeezing in a way that made his eyes damn near cross, and then went to work rolling on the condom. Then she climbed back on top of him, kissing him as she adjusted the angle and plunged down on top of him.

Holy mother of God. He gripped her hips, holding her sealed to him, taking a second to simply enjoy this moment. With her eyes half-closed and her body rolling as she took him deeper, she was a vision straight out of a fantasy he hadn't even been aware of before now. He coasted his hands up over her sides to cup her breasts, rolling her nipples between his fingers as she moaned.

She rode him as if she had all the time in the world, as if she didn't want to miss a second of it. Like she was savoring the feeling of him inside her just as much as he was. "Fuck, angel."

She let her head fall back, her body arching to take him deeper yet, her breasts bouncing each time she sank onto his cock. "God, this feels good, Teague. I never want this to stop."

"Me either." He pulled her down to kiss her, the truth slashing through his chest.

He'd gone and fallen for his fiancée.

CHAPTER THIRTEEN

Callie never thought it could be like this. She lost herself in the sensation of Teague's hands on her hips, his cock filling her completely, the jagged sound of their breathing intermingling in the shadows of his room. Then he reached between their bodies to stroke her clit with his thumb, and her entire body caught fire. "Oh God."

He did it again. She closed her eyes and gave herself over to the delicious pleasure building in her core. Each stroke of his thumb was timed to her sliding down his cock, and it pushed her closer and closer to the edge. "I can't—"

"Yes, you can." He caught her moan with his mouth. "Come for me, Callie."

Hearing her name on his lips like *that*—almost worshipful and yet so damn possessive—sent her hurtling into oblivion. She clutched his shoulders and cried out, her hips bucking. She was vaguely aware of his fingers digging into her hips as he followed her over the edge, and then she slumped down, careful to roll onto the bed instead of his chest.

Teague immediately tucked her against him, his legs tangling with hers, as if he couldn't stand the new distance any more than she could. "Damn, angel."

Her laugh was a little hoarse. "I couldn't agree more." She had expected to feel the peace she'd come to associate with orgasms connected with Teague, but it was slow in appearing this time. Instead, the realization that she truly *cared* about this man had rooted itself deep in her being. She kissed him, fear threatening to ruin the moment. She remembered all too well how it had been when Ronan died. It might be a different type of feeling that Teague induced, but the threat of loss was equally devastating.

She held him tighter. "I don't know what I'd do if something happened to you." It didn't make the smallest bit of sense for her to have such strong feelings for this man after such a short time, but she couldn't deny it. She wasn't even sure she wanted to try.

There were worse things in the world than beginning to fall in love with her future husband.

He kissed her forehead. "Nothing's going to happen to me."

"Says the man who looks like a human punching bag."

Against all reason, he laughed. "Fair point. Fine— nothing *else* is going to happen to me."

"You can't promise that."

He tensed, his hand stilling where it had been running through her hair. "I won't lie and say I can, but I'll do everything in my power to see our wedding day. I said that before, and I meant it." His hand resumed its movement, soothing her despite her worries. "I have a plan."

"That sounds detailed and well-thought-out."

His laugh rumbled against her cheek. "I'm going to find who killed Brendan."

Her heart stopped beating and her breath stilled in her lungs. Callie opened her eyes, a strange buzzing in her ears as she stared at the off-white wall next to the bed. Teague was looking for Brendan's killer. Her fingers curled, instinctively withdrawing, but she made herself relax against him again.

"James can't guarantee anything—naturally—but it's the best bet to call Victor's vendetta off. If he's trying for peace, then my family can't attack without looking like they made the first move. They lose the moral high ground and potentially their Sheridan support."

The words finally penetrated the numb feeling threatening to suck her under. "You make it sound like the O'Malleys wanted this war."

"I'm not so sure they didn't."

He sounded so grim, she risked raising her head to meet his eyes. "Surely not."

"Angel, I say this because you're going to be running the Sheridan empire before too long, and because I care about you—don't ever underestimate either my father or Aiden." He said his brother's name like a curse. "They'll do whatever they think necessary to bring more power under our control, and to hell with the potential consequences."

It was obvious he'd recently been disillusioned on that front, or the bitterness would have faded by now. "I'm sorry."

"It's not your fault."

Guilt flared, bringing with it the horrible mix of fear and panic. Teague was looking for Brendan's killer—for *her*. What would he do if he realized he'd just made love to the very person he intended to turn over in his attempt to stop this war? Would he drag her from the bedroom and drive straight there?

Oh God, this is my worst nightmare come to life.

"Angel? Callie, what's wrong?"

"Nothing." The response was so automatic, it was out before she'd fully registered the question.

And, damn it, he knew it. He frowned, searching her face. "You're lying."

She had to put a stop to this conversation, sooner rather than later. Teague wasn't stupid. The longer they spoke, the greater the chance she'd slip up and say something to help him connect the dots. She couldn't allow that to happen. Callie moved to kiss him, but his grip tightened in her hair, keeping her scant inches from making contact.

"Tell me what's wrong."

She could actually see the peaceful oasis they'd created crumbling around them. "I'd rather not talk about it."

"Just like the bruises." His gaze fell to her throat, tracing the pattern that had long since faded away to nothingness.

"Teague, please."

He seemed to be debating pushing her further. A small treacherous part of her almost welcomed it. The memory of Brendan's death was like a festering wound inside her, poisoning everything around her. It would feel so good to share the burden.

But she couldn't risk it.

She cared about Teague, but she wasn't sure she could trust him—not with this. Because he was right in thinking that there was a good chance the identity of Brendan's killer would put a stop to this entire mess. If she had a little less self-preservation and responsibility to her people, she might have even considered turning herself in on her own.

"You can trust me, Callie."

Maybe. She knew he cared about her, but caring about someone he met a few short weeks ago and putting them before the family he so obviously loved, despite his issues with his father and older brother...Those were two very different things. She *wanted* to tell him. But she couldn't risk it. "It's that not simple." Nothing was simple anymore.

"You're going to be my wife." Tension ran through every muscle of his body, though little of it showed up in his voice. "You're safe with me."

"I know." In every way that counted—except this one. She couldn't expect him to put her before his family, and the fact that she wasn't sure he would was enough to keep her silent. She lifted her head. "I *do* feel safe with you, Teague. I haven't felt safe in a long time. Can't we just leave it at that?"

He stared, and she held her breath, hoping like hell that he couldn't read every thought dancing across her face. "One day you will tell me."

If she did, it would be the end of them. She was sure of it. Callie forced a small smile. "Yes." She hoped he couldn't tell she was lying through her teeth, because she didn't want to fight. No, she wanted their reprieve back with a desire that bordered on desperation. So she kept going, words spilling out. "I promise. I'll tell you one day."

He didn't look particularly happy to be put off, but he finally sighed. "I just want to keep you safe."

An impossible need considering their current circumstances—Brendan aside—and they both knew it. She pressed a quick kiss to his lips and settled back against him. "I'm as safe as anyone can be in this world."

"That's what I'm afraid of."

* * *

Teague woke up to find Callie gone. He rolled over, staring at the ceiling, not bothering to check the rest of the apartment. She wasn't here. Their conversation last night had been enough to send her fleeing, and he wasn't sure if he should be pissed or grateful that she'd waited until he was asleep to sneak out like a thief in the night.

He'd almost forgotten that she was keeping things from him, and he couldn't face down a threat he couldn't see. Whoever had put those bruises on her throat was a threat. There was more to it, something he couldn't shake the feeling he was missing…but that might be paranoia talking. Their current situation was enough to create anxiety in even the calmest of people. It could very well be only that bringing the fear into her blue eyes.

But he didn't think so.

It was obvious she wasn't going to open up to him, so he had to try a different tactic. Time to bring in the big guns. He reached for his phone and typed out a quick text to his older sister. *I'll be home in twenty. Need to talk.*

Her reply was almost instantaneous. *I'll be in the attic.*

The attic? Was she hiding up there? Worry he didn't have time for and couldn't afford rose. He hadn't forgotten the increased pressure their father had put on her to make her decision. It seemed like the lesser of the issues they were facing, but it wasn't to Carrigan. He had no doubt that was the fear at the forefront of her mind at all times.

And he'd left her to deal with it alone.

He showered quickly and threw on a pair of jeans and a faded T-shirt. Since it was early on a Friday, there was some small hope that he wouldn't run into his father— or older brother. Teague grabbed his keys, the weight in his chest only heavier with every second that passed. As much as he wanted to rage at Aiden and demand to know when the hell he'd gone and changed, he couldn't do it. Aiden was as much a victim of their father as any of them were. If he had to become a modern version of the man himself to survive... Teague couldn't hate him for that. He just wished it wasn't necessary.

Wishing never changed a damn thing, though.

He made it home in record time, the traffic surprisingly light. But when he shut the car off, he sat there and listened to the engine tick, the heat of the day slowly seeping in from outside. Bringing Carrigan in meant potentially making Callie vulnerable. He didn't think his sister would betray her, but then he hadn't thought Aiden would willingly orchestrate a situation guaranteed to bring them to war. His sister might love him, but would she throw his fiancée under the bus if it meant a measure of freedom for her?

Without a doubt.

He closed his eyes and took a deep breath. Damn it, it was like choosing between the frying pan and the fire. It seemed that no matter where he turned, there was potential danger. He didn't like thinking that his siblings—the only people he trusted in this world—weren't actually worthy of that trust.

A knock on the window had him damn near startling out of his skin. He opened his eyes to find Devlin standing outside the car, watching him with concern. "Are you okay?"

"I'm fine."

"You're not going to roll down the windows and start the engine, are you? Because in a garage this size, I don't think it's possible to actually inhale enough carbon monoxide to actually die."

Against all reason, he laughed. "Thanks for the tip."

"Anything for my most tormented brother." Devlin opened the door. "In all seriousness, what's going on? You look like you have the weight of the world on your shoulders and you just realized that you can't carry it."

That was exactly how he felt. Trust his youngest brother to cut to the heart of the matter. He'd always been too perceptive for his own good. Even though his first instinct was to beg off or make a joke to deflect the whole conversation, Teague found himself telling the truth. It was something that had been happening more and more with Devlin as he got older. "I'm worried. There are bigger things at stake, but Callie is keeping something from me that might be dangerous."

Devlin's dark eyes studied him. "We all have our secrets."

Did he know about Finch? As soon as the thought

crossed Teague's mind, he discarded it. There was no way anyone could know—especially Devlin. But the flicker of unease wouldn't dissipate. "I want to keep her safe. I can't do that if I don't know where the threat is coming from."

"If she's not telling you, there's a reason."

"She doesn't trust me." He'd known that, at least in theory, but saying it aloud seemed to make it real. Callie didn't trust him. He rubbed a hand over his mouth.

Devlin's smile was a little bittersweet. "And what have you done to earn that trust?"

That was the question, wasn't it? He cared about her, but did he trust her completely? Teague climbed out of the car and shut the door. He'd feel better if he knew what she was hiding, but that wasn't a good enough reason to pry the information out of her. Damn it, he was fucking this up. He shook his head. "When did you get so smart?"

"When you have five older brothers and sisters, you learn fast on your feet."

Teague laughed. "I won't pry the information out of her. I promise." It would mean that much more when she finally trusted him enough to tell him the truth. But that didn't mean he couldn't still talk to Carrigan. With his mother in full wedding planning mode, it was only a matter of time before she dragged his sister to ambush Callie again.

"She seems nice." Devlin snorted. "I know that's kind of stupid to say, but it's the truth."

"She is nice." And gorgeous and passionate and smart. Fuck, he really was head over heels for the woman. He didn't know if it was a good sign or a bad one that he didn't care that he'd gone and lost his mind where she was concerned. He opened the back door and led the way into the house. "Do you want to get drinks with us sometime and actually get a chance to have a conversation with her?"

"Yeah, I would. Though don't say that too loudly in here or you'll bring all three of our sisters down on your head, demanding the same thing."

And, just like that, an idea spawned. He grinned. "Devlin, you're brilliant."

"You're not the first to say that." He gave Teague a playful push. "Now go hatch your plans. I have a paper due Monday that I need to work on."

"Better get an A." Another thought occurred to him. "Hey."

Devlin turned. "Yeah?"

"You want to get a beer tomorrow?" He suspected he'd been neglecting his siblings recently, and he damn well knew it for sure when his brother's face lit up.

"That'd be great. I'll let Cillian and Aiden know."

It was on the tip of his tongue to tell Devlin not to, but the truth was he had to face Aiden eventually. And Cillian might drive him up the wall, but he was still family. "Good. We'll go down to Jameson's and have a few beers." He waited for his brother to disappear through the doorway before he made his way up to the attic.

Carrigan looked up from a giant box she was digging through when he climbed up the last step. "You're late."

"I was talking with Devlin."

Her entire expression softened at the mention of their youngest brother. "He's really kicking ass at school."

"Good." Though they both knew he wouldn't get a chance to use that web design major any more than Teague would use the master's degree in business that he was working on in his spare time. "How are you doing?"

She raised her eyebrows. "I'm the same as I've ever been." Which wasn't a damn answer.

He crouched down to peer into the box holding her attention. It was filled with what looked like embroidered handkerchiefs. "What's all this?"

"Mother Dearest has me on a wild-goose chase, looking for Grandma Donaghue's second-favorite blue handkerchief to give to your fiancée for the wedding."

"Second-favorite?"

She shoved her hair back from her face and adopted a stern look and a tone terrifyingly similar to their mother's. "Of course, Teague. We can't be giving that Sheridan girl the best of the best, now can we?" She rolled her eyes. "I've been up here for two hours. Did you know we have *four* boxes this size filled with handkerchiefs? Why in God's name would we need so many?"

They shared a look and said the word at the same time. "History."

Teague looked around the dim attic. "I haven't been up here in years."

"No one has. That's the point of it being an attic. The only things up here are boxed-away memories and maybe a ghost or two." She dug deeper into the box. "But you didn't text me because you were dying to dig through family heirlooms."

No, he hadn't, but he looked around the attic, and couldn't help seeing it as a physical reminder of everything they had to lose. It was entirely possible that

Callie's secret wasn't something that could potentially be a grenade, but he wasn't about to place bets on it. Life was far too willing to rise up and kick him in the teeth for him to hope for the best. "How did things go with Callie last week?"

She sneezed when a cloud of dust rose out of the box. "She's not what I expected, but I suppose I was a little biased. She managed to placate our mother without insulting her, which is something I've never pulled off, so she's smarter than I gave her credit for. Prettier, too."

High praise coming from his sister. "Do you like her?"

She shrugged. "I don't hate her."

He suspected it was as good as he was going to get. "I'd like you to take her out—spend some more time with her. She's going to be family, after all."

"If you're trying to endear her to me, comparing her to family isn't the way to go about it."

He laughed. "*I'm* family."

"My point stands." But she was finally smiling. "But since you are my second-favorite brother, I will see about some sisterly bonding time."

"I appreciate you—" Then he stopped to consider her words. "Wait—second-favorite brother?"

Her smile widened. "You're great and all, but Devlin is—"

"Devlin. Yeah, I get it." He reached into the box and grabbed a scrap of blue that had caught his eye. "Is this it?"

"Oh, thank God, yes." She took it out of his hand and frowned at it. "It doesn't look like much. But, back to Callie, don't worry about it. The girls and I are taking her out tomorrow night."

He sat back. "You already planned this before I asked you to, didn't you?"

"I'm sure I have no idea what you're talking about." She pushed to her feet and dusted off her skirt. "That fiancée of yours is wound too tight. She needs a little loosening up."

Considering he knew exactly what kind of activities Carrigan enjoyed to loosen up, that wasn't comforting in the least. Callie was so restrained and proper—at least outside the bedroom. He couldn't imagine her in the clubs his oldest sister liked to frequent. Not to mention... "You're not taking Keira, right?"

Her green eyes were all innocence. "Keira isn't twenty-one. Would I really take her to a place that might corrupt her innocence?"

"Yes, you would." He crossed his arms over his chest. "And I don't see Sloan volunteering for that sort of thing, either."

"Brother, you constantly underestimate me. It will be as good for Sloan to get out of her shell as it will be for Callie. Now, run along. I have things well in hand."

"That's what I'm afraid of." But he recognized a losing battle when he saw one. Carrigan would do what she wanted, despite his wishes. She always did. The only saving grace of the whole clusterfuck was that his sister had perfected getting in and out of these places without being caught. There was no reason to think her perfect record would be ruined tomorrow. No reason except that nothing had gone right in recent memory. He rose. "Be careful, Carrigan. Please."

She opened her mouth like she was going to deliver a flippant reply and then closed it. "I always am."

It would have to do. He paused to ruffle her hair like he used to when they were kids, her outraged shriek music to his ears. He ducked out of the attic and headed to his room. There was a lot to accomplish today. If he couldn't ferret out Callie's secret, the least he could do was keep pulling at the string of information about the identity of Brendan Halloran's killer.

CHAPTER FOURTEEN

When she'd agreed to spend time with Teague's sisters, Callie had anticipated a spa day or something equally relaxing. She'd said yes because she needed that relaxation desperately. Instead, she was near Fenway Park, being towed through the front door of what looked like a warehouse. She glanced at the two younger women who'd been introduced as Keira and Sloan—more sisters—but they didn't look the least bit surprised to find themselves in a club packed with gyrating bodies with music so loud she could feel it in her blood.

Carrigan led the way around the dance floor and up a set of rickety-looking stairs. She grinned at the man guarding the top, leaning forward to speak directly in his ear, her hands resting on his chest. Callie couldn't hear his laugh, but she was grateful when he stepped back and allowed them through the door. Inside, it was moderately quieter—at least the point where she could almost hear herself think. She turned to Carrigan. "This isn't what I had in mind."

"Maybe not, but it's what you need." She turned and strode over to the bar on the back wall, manned by a woman who could barely be seen over the counter.

"Why don't you sit down? You look a little shell-shocked." Keira guided her to a U-shaped couch built into the wall. It afforded a small amount of privacy, more than she'd expected because this room was only half-full.

She shot the woman a look. "Are you even old enough to drink?"

"My ID says I am." She gave a cheeky grin and dropped down next to Callie, dragging Sloan behind her. "This is great. Carrigan never lets me tag along when she slips her leash."

Things started to fall into place. This wasn't about her at all—this was about Carrigan. She couldn't even blame the woman for using any excuse she could come up with to find a legitimate escape from the gilded cage she lived in. Callie knew all about that, being how she was trapped in one of her own. She relaxed back into the seat. She'd been considering making her excuses and getting out of here, but it was the least she could do to stick around for a little while longer. She might not be free in any sense of the word, but it wouldn't hurt to let these other women have a little taste of it.

Carrigan reappeared with four shots in her hands. "Let's start this night off right."

Oh dear God, this is going to go sideways fast. But she'd already decided to stay, so she took the glass and held it gingerly between her fingers. Carrigan sat across from her, next to Sloan. "Here's to the men who love us, the losers who have lost us, and the lucky bastards who have yet to meet us."

Keira laughed. "Hear, hear!"

They took their shots, and Callie didn't miss the sick look on Sloan's face. Apparently the woman wasn't much of a drinker—or a partier, since she looked a half a second from bolting. It was enough to make Callie want to hug her, or offer some meaningless words of comfort. Carrigan must have noticed as well, because she put her arm around her sister in a half hug. "I know this isn't your choice of a good time, but you need to stretch your boundaries a little."

"For real, Sloan. You're in danger of becoming that weird sister in the attic who only haunts the halls at night."

Callie started to smile, but the expression died when she realized neither of them were joking. There were emotional undercurrents in this conversation that she barely understood, so she kept silent and watched it play out.

Keira jumped to her feet. "I know just the thing to get out of your funk. Come on, let's go dancing."

"I don't—" The rest of Sloan's words were lost when her younger sister yanked her to her feet and through the door leading back the way they'd come.

Carrigan sat back and crossed her legs, making the tiny dress she wore ride up to indecent lengths. "Sisters."

There was so much meaning and history in the word. "I always wanted one." Though she'd been happy tagging along behind Ronan on his many adventures when they were children, she'd always longed for someone who would rather play dolls than sword fight with sticks.

"They're both a blessing and an enormous pain in the ass." Carrigan shrugged. "But the same could be said for most families."

The bartender appeared, two drinks in her hand. She set them on the little table between them and disappeared before Callie could get out a single word of thanks. She picked up the glass, examining the mix of bright colors. Her first sip found it pleasingly sweet and fruity. "This is good."

"Miami Iced Tea. It only takes two to get your head into exactly the right kind of place." She drank deeply with great relish.

In that case, Callie was going to have to be careful. She didn't drink often enough to build up the kind of tolerance necessary for both the shots and mixed drinks, and she didn't trust this situation enough to indulge freely. "Good to know."

"My brother likes you, you know."

She knew, but hearing it still made her entire body go warm. "I like him, too."

"Good." Carrigan took another drink. "Because if you hurt him, I will have no problem taking you into a back alley and cutting your heart out." It was delivered in exactly the same careless tone that she'd said everything else, and for a long moment Callie was sure she'd misheard her. But then the woman turned those pale green eyes on her and she knew she had it right. As ruthless as Teague could be on occasion, he didn't have anywhere near the degree of cold that his sister obviously possessed. Then Carrigan blinked and the look disappeared, replaced by a light, teasing expression. "Do you dance, Callie?"

"Yes." She answered without thinking, still marveling at how completely the woman went from icy to warm, and how little effort it seemed to take. This was a person who wore masks with such regularity, there was no telling what she was really like.

Though Callie would bet the cold threats were closer to the truth than the carefree smiles.

"Perfect. Finish your drink and let's go join my sisters before they get into trouble."

She took a sip before she realized she was obeying. "If you're worried they'll get into trouble, why did you bring them here?" Maybe she should have begged off on this outing as soon as she realized what they planned. Though her father had always taught her that recognizing a threat was important, and she couldn't shake the feeling that Teague's older sister was exactly that.

Carrigan's grin was downright wicked. "Sometimes a little trouble is good for the soul."

* * *

Carrigan slid into the mass of dancing people, feeling like she was coming home. In here, surrounded by strangers, with the music so loud there was no chance of conversation, it didn't matter that she was an O'Malley or that her future was less than certain.

She was blissfully—if temporarily—free.

She dragged Callie behind her and worked her way toward where she'd seen Sloan and Keira from the balcony above. They'd been directly in the middle of the seething mass—something she suspected was her youngest sister's doing, because God knew Sloan wouldn't set foot on a dance floor without being forced. She'd much rather find a relatively quiet nook and watch the drama going on around her than to actually participate in them. Well, that was too damn bad, because tonight she was participating whether she wanted to or not.

People were packed in like sardines, making it a struggle to get through, but she relished the contact. It seemed like the only time she got touched was when she was out here and surrounded by strangers. She always managed to convince herself that she didn't need it, but then she'd slip her cage and prove herself a liar on the dance floor. The truth was she was well and truly skin-starved.

It was enough to make her do truly foolish things.

They found Keira first, her arms above her head, her eyes closed as her hips moved to the grinding beat. There were no less than three men around her, circling like sharks. Carrigan cut through them and wrapped her arms around her, laughing as she pulled her away from them. She glanced over to where Callie had found her other sister and towed her to safety as well.

Carrigan let go of Keira and crossed to Sloan. She leaned in close because she wanted her sister to actually hear. "Are you okay?"

"Mostly."

She might actually be okay, or she might be saying the right words so as not to make waves. Carrigan leaned back and looked her over. She was a little pale and her eyes were a little wide, but she wasn't searching for the exits. "If you want to leave, just tell me. I'll make sure you get in a cab safely."

"I'm fine. Go dance. You need this more than I do."

The truth was a bitter pill stuck in her throat. She *did*

need this, and she was just selfish enough to drag her sisters and Callie into it in order to justify coming here. Actually, selfish didn't begin to cover it, but she wasn't going to apologize. For all the love her siblings bore her, there was no one in this world who'd put her happiness and emotional needs above all others. That was her responsibility and hers alone. If she had to be a selfish bitch to meet those needs, so be it.

She checked on Keira and Callie, but they were fine, both dancing with grins on their faces. So her brother's fiancée could let loose. Good. She'd seen Callie's face when she talked about Teague. The woman was over the moon for her brother, and as happy as that made her, she couldn't kill the little sprout of jealousy that rose. Teague would finally get his happiness, and he would finally stop trying to take his sisters away and save them from this life. It had been a vain hope in the first place, but she still mourned its death. But it just reinforced her belief that no one would take care of her except *her*.

"I'll be right back." She didn't wait for Sloan's response before slipping through the crowd, taking her time working her way to the bar on this level, pausing to dance with this man and that and then moving away before they realized she was leaving.

The bar itself was nothing fancy—a counter of faded wood that kept the masses from getting to the wall of liquor on the other side—but it fit the club itself perfectly. She leaned over, trying to catch the bartender's eye, dipping down a little more than necessary to flash him a generous slice of cleavage.

"Good luck. I've been waiting for fucking ages."

She glanced over and froze, her breath stalling in her

lungs. The man who spoke was big enough to give even her brothers pause, and had an air about him that promised more danger than she could possibly handle. It wasn't his plain white T-shirt or faded jeans that gave that impression, and even his short, scruffy beard and long blond hair wouldn't make her give him a second look. No, it was blazingly apparent in every line of his body, in the way he held himself as if ready for a fight to break out at any second, and the way his cold blue eyes searched the room for a threat before finally landing on her again, making her treacherous heart skip a beat.

This man was danger personified.

And she wanted him.

Carrigan leaned against the bar, taking her time looking her fill. The stranger sure knew how to fill out a shirt, and the clean-cut clothing only accented his rugged looks. He would be perfectly at home on a Harley if she had to guess. A biker. Her mouth practically watered at the thought. She leaned in to him under the pretense of wanting to speak, taking the opportunity to run her hand up his chest. Yeah, he was more cut than a damn diamond. "Hey there."

He moved back enough to search her face. Whatever he was looking for, he must have found, because he closed the distance, his short beard scraping against her cheek as his lips brushed her ear. "You look too classy for this joint."

"Looks can be deceiving."

"I sure as fuck hope so." His hand settled on the small of her back, a slight nudging that she could have resisted easily. She didn't. Instead, she let him guide her closer yet, until the front of their bodies pressed against each other. The fabric of her dress was so thin, it might as well not have existed. She could almost feel the calluses on his palm, and she resented the hell out of the barrier.

"You want to take this somewhere more...private?"

His laugh rumbled in her ear. "You read my mind."

A quick glance at the dance floor showed no sign of her sisters or Callie, but she had no illusions that they wouldn't come looking for her if she was gone too long. So she wouldn't be gone too long. She grabbed the stranger's hand and led the way back toward the bathrooms. Bypassing them, she tried the door to the old, unused storage closet. He raised his eyebrows, and she shrugged. "The lock's been broken for years, and the owner's too cheap to replace it."

"It's enough to make a man wonder how often you make the trip back here."

She smiled, even though the comment stung. It didn't matter what this man thought of her. He didn't know a damn thing about her life or what she went through on a daily basis. She was entitled to getting her freedom where she could find it. "And yet it's benefiting you, so maybe you shouldn't ask too many questions."

"You're right. I need this tonight."

Before she could wonder at his words, he was on her, dragging her against his big body and taking her mouth like there was no question of it being his. She opened to him out of reflex, half expecting some sloppy drunk fumbling, but he only tasted faintly of whiskey.

And there was nothing sloppy about the kiss.

He tasted her mouth, seeming to sample her before he groaned and *took* her. His tongue clashed with hers, demanding something she wasn't sure she could give.

Her head spun at the sheer unexpectedness of pleasure coursing through her body, brought on by the feel of him against her and his intoxicating taste in her mouth. He guided her back to the bare wall and pinned her there. She was so lost in the kiss, she didn't realize his hands were moving until one slipped up her dress and yanked her panties off. They hit her knees and then he was parting her, slipping a finger inside.

Holy shit.

He kissed down her throat, still working her with his finger, relentlessly shoving her toward an orgasm. She tangled her fingers in his hair, not sure if she was pushing him away, pulling him closer, or simply hanging on for the ride. He used his free hand to slide her dress off her shoulders, and then his mouth was on her right breast, his teeth against the sensitive skin as he worked his way to her nipple. A second finger joined the first between her legs, and she couldn't stifle her whimper.

The stranger looked up, his blue eyes glinting in the near darkness. "You're close, lovely, but you're not coming until it's on my cock."

Her mouth worked, but no words came out. He slowed his fingers' movements, sliding up to circle her clit. Her entire body tightened at the touch, reacting even as her mind tried to catch up with his words. They were so...possessive. There was no room in her life for another possessive and dominant man, even for such a short time as this.

But then he kissed her again, and she threw caution to the wind. It was one night. She'd never see him again. She never even had to know his name. He broke away, his hands withdrawing from her body. "I'm going to fuck you, lovely. If that's not what you want, now's the time to speak up."

In answer, she went for the button on his jeans, and carefully drew down the zipper. A condom wrapper crinkled as she took his cock into her hand, the feeling of it bringing out another whimper. He kissed her neck, moving her hand so he could roll on the condom. "I love that fucking sound. It makes me crazy for you."

She wasn't sure she'd ever made that sound before. Every other time she'd sought escape in the arms of a stranger, *she'd* been the one in control and driving things. There was no control to be had tonight. He lifted her, spreading her legs, pinning her against the wall so she was helpless to do anything but take whatever he chose to give. "Last chance."

"Oh my God, just fuck me already."

His white teeth flashed in a grin. "Your wish is my command." He shoved into her in one movement that stole her breath, stole her thoughts, stole her very soul.

Before that thought could truly terrify her, he moved again, sliding in and out of her, rolling his hips in a way that hit that sensitive spot. Normally, she had to come at least once before she could orgasm from penetration alone, but he had her primed and ready before he ever brought his cock out. And now...

Now her body sparked with pleasure, promising an orgasm to end all orgasms.

She started to reach for him, but he shook his head. "Arms above your head. I want to see you."

He couldn't see more than shadows...could he? It didn't matter, because the command stripped her bare in a way that had nothing to do with the physical. She obeyed.

"There's my girl." He started moving again, slower this time. "You're so hot and tight around me, lovely. And that whimper? Fuck, I could spend hours coaxing that sound from those sweet lips. Would you make it again if I went to my knees for you and sucked that sensitive little clit into my mouth?"

The pleasure that had been building with each stroke exploded at his words, and she shrieked. The sound barely escaped her mouth when his hand was there, muffling her cries as he closed the minuscule distance between them and kept fucking her, drawing out her orgasm until all she could do was cling to him and take it. He came with a curse, grinding against her, and nearly sending her over the edge again. "Damn."

She slapped his shoulder. "Let me down." That had been too intense, too possessive, just too damn much. She hadn't signed on for this quaking through her body when she'd offered to bring him back here. Her life was already enough of a mess without some stranger pulling at her in ways she didn't know how to cope with.

He didn't move. "Tell me your name first."

"No." She wiggled, but she wasn't getting anywhere with him wedged between her thighs on one side and the concrete wall on the other. Against all reason—and her better judgment—the thought sent a bolt of heat directly through her. Part of her didn't want him to let her go.

Which meant she had to get the hell out of here. *Now.* "Let me go."

"Your name, lovely. I can stay here all night." He thrust a little and, to her horror and traitorous desire, she could already feel him hardening in her again. Part of her wanted to keep silent and go another round, but panic reigned supreme. This hadn't been the escape she was hoping for. No, this man made her feel branded—like she was *his*.

If he could do that after a single time, she didn't want to know what he could do after two.

So she answered him. Anything was better than being held in his power a second longer. "Carrigan." It never even occurred to her to lie, but as soon as the name was out of her mouth, she regretted it. It was yet another mark of the way this man was different from the others, and she didn't need the reminder.

"Unique name. I feel like I've heard it…" His eyes went wide and he backed up so fast, she would have fallen if he hadn't closed the distance just as quickly and caught her. "No fucking way. You're Carrigan O'Malley." He cut in before she could say anything. "Don't bother denying it. You've got the same coloring as Teague. I would have noticed it sooner if it wasn't for the eyes."

She pushed against his chest, gaining a few precious inches. "Who the hell are you?"

"Well, lovely, I'm a token of your shitty luck tonight." What she could see of his expression in the low light made her heart go cold. "I'm James Halloran. And you're coming with me."

"No!"

"You don't have a choice." He moved faster than she could have anticipated, throwing her over his shoulder. She shrieked as he opened the closet, sure someone would hear and come investigating, but the music drowned the sound out. Beating at his back didn't do a damn bit of good, either.

He pushed open the side door, the chill night air shooting straight up her short dress. She screamed again—out here at least, there wasn't the music to contend with—and struggled harder. It didn't matter. His arm was a band around the back of her thighs, sealing her to him. He started jogging, the bouncing driving the air from her lungs and preventing another cry for help.

She heard a man call his name and then he dumped her in a trunk. Carrigan shoved her hair out of her eyes, in time to see something like regret on his face before he slammed the trunk closed, leaving her alone in the darkness.

CHAPTER FIFTEEN

Sweat dripped down Callie's body, and her muscles shook from dancing for so long. She glanced at Sloan and Keira, and found them both flagging as well. How long had they been out here? She touched both their arms and jerked her chin toward the bar. They nodded, looking as wilted as she felt. Wilted and happy. Threats from Carrigan aside, apparently she'd been right—Callie needed this more than she'd needed a spa day. Out in the middle of the dance floor she was just another woman with no past and no future, the music driving every single thought and worry out of her mind.

But now it was time to come back to earth.

They made their slow way to the bar, and Callie looked around, trying to pick Carrigan out of the people standing there, and came up with nothing. She turned back to yell in Keira's ear, "Where did Carrigan say she was going?"

"She didn't. Hold on." Keira trotted over and flagged

down the bartender. They spoke over the bar for a few minutes, and then she trotted back. "Carrigan was here, but she left with some big, blond guy. I'll text her and we'll just meet her back at our place."

Callie frowned. The woman had seemed far too protective to just up and leave her sisters to fend for themselves, especially when she so clearly didn't trust Callie. "Are you sure she left with a man voluntarily?" There were more dangers now than there had ever been. She cursed herself for letting Teague's sister out of her sight.

"Oh yeah." Keira grinned. "They were practically making out here at the bar and *she* was the one leading the way when they left."

Small mercies, though it didn't reassure her as much as she'd like. If Carrigan was safe, then she was incredibly selfish to abandon them like this when it was her idea that they come here in the first place. She took a deep breath, and wrinkled her nose at the overwhelming scent of sweat and alcohol. "Let's get out of here." Both women nodded, so she led the way through the front door and hailed a cab.

The silence pounded against her ears much the same way the music had. She shook her head. "That was fun."

Keira grinned. "The funnest. I'll have to blackmail Carrigan into bringing me along next time she goes."

"Keira." Sloan sighed and typed away at her phone. "I let her know we left." She seemed to sink into the worn seat of the cab, as if it had taken all her energy to get through the night and now she was done.

The rest of the ride passed quickly, Keira filling the silence with chatter about the songs and the club and the men she'd been far too interested in for Callie's state of mind. She knew the girl was eighteen and legally an adult, but she couldn't shake the protectiveness. Keira was just so fresh faced and young in a way Callie hadn't felt in too many years to count, despite not being that much older than her. Innocence was something to be protected in their world because it came around so rarely.

The sisters poured out of the cab and stopped before shutting the door. Keira smiled. "I'm glad my brother is marrying you. You two are good for each other."

It didn't matter that she'd come up with that decision after a night of their barely talking—it still made Callie's chest warm. "Thank you."

Keira danced away, singing the last song they'd danced to. Sloan hesitated. "She's right. Teague takes too much responsibility for everyone around him. He needs someone to look after him as much as he looks after all of us."

The warmth in her chest spread, quickly doused by reality. "I'll do my best."

"I know you will." And then Sloan was gone, following her younger sister into the house.

Callie rattled off the address to her home and sat back, feeling like she'd just lied through her teeth. She *did* want to keep Teague from danger, but it was her fault that he was in danger to begin with. Worse, he was looking for her and didn't even know it. She rubbed a hand over her chest, but it did nothing to stop the ache starting there. Last night they'd shared something. They'd talked—really talked—and he'd brought her to heights she hadn't thought possible and held her afterward like she was the most precious thing he'd ever possessed.

And she was lying to him.

The cab stopped on her street and she paid the driver before stepping out into the night. The cool air felt heavenly on her heated skin, but her reprieve that had come from the dancing was over now, and her worries were all too eager to come crashing back in. She still had no idea what she was going to do, and every day that flew by brought the increased risk of someone getting killed because she was too much of a coward to turn herself over to the Hallorans.

She dialed her phone before she could think better of it. It barely rang twice before Teague picked up. "Hey, angel. How are things going with my sisters? They haven't made you reconsider saying yes at the altar, have they?"

"No." She laughed a little. If she were any less selfish, she'd tell him the truth and accept the consequences, but she couldn't make herself give Teague up. She could pretend it was because she didn't want to hurt him, but it wasn't the truth. If he knew what she'd done, he'd never look at her the same, and she couldn't stand the thought of never seeing that wonderful combination of heat and caring in his eyes. "I just dropped Sloan and Keira off safely at home."

"Did you have fun?"

It said something that he didn't ask where Carrigan was. Maybe she was paranoid to be worried about the woman—none of her actual family seemed that concerned. "Yeah, I actually did."

"Good." The noise in the background almost drowned out the approval in his voice.

"Where are you?" The question was out before she could think better of it.

"Down at a pub with my brothers." He hesitated. "I didn't realize how much I needed this time with them until I got it."

She'd known he cared for her—he'd have to be a liar of exceptional proportions to treat her the way he did and *not* care—but she appreciated each small vulnerability he revealed almost more than the outstanding sex. Because he was allowing her inside, and she'd been around him enough to know he didn't do that with just anyone. Callie smiled. "I'm glad you're getting it, then. Go have fun. You need it."

"Come out with me tomorrow. Let's get out of town for a few hours. Maybe go down to New York."

She smiled. "That sounds like heaven."

"Then it's a date. I'll see you tomorrow, angel."

"See you tomorrow. Be safe."

He laughed. "Always."

* * *

Teague hung up the phone and turned to find Cillian mocking him. His brother froze, and then a slow grin spread over his face. "Man, you are so pussy whipped, it's almost cute."

"Fuck off." He dropped back into his seat and eyed the shots that had been delivered while he wasn't paying attention. "More shots?"

"Shots are what real men take when they're not calling their girlfriend every five minutes to check in."

Aiden leaned over and casually slapped the back of Cillian's head. "Now's a good time to stop talking."

They raised their shots, all grinning like fools. He wasn't sure when they all grew so busy that they had no time for each other, but it had been longer than he could remember since they did anything like this, anything *to-*

gether. Teague took the shot, the whiskey barely burning his throat. "We should do this more often."

Cillian started to make some smart-ass comment, but Devlin cut in. "We should."

"If you can leave that college you love so much long enough to come hang out with us." Cillian laughed, a little too loudly. "College is meant to be enjoyed, little brother. You go for the women, the parties, and the sheer self-indulgence. You don't go seriously."

"No, that's what *you* do in college." Teague snorted. "How's that degree in accounting treating you?"

"Hey, I like numbers. It was the easiest major I could pick that got our father off my back." Cillian leaned over and gave him a stern look. "All I need are some sexy-ass glasses and I'd make a wicked accountant."

Given his trendily tousled hair, ridiculously expensive suit with the brightly patterned tie, and tattoos, Cillian couldn't look further from the old man who did the family's books. But he was right that their father wanted to pad the future with family in every way he could—including setting up one of his sons as bookkeeper to keep every responsibility in-house that he possibly could.

"Unlike you, Devlin's in college actually making something of his life." Aiden swiped at Cillian halfheartedly. "Some of us take things more seriously than you—and by some, I mean all of us."

"Asshole."

"You know it."

Devlin took a drink of his beer. "The only difference between us is that I like school."

"Nope." Cillian shook his head, and then did it again like he had water in his ear. "No, they're right. I enjoyed fucking around, and I had a whole hell of a lot of fun, but you're actually going to go on and accomplish something."

Well, shit. They were in danger of getting morose. Teague elbowed Cillian. "You're never *not* fucking around."

"Damn straight."

"Then we toast." Aiden lifted his beer, his eyes a little glassy. "To those of us who fuck around. And to Devlin, the best of us all."

Teague and Cillian raised their glasses, blatantly ignoring the embarrassment on their youngest brother's face. "To Devlin."

Of them all, Devlin had the best chance to be as free as anyone could be in their family. There were five siblings between him and the position of heir, and he wasn't female to be traded to an allegiance. It would take some arguing, but he could probably convince their father to let him get a job doing something he'd truly love.

Aiden slouched in his seat, his back popping. "Someone has to get out, Devlin. It might as well be you."

"You say that like all your future is set in stone. It isn't." Devlin set his beer back on the table, untouched. "You can change things. All of you can."

The only changing going on these days was for the worse. Aiden was turning into their father, Teague was almost drowning in a war he couldn't seem to get ahead of, and Cillian...Well, with Teague married and safely positioned for the glory of the O'Malley clan, their father would turn his gaze onto the next eldest child. Cillian's days of freedom were nearly at an end, even with his plans to step up and take over the family books.

He hadn't realized he'd spoken aloud until Cillian laughed, sliding sideways in his chair. "That just means I have to enjoy life to the fullest before it all starts crashing down around me."

Devlin shook his head. "You're hopeless. All of you. What happened to our sticking together, to us versus the world? You sound like you've given up."

"And you sound like you haven't been drinking nearly enough." Teague peered into his brother's beer. It blurred for a moment before snapping into focus. "Are you *sober*?"

"Someone has to be there to make sure you lot don't end up lost and passed out in a back alley."

Teague turned to Aiden. "You hear that? He's not even drunk." Hell, *he* shouldn't have drank so much tonight— he hadn't planned on it when he'd agreed to this—but the nostalgic feeling of being surrounded by his brothers had made him careless. He shook his head. "What time is it?"

"Time for you to get a watch." Cillian snickered. "God, I crack myself up."

"That's because you're an idiot." Teague flicked a peanut shell at him. He glanced at his phone and grimaced. It was well after one in the morning. "We have Mass in seven hours."

They all exchanged looks. Cillian shrugged. "Not like I haven't shown up hungover for Mass before."

"There's a difference between showing up hungover and showing up still drunk." Aiden rose, wobbled a little, and then straightened. "I'll take care of our tab."

"I guess that's that." Cillian drained his beer and stretched. "I've got to use the pisser."

Teague watched him stumble off. "Our brother is a serious winner."

"Leave him alone. We each deal with this stuff in our own way."

That was the damn truth. It just seemed like stress, and their family bullshit didn't touch Cillian the way it did the rest of them. But what did he know? He and Cillian had never been particularly close—responsibility weighed on Teague too heavily and his younger brother too lightly for them to do more than aggravate the hell out of each other. He glanced at Devlin. Maybe he was right. "How'd you get so smart?"

"I learned from the best." He grinned. "Now, let's get you home so you're not a mess for your woman tomorrow."

They'd specifically picked a pub they could walk back from, though he wasn't sure the few blocks would be enough to sober them up before they got there. Teague collected Cillian and handed him off to Aiden. The walk through the brisk night air would hopefully balance out the short distance before they actually reached the front door. His mother didn't bother to yell at them, but she could send all four of them to their knees with a look of profound disappointment. "I'd like to be able to do that someday."

Devlin looked over. "Do what?"

"That thing our mother does with her face when we've screwed up."

Aiden snorted. "Good luck with that. She's had an entire lifetime to perfect that look." He cursed when Cillian swerved and started singing "Kiss Me, I'm Shitfaced" at the top of his lungs. "Damn it, shut up. You'll get the cops called on us for sure."

"That's *sure* to get us the look from Mother." Teague

laughed. Headlights cut through the night, blinding them. Devlin yanked him back onto the sidewalk, waiting for the truck or whatever it was to drive past.

Except it didn't.

A car door opened in the sudden silence of the night. Behind him, Aiden cursed, but Teague still didn't get it...until a man stepped in front of the headlights, a gun in his hand. *Shit.* He backpedaled, keeping a death grip on Devlin's arm. He was vaguely aware of Aiden doing the same thing with Cillian, but he couldn't tear his gaze away from the man. "Don't do this." He raised his voice. "This is a mistake."

"The mistake is yours, fuckers."

The first bullet tore into the brick next to him, surreally loud. He dropped to the ground, dragging Devlin with him, cursing himself to hell and back for not getting them a damn cab. The shots kept going for what felt like an eternity, but was most likely a few seconds.

A second voice joined the first. "Let's get the fuck out of here."

"I need to—" A footstep in their direction.

"*Now.*"

The door slammed and the SUV peeled out, flying down the street just as sirens cut through the night. Teague slowly pushed himself up. His ribs hurt like someone had dealt him a vicious blow to the chest, but nothing felt worse than bruises. "Aiden?"

"We're good."

"Thank Christ."

A low groan brought his attention around to Devlin. He frowned. "You okay?"

Another groan, this one eerily wet sounding. It took

his brain a second too long to process what he was hearing. He crawled to Devlin's side, nearly falling over himself in his hurry. "Devlin?"

He lay on his back, his hands clutching his chest. Teague lifted one, finding it soaked with red. "Fuck, fuck, fuck. Aiden!"

His oldest brother was there in a flash, covering Devlin's hands with his own and pressing down. "9-1-1, Teague, now."

His fingers, slick with blood, slid over the screen of his phone. Teague had to take a deep breath, wipe them off, and then dial. He gave their location and information to the operator and then tossed the phone to Cillian. "Keep talking."

Teague dragged off his shirt. "Here, use this."

They moved Devlin's hands and put more pressure on the wound. In the streetlights, his eyes looked strange and glassy, like he wasn't seeing them at all. His hands fluttered against Teague's, the little spasms ripping his heart to shreds. "Hang on, just hang the fuck on. The ambulance is coming."

"Cillian, tell them to hurry the fuck up!" Aiden's hands joined Teague's. "Devlin, it will be okay. It's got to be okay."

The fear and dread in his brother's voice hit Teague almost as hard as the blood now trickling from the corner of Devlin's mouth. He took one last wet gasping breath, and then lay still. "No. No, no, no, no, no." He stopped clutching the now-soaked shirt and lifted his youngest brother's head. "Stay with us. Goddamn it, Devlin. No!"

This couldn't be happening.

It had to be a nightmare. In a second he'd wake up,

shudder at his overactive imagination, and reassure himself that reality would never be so cruel.

Except he didn't wake up.

Red and white lights flashed over Devlin's still face, and then Teague was pulled away by men in white uniforms. He struggled, fighting off their hands. "Not me, *not me*. Help Devlin."

A third man looked up from where he knelt, his fingers against Devlin's neck. "I'm sorry. There's nothing we can do."

Teague's legs went out from under him, and he slumped to the ground. "Where were you? Why didn't you get here quicker?"

One of the paramedics shook his head. "We got here in record time—" His partner stopped him with a hand on his arm.

Aiden dropped next to Teague. "I . . ."

"I know." He couldn't stop looking at Devlin, half expecting him to sit up. The sound of throwing up finally made him tear his gaze away, only to find Cillian puking in the street. That got him moving—anything to hold off reality for a little while longer. He knelt next to Cillian and put his hand on his back. "It's okay."

But it wasn't. He couldn't shake the feeling that it'd never be okay again.

Tears streamed down Cillian's face. "He's gone. Goddamn it, it wasn't supposed to be like this. Not *Devlin*."

Not Devlin. The only one of them who might have actually succeeded in getting free. Not Devlin, the kindest, smartest man he knew. No, not even a man. He was barely twenty. He couldn't even legally drink yet. His life had been laid out before him, there for the taking.

Now he was gone forever, snuffed out in a war that wasn't his.

Cillian's head hung between his shoulders, hiding his expression. "It was the Hallorans."

"Not now." He couldn't deal with talk of the future, not when their entire present was being systematically ripped to shreds. Something occurred to him. "Someone has to call our parents."

And tell them Devlin was dead.

CHAPTER SIXTEEN

It went off without a hitch."

Callie sat next to Papa while John gave his report. There had been significant damage done to the Hallorans' property, no casualties, and they slipped away into the night before the Hallorans showed up to investigate. She leaned forward in her chair. "The night guards?"

"We incapacitated them like you ordered."

Her breath left her in a nearly inaudible sigh. *Thank God.* The attack had been a necessary evil, but getting a low-level guard killed for no reason would have weighed heavy on her conscience. They had parents, possibly even children. They didn't deserve to be dragged into this. In an ideal world, no one would die before they got this conflict resolved.

But this wasn't an ideal world.

She cleared her throat. "Well done."

"Get some rest." Papa waited for the man to leave the office before he turned to her. "You were right."

Pleasure at his approval threatened to go to her head. He'd never withheld it from her growing up, but it had always been something she strived for. She didn't let it guide every choice she made these days, but the need to make him happy was always there in the back of her mind. "There are more ways to hurt someone than taking their life."

"Halloran doesn't feel that way. He'll strike back, and he'll strike back to hurt." He suddenly looked tired, the lines around his mouth and eyes deepening. "Stay close, Callie. I couldn't bear it if you..."

One more reason she couldn't turn herself over to the Hallorans. If something happened to her, the last of her father's children, it might actually kill Papa. She covered his hand with her own. "I'll be careful, but you know as well as I do that I can't hide away in the house like a princess in a tower. This won't be the last conflict, and the men need to see that I can lead."

"I know. Good lord, Callie, I know that." He pinched the bridge of his nose. "You're more than capable of leading, but I'm human. I want to protect my daughter."

"I understand." But there were no guarantees. Papa knew that. It had been decades since the Sheridans warred with another family. All she remembered of it was her mother taking her and Ronan out of town and a wonderful summer spent in the country. She hadn't understood then the new lines around her father's face when they'd returned.

She did now.

She squeezed his hand. "It won't be like before." It

wasn't a promise she could make, but that didn't stop her. Last time, he'd systematically killed the head of the MacNamara clan, and all three of his grown sons. She couldn't allow him to make that decision again. He had enough deaths on his soul.

Hell, *she* had enough deaths on her soul, and they totaled out at one.

But she would add as many as it took to save her father from more—and to save Teague from adding any at all. She glanced at the clock on Papa's desk. It was approaching noon and she still hadn't heard from him. Worry flickered through her, but she firmly ignored it. When they'd spoken last night, it was clear he was drinking with his brothers. It was entirely possible that he was sleeping off an epic hangover. There was no reason for the hairs to be rising on the back of her neck. She pulled her hair over one shoulder, combing her fingers through in it in an effort to distract herself.

"You're strong, Callie. You'll get through this."

"We both will," she said firmly. She was nowhere near ready to take over the family. The sheer amount of responsibility her father shouldered on a daily basis was staggering. She could do it. She knew she could. But it meant her father was no longer strong enough to do it himself. She wasn't ready to acknowledge that, even if he was.

Her phone vibrated in her pocket. "Excuse me." She slipped it out, finding a text from Teague. Three little words, but every cell in her body cried out in warning that something was terribly wrong.

I need you.

It was tempting—too tempting—to act like he was

talking in a physical way, but instinct said that wasn't the case. Something had gone terribly wrong. She typed out a quick reply. *Where and when?*

His answer confirmed her worry was founded. *My parents' home. Now.* Callie pushed to her feet. "I've got to go."

"Is something wrong?"

Yes! She made an effort to keep her voice calm and her body relaxed, even though all she wanted to do was tear out of the room and rush to Teague's side. "I don't know."

Papa nodded. "Take Micah and one of the other men with you."

"I will." It wouldn't slow her down much, and the added safety was necessary, even if only to get her to Teague's side without interruption. She pressed a kiss to the top of her father's head and strode from the room. It took seconds to grab her purse and text Micah to meet her in the garage. He was there before she was, dangling the keys from the SUV from his fingers.

"Do you want to drive, or should I?"

She was so rattled, it was entirely possible she'd end up wrecking the damn car. "It'd be best of you do. But, Micah, drive *fast*."

He nodded and opened the door for her. Another man, one of the new recruits whose name she couldn't quite place, slipped silently into the backseat. No one said a word as Micah pulled out of the garage and onto the street.

Callie took a deep breath. "To the O'Malleys'." She kept checking her phone, but there was nothing new from Teague. She resisted the urge to text him again and ask what was going on. Barely. She'd find out soon enough.

That wasn't nearly as much of a comfort as she'd have liked it to be.

She shouldn't be remotely surprised that the O'Malleys' home was on Beacon Hill. They might not be able have a legitimate claim as Boston's elite, but they certainly reeked of new money parading as old money. Still...

She stepped out of the SUV, unable to stop herself from feeling intimidated. The front door towered over her, seemingly ready to gobble her up the moment she missed a step, the tree-lined street giving every brownstone an aura of hushed secrecy. She tried to dismiss the feeling as pure fancy, but she couldn't quite shake it. She looked at Micah.

He frowned. "Don't even think about it. We're going in with you."

It might be cowardly to feel the level of gratitude flowing through her at his words, but she had no idea what she was walking into. She didn't *think* she'd be in danger from anyone in the O'Malley family, but she couldn't be sure. And, because she couldn't be sure, she allowed Micah and the other man to fall in behind her as she climbed the steps to the massive door and raised her hand to knock.

It opened before she made contact. Considering the sheer size of the house and how it brought to mind old money, she half expected to see a butler. But it was Keira who stood there, her hazel eyes bloodshot and her face red and swollen from crying. "Callie."

That was all the warning she got before the girl threw herself into Callie's arms. She looked over her head at Micah, who shrugged. Apparently he was done helping.

She smoothed down Keira's dark hair, trying to breathe around the stranglehold she had on her ribs. "I'm here. What's going on?"

"It's so horrible." Her body shook. "It's Devlin. He's…"

She didn't need to finish the sentence for Callie to understand. She knew this grief, recognized it on an intimate level. Shock nearly sent her to her knees. *No. Oh no, no, no.* She hugged the girl tight. "I'm so terribly sorry."

Keira only cried harder, her entire body a giant clench as she lifted her head. It only took one look in her eyes to realize this was surface reaction. There was a part of the girl who hadn't caught up with the news yet and, when it truly hit, the results would be devastating. And it could happen at any time. Callie gently guided her into the house. "Where is everyone?"

"The living room." She sniffed.

"Can you show me?"

"Yeah." Keira straightened her shoulders, and Callie could actually see her drawing her walls around her. It was slightly terrifying to watch. The girl had lost the shine of innocence that she'd had only last night. Now there was a hardened, brittle feel to her that made Callie's heart ache.

In this world, everyone had to grow up sometime, but she hated that this happened to *any* of them—especially to the starry-eyed girl who'd danced and laughed and had the time of her life just twelve short hours ago.

She followed Keira through the house, taking in the dark woods and deep green on the walls. This place practically screamed masculine power, and the feeling of being swallowed whole came back with a vengeance. *This* was the place Teague had grown up in? She couldn't begin to imagine children playing in these halls, or getting into the kinds of trouble that only young kids seemed to find. It was all so... uptight.

Her home was a similar size, but aside from Papa's office and the single room they kept spotless to receive important guests, it felt more lived in. Comfortable. It was the kind of place where a person could prop their feet up and relax. Exactly the opposite of this place. She glanced down at the floor, half-sure she'd tracked dirt all over the spotless wood floors.

She was focusing on the house so she didn't have to think about the scene she was going to walk into. She knew that. It was easier dealing with the decorating than with what was coming. Teague's brother... Old hurt rose, no less potent for the months that had passed. *Oh, Ronan.* She knew all too well what the people in this house were feeling right now, and there was a very large part of her that wanted to turn on her heel and get out of here as fast as she could run. She didn't want the memories, didn't want the grief, didn't want the tears.

But Teague needed her.

She lifted her chin and kept her steps steady as they turned a corner and approached a pair of double doors. Raised male voices gave her pause. She recognized Teague's, even through the fury and pain it held. "This is what you wanted, Aiden. War. Are you happy now?"

"This isn't what I wanted." This voice was quieter, but no less full of poisonous emotions. "This was *never* what I wanted."

"That's what war is. Death of the people you care about. I swear to God—"

Keira opened the door. The room was large with soulless—and no doubt horrendously expensive—art covering the walls and a carefully arranged set of white couches dominating the space. Not that anyone except Sloan was currently utilizing the furniture. She sat with her knees pulled to her chest, her gaze a thousand miles away. There was another man—a brother if his similarities to Aiden were any sign—standing well back, a bottle of what looked like whiskey in his hands.

And there was Teague, standing toe to toe with his older brother and looking ready to go several rounds. He stopped when he saw her, his dark eyes containing so much pain, she was helpless to resist going to him. She stepped into the room, and glanced over her shoulder to keep Micah and his partner out. He nodded, though he didn't look happy about it. Callie turned back to find Teague directly in front of her.

She reached out to touch him, but hesitated. He didn't appear as brittle as Keira, but that didn't mean he wasn't. Before she could decide whether to make contact or not, he took her hand and pulled her into his arms.

"You're here."

She hugged him like he'd fly apart if she let go. "I'm here."

He stepped back, but took hold of her hand. "Aiden, we're not done."

The man he'd looked about ready to come to blows with dropped onto the couch across from Sloan. "I figured."

Teague nodded and led her out of the room. He didn't say a single thing as they passed through yet more halls, finally climbing a narrow set of stairs and slipping into a room that must be his. She didn't get much chance to look around, because he shut the door and then she was back in his arms, his hold so tight, she thought she heard her ribs creak. "What can I do?"

"Just hold me." His voice was thick against her temple. "I need a few minutes."

"Okay." She could do that. Words wouldn't do a single thing, but if this gave him any kind of comfort, she was more than happy to hang on to him until night fell and reality called. He nudged her back to the bed in short little steps and sat down, pulling her into his lap.

"It was my fault."

She tensed. "It couldn't possibly be."

"Cillian was drunk. We all were. I thought it'd be brilliant to walk home." He sounded like a man kissably close to rock bottom. "They caught us less than two blocks from the pub."

Her heart stopped. "They?" Even as she asked, she knew what the answer was. She'd been a stupid fool not to consider it before. If something happened to Teague's youngest brother, there was one likely culprit. God, she never hoped she'd be wrong so much as in that moment.

"The Hallorans."

She closed her eyes, the weight on her shoulders threatening to crush her. If Teague was looking for someone to blame, he had to look no further than the woman in his arms. *Her fault.* Her actions had put this whole thing into motion, and now his little brother's death was on her hands.

If Teague found out, he'd never forgive her.

She wasn't sure she'd ever forgive herself.

* * *

The tide that had been drowning Teague since he realized Devlin would never follow through on his many dreams retreated slightly with Callie in his arms. It wasn't gone. He knew that. He didn't *want* it gone. To move on his with life as if nothing was wrong would be unforgivable. There was a gaping hole in his chest and it didn't show signs of closing anytime soon.

He closed his eyes and inhaled Callie's rose scent. "Devlin was…" His throat tried to close.

She hugged him tighter, careful of his bruised side. "You don't have to talk if you don't want to."

"I know. I want to. I need to…" He didn't even know. His life hadn't been untouched by pain up to this point, but calling what he was feeling pain was a gross understatement. There was an abyss inside him that had never existed before, ready to swallow him whole.

She nodded against his chest. "You want to remember him how he was in life, not how it ended."

"Yes." That was it. That broken, bloody body wasn't his brother. Everything that made Devlin *Devlin* fled the moment he took his last breath. *Fuck, this never should have happened. I should have protected him, gotten him and the girls out of town and safe until I knew the danger had passed.* The wound in his chest pulsed in agony, the abyss opening wider. He'd been damn near cocky, sure that he'd find the identity of Brendan's killer before something terrible happened.

The price he paid for being wrong was too high.

"I'd do anything for a time machine to take me back a week."

"I know." The quiet grief in her voice snapped him temporarily out of his spiral. Because she *did* know. She'd lost her brother less than a year ago. It hadn't been in violence, but that really didn't make a difference when someone so young was suddenly gone, taken too soon.

"Does this feeling ever go away?"

Callie shifted. "There will always be bad days, I think. Days where you wake up and forget that he's gone, and then the realization hits and it's every bit as bad as what you're feeling now. But there will be good days. At first they're so few and far between it's like they don't exist at all, but then one shows up and it's this soft ray of sunshine in the midst of a hurricane. You barely notice it, and then it's gone. And then, sometime not too long after that, another one shows up, and another, until the balance shifts and you have more sunshine than storm."

The sheer amount of time he'd be forced to deal with this feeling was nearly overwhelming. Teague closed his eyes and took a deep breath. Devlin deserved it. He deserved to be mourned. Life couldn't just go on as it had before, with only the slightest of hiccups. "He'll never finish his degree. He'll never get to backpack through Europe and have that great adventure he'd been dreaming of since he was a kid. He'll never fall head over heels in love with a pretty girl and lose his heart. He'll never have kids."

She leaned back and framed his face with her hands. "I know there's nothing I can do to make this right, Teague. I am so terribly sorry."

There was a strange weight to her words. He looked into her blue eyes, trying to understand it. "This has to be answered, angel. You understand that?"

Her eyes shone in the low lamplight. "There's nothing we can do to stop it now, is there?"

"No." Part of him howled for blood to repay the loss of Devlin's future. It didn't matter that James used to be a friend. His brother was dead, and that demanded retribution. The other part of him? It just wanted this to end. Devlin's death was horrible—he didn't know if he'd ever fully recover—but if more of the people he cared about died?

If *Callie* died?

"Marry me." He didn't realize he was going to say the words until they hung in the air between them.

She blinked. "Excuse me?"

"Marry me." When she still looked uncertain, he plunged ahead. "I wanted to wait until this was over, and get a real fresh start with you that wasn't tainted by this war brought on by our fathers and a situation outside our control." Her expression flickered, but she didn't say anything, so he kept going, "But it's not going to end. There will always be the next conflict, or something showing up to drag us deeper, whether we want it or not. I care about you, angel, and I'd never forgive myself if I spent another day without us being husband and wife."

Her mouth opened, closed, and opened again. "That was some proposal."

"It was the best I could come up with on the fly." He kissed her, soft and sweet. "Marry me, angel. Tonight."

"There's a three-day waiting period to get a marriage license." She sounded uncertain, but not panicked.

"I know a judge." He smoothed his thumbs over her cheekbones. "Say yes."

She hesitated still. "This won't bring Devlin back, Teague."

The loss rose up, ready to swallow him whole. There was no fighting it, no resistance strong enough to keep it at bay, even in Callie's presence. He took a shuddering breath. "I know. I wanted to marry you even before this happened. This just made me realize that I can't take the future for granted. There's no guarantee of tomorrow, not even for us." He shifted her off his lap and went to one knee before her.

"Teague—"

"Marry me, angel. Today. Right now." He took her hand. "Say yes and I'll spend the rest of my days doing my damnedest to protect you from harm and make you happy. I'm not perfect and I'll fuck up, but say yes and I'll never hesitate to apologize, and I sure as hell won't ever lay my hands on you in anger. Just *say yes.*"

She pressed her free hand to her mouth. "Yes." At first, he was sure he'd misheard her. But then she nodded, her eyes shining with unshed tears. "You're right. There are no guarantees but...I want your ring on my finger and you in my life for as long as we're granted. Not because of your family or my family or consolidating power or any of the other reasons that originally drove us to agree to this marriage. I want you, Teague. I *choose* you. "

CHAPTER SEVENTEEN

James stalked through his house, ignoring the way his conscience seemed to dog his heels. The time for regrets and second-guessing had passed. His fucking idiot of a brother had solidified that when he'd decided to prove his worth by killing one of the O'Malleys. There was no taking that back, even if James never would have given the order himself. It didn't matter that he'd planned on using O'Malley's oldest daughter as leverage to stop this shit in its tracks.

O'Malley's oldest daughter.

Carrigan.

He turned the corner, picking up his pace when he heard male voices in the room he'd left her. Goddamn it, nothing was going right. He threw open the door, finding Ricky and two of his men circling Carrigan where she was cuffed to the chair. James didn't like the look on their faces one fucking bit.

Ricky leaned in, close enough to touch. "I killed that piece-of-shit brother of yours. I shot him down in the street."

Fuck.

She flipped her hair, hitting him in the face. "Liar."

He jerked back. "Bitch, I'll show you—"

"*Enough.*" All four of them froze, and James didn't blame them. He barely recognized the growl as his own voice. It sounded like it'd come from someone else.

From *Brendan.*

Before that realization could really freak him the fuck out, he strode into the room. "You three, get out."

Ricky leered, though he didn't look nearly as confident as he had two minutes ago. It was all a song and dance for his boys—show no weakness—just like their old man taught them. But he was scared of James now. "I'm just giving the bitch what she deserves."

Don't call her that. He clenched his teeth to keep the words internal. "Get Out."

Ricky hesitated, and finally laughed. "You want her first. I get that. But me and the boys want a turn when you're done."

What the hell had happened to his sweet little brother who needed protection? He didn't recognize this man— this monster. But then, James barely recognized his own reflection in the mirror anymore. Brendan's death had changed all of them for the worse.

It didn't matter, though. Brother or not, the only way Ricky would lay a hand on Carrigan was over James's cold, dead body. He waited, letting that truth seep over his little brother's face. Ricky's eyes went wide, and he practically scrambled out of the room.

The door shut, and James sighed. He'd pay for this later, just like he'd paid for taking the whip to his brother's back. Maybe Ricky still would have gone after the O'Malleys personally...but maybe he wouldn't have. He finally looked up to find Carrigan watching him. She didn't look particularly afraid, which would be what he'd expect of a woman held captive by her enemies.

No, she looked furious.

"You have me here, so what's the plan? A little torture, maybe with some rape thrown in for shits and giggles." Her voice didn't waver, and hell if he didn't respect her for it. She must have been terrified out of her damn mind, but she wouldn't show a single slice of weakness that could be used against her. It had to cost her to keep it hidden—he of all people knew the cost of keeping that kind of thing locked down.

"No." He moved around behind her to check the cuffs. They were tight enough that she couldn't squeeze out, but they weren't rubbing her wrists raw. He fished the key out of his pocket and unlocked them. He couldn't leave her here, because he couldn't afford to be here with her every second of the goddamn day, and it was glaringly obvious that he couldn't trust her with anyone else. "Come on."

"Thanks, but I'm good."

He ignored her, hauling her to her feet by her upper arm. It felt wrong—so fucking wrong—to manhandle her when he couldn't get those stolen moments at the club out of his mind. James shook his head, as if the motion could dislodge the feeling of her clenched tight around his cock.

It didn't help.

He wanted her again, more than he'd wanted any

woman he'd ever been with. It didn't make a damn bit of sense, but even having his hand on the bare skin of her arm was enough to have his body roaring to life. Only ironclad control kept him from showing exactly how deeply she affected him.

She was the one woman he couldn't have.

He marched up the stairs and threw open the door to his room. It was the only place in the house that he'd guarantee no one would fuck with when he wasn't around, so it was a solid choice. But he couldn't shake the almost primal satisfaction of seeing her surrounded by everything *his*.

Damn, he was losing it. He had to get his head on straight, because one fuck—even as mind-blowing as it'd been—didn't change a thing. She was the daughter of the enemy, and he'd just kidnapped her. There was no possibility under the sun in which she didn't hate him.

Carrigan walked farther into the room, and he couldn't help noticing exactly how little that tiny excuse for a dress of hers covered. It barely touched the bottom of her ass, and that curve was enough to make what little blood was left in his brain course south.

"Stop staring at my ass." She stopped next to his dresser, seemingly fascinated by the shit thrown across the top.

He crossed his arms over his chest. "Does your daddy know you leave the house dressed like that?"

She snatched the lamp off the dresser and spun. James barely had time to register to move when she threw it at his head. He got his arm up just in time to take the blow but, fuck, that hurt. Carrigan wasn't done, though. She snatched the heavy ashtray he used to keep change in and flung it at him. "My *daddy* is going to skin you alive when he finds out what you've done." A boot hit him in the shoulder. "And I'm going to enjoy watching."

That was enough of that shit. He caught the second boot and dropped it just as she grabbed the second heavy lamp on the opposite side of the dresser. "Don't you fucking dare."

"Or what?" She brandished it, moving a step closer. "You're going to hurt me? Please. I know how this works, *James*. It's going to happen anyway."

He hated that she said his name with such venom, but he wasn't about to become her whipping boy—deserved or not. "Drop it."

"I don't think I will." She swung it at his head.

He caught her wrist and wrenched the lamp out of her hand. "Christ, just stop."

"Just lie back and take it, and it'll be over soon? Not fucking likely." She fought harder, trying to break away, but he wasn't about to let her get access to more shit to throw at him. James dragged her to the bed and tossed her onto it. He cuffed her hands to the headboard before she had a chance to hit him again.

It was only then that he registered exactly how terrified she was. He froze, taking in the little shudders working their way through her body and her too-wide green eyes. "Carrigan—"

"Just do it, okay? Just . . . get it over with."

He jerked back. "I'm not doing shit."

Her eyes were full of accusations and her anger practically crackled against his skin. "You have me here and helpless. You don't have to play that role anymore."

"I'm not playing a role." Even if he felt like it more

often than not in the last few days. "No one is touching you." He'd fucking kill them if they did.

"Whatever you say."

It bugged him that she didn't believe him, like a piece of sandpaper beneath his skin, scratching away every time he breathed. "You're safe here."

She laughed in his face. "And you're obviously delusional. I'm not safe." There was something in her words, something that made him wonder if she was talking about this specific situation or in general.

There was nothing he could say to change her mind. Hell, he didn't blame her for expecting the worst. He knew the reputation his old man had for prisoners, especially when he wanted to prove a point. It didn't matter their gender, either.

But he still found himself wanting to reassure her. "Carrigan." He waited for her to meet his gaze. "You're safe here. I swear it."

She turned her face away. "You know better than to make promises you can't keep, Halloran."

* * *

Callie kept telling herself that it was time to come clean. Saying "I do" to Teague without his knowing about Brendan was selfishness of the highest order. There was no way he'd marry her if he knew the truth.

But she couldn't make herself say the damning words.

She wanted everything she'd said before. She wanted Teague. He'd been with her every step of the way through this nightmare, even if he didn't know the full story, and he'd proven time and time again that there was no better man in the world out there for her. She couldn't let that go. She cared about him too much.

She wasn't particularly proud of that realization.

She knew how she'd feel if the fault of Ronan's death had been laid at the feet of anyone else. There was no forgiveness. Not for that. She might not have been out for blood, but she would have effectively cut the responsible party off from everything they cared about. She would have done her best to break them. She couldn't expect Teague to react any differently, no matter how much her very heart cried out that she could trust him. She'd been responsible for his brother's death. It didn't matter if it was indirectly or not.

He opened the door for her, his dark eyes filled with things unsaid. "Are you ready?"

No. She opened her mouth, ready to spit the damning words at his feet, but then he kissed her. Teague's lips moved against hers as if she was his last bastion of hope in a world gone mad. She clung to him, trying to keep from losing herself. It was a lost cause. Her control always was when it came to this man. She would do truly unforgivable things to keep him at her side. She was proving that right now.

Selfish. Stubborn idiot. Coward.

Teague rested his forehead against hers. "This is the only bright spot in the clusterfuck we're currently neck deep in."

Just like that, all her good intentions went up in smoke. She couldn't walk away from this man, even if she wanted to. And she desperately didn't want to. She'd deal with the fallout when she was forced to, and not a moment sooner. She pressed a kiss to his cheek. "Shall we?"

"Definitely. I'm not giving you a chance to get cold feet." He took her hand as she slid out of the car and shut the door behind her. "The judge already signed the paperwork, so we're good to go."

They walked into the courthouse. Callie had been here a few times over the years, but it felt different now. She would be walking out the doors as a married woman. Trying to wrap her head around that fact just gave her a headache. So she didn't think about it. There were far too many things she tried not to think about these days.

She occupied herself with filling out the paperwork, and then they were being ushered back to say their vows. The dim little room wasn't anything like she imagined their families had wanted for them. There was no bouquet, no family, no elegant white dress. She wouldn't dance with her new husband, staring up into his eyes and feeling her heart full nearly to bursting with love. It was strangely fitting.

Teague repeated his vows after the minister, his gaze never leaving hers. His thumb stroked soothing circles on her knuckles, as if he knew exactly where her mind had gone. He finished with, "Till death do us part."

Now it was her turn. She spoke her vows through numb lips, unable to summon even the smallest reassuring smile for him. Marrying Teague was what she wanted, but the fear that worked its insidious way through her threatened to send her to her knees. *He will never forgive me*. Her last words came out as barely more than a rasp.

The minister moved on, his voice so monotone, he could have been reading from a phonebook. He did manage a smile as he pronounced them husband and wife, but it was a cynical one. He patted them on the shoulders. "Good luck."

Callie blinked. That was...uplifting.

She let Teague tug her over to where Micah and Emma stood in the first row. Emma's eyes were shining, but her son didn't look any happier now than he had been when Callie first asked him to stand as one of the witnesses. He shook Teague's hand, but his attention was solely on her. "Your father isn't going to be happy."

"I know." But, as much as she didn't want to hurt Papa, she refused to let anything stand in the way of their doing this today. Her father most certainly would have objected. She turned to Emma and took her hands. "Thank you for being here."

"I can't believe it. I knew you were all grown up but..." She wiped a tear from the corner of her eye. "Your mama would be proud of you, and your papa will be fine."

Words tried to stick in her throat. She doubted her mother would be proud of any of the things she'd done, but marrying a man she cared about in the courthouse instead of having a fully Catholic wedding was the least of her sins. "Thank you, Emma."

Teague's arm settled around her waist. "We should go."

She nodded. "Micah, we're going to Teague's apartment." He'd proven his loyalty to her time and time again. She wasn't going to compromise it further by running off with her new husband and making Micah search for her.

He nodded once and then stood with his mother and watched them walk out of the room. She was half-sure she felt his gaze on the back of her neck even after the door closed between them, but it was most definitely her guilt talking. They made their way through the building and out into the light. She couldn't breathe any better out here, despite the fact that there were no walls to close in around her. She pressed a hand to her chest.

Oh God, what have I done?

"Angel?"

She looked up, the tired happiness on his face grounding her further. This was why she'd agreed to marry him—she'd never met a man who made her feel so incredibly safe and wanted and cared for. No matter how twisted up inside she felt, she wasn't simply going through the motions for the sake of their respective families. She wanted Teague as her husband. She just flat-out wanted him.

That was it. The one thing guaranteed to quiet her mind and silence her worries. She *chose* him. It made all the difference in the world. She stopped next to his car. "Take me home, Teague."

"With pleasure." He held the door open for her and moved quickly around to slide into the driver's seat. There was no need for words—especially when she didn't trust herself not to say something she couldn't take back the second she opened her mouth—but she slid her hand back into his.

The trip passed far too quickly and not quickly enough. There was so much left unsaid between them, even beyond her confession that she never quite managed to actually confess. He turned the car off. "It will be okay, angel."

It was a false comfort, and they both knew it. She gripped his hand too tightly, but she couldn't make herself loosen her hold on him. "I'm afraid." Those words cost her, but she fought to get the rest out. "This isn't over, Teague. I feel like it's just getting started." *All my fault.*

"I won't let anything happen to you."

It wasn't lost on her that he'd just lost a brother and *he* was comforting *her.* God, this was pathetic. She had to get herself together. She was better than this. She had to be. "It's not just me that I'm worried about."

"I know. We'll put a stop to this. I promise."

Words. They were just words. They shouldn't have the ability to calm her when she knew that he had as little control over this situation as she did. No matter what happened tomorrow, they had tonight. It would be enough. It had to be. She tried for a smile, but it felt broken on her face. "Are you going to carry me over the threshold?"

"Of course."

The trip up to his apartment door was a blur. Now that they were so close to being able to shut the door between themselves and the rest of the world, she moved more quickly, needing to surround herself with him. Teague swept her into his arms and opened the door in one smooth move. He kicked it shut as soon as they were through, leaving them bathed in the shadows of his apartment.

And then he just stood there, looking at her like she was the most precious thing in the world to him. "I'm going to be the best damn husband to you that I can be, angel. I can't promise you much else with all the bullshit going on, but I can promise you that."

He meant every word. Teague wouldn't hesitate to put himself between her and the rest of the world. She fisted her hand in the front of his shirt, her heart beating too hard. *I love this man.* As if just waiting for her mind to come to terms with the realization, the feeling swelled inside her, filling her completely, making it hard to breathe.

I love him.

She couldn't say the words aloud. Not yet. But she could show him.

So she kissed him, slipping her tongue between his lips the second he opened for her. He didn't miss a step on his way to the bedroom, until he stopped next to the bed and let her body slide against his as he set her on her feet. He tangled his hands in her hair and tipped her head back, taking control of the kiss, gentling it to the barest brushing of their lips, as if he fully intended to take his time.

As if she was priceless.

She shivered. She wasn't priceless. She wasn't...He nipped her bottom lip, effectively bringing her back to the present. "Stay with me, angel."

"Always." A promise she couldn't make, but this was the day for them. She unbuttoned his shirt, going slowly, relishing the way his chest felt beneath her fingers. The bruises looked better today. He was healing. He'd be okay. Thank God. All too soon she was at the waistband of his slacks.

His hands caught hers. "Not yet."

She didn't get a chance to argue, because he bent to unzip the side of her dress and then pulled it off, leaving her in only a pair of white panties. Teague's breath hissed out. "A month or a hundred years, I'll never get tired of seeing you like this." He traced a finger down her sternum, the look in his eyes stealing her breath. "Angel, I don't deserve you."

It was *she* who didn't deserve *him*. She opened her

mouth to tell him as much, but he hooked his finger in the top of her panties and towed her to close that last inch between them. The feeling of her skin against his chased every thought from her head. She let herself run her hands up his chest, marveling at the muscles that tensed beneath her touch. She stopped at the tattoo over his left pectoral, a twisting oak whose roots worked down his side and whose branches covered his shoulder. "Will you tell me about this one?"

"I'll tell you about anything you want." He kissed her again, backing her to the bed and gently laying her on the mattress. "After." He moved down her body, stopping to pepper her breasts with almost worshipful attention. She dug her fingers into his hair, simultaneously wanting him to do more and never move, all at the same time. He sucked her left nipple into his mouth, raking it gently with his teeth.

"Oh God."

He chuckled against her skin, and her entire body went tight as he pulled her panties off and settled between her thighs. "Do you know how much time I spend thinking about doing this to you?"

"Tell me," the command escaped before she could think better of it, but she was so happy it did the second he started talking.

"You *consume* me, angel. It's the most welcome kind of distraction, but I can't get through an hour without thinking about you. Thinking about this." He dragged his tongue over her center, circling her clit.

She thought about it, too. But more than the sex, she thought about *Teague*. Callie closed her eyes and gave herself over the feeling of his tongue driving her closer and closer to orgasm. In this moment, she didn't have to make decisions about the future. She didn't have to contend with the riot of feelings in her chest, all centering on this man. She didn't have to do anything but *feel*.

With one last long lick, he drew back, a smile spreading over his face at her involuntary sound of protest. "Impatient."

"Tease." She watched him unbutton his pants and shove them off. He grabbed a condom from the nightstand and rolled it on, his gaze on hers. She shifted, her skin too tight, her body feeling like it was a thousand degrees. "Come here."

"With pleasure." His weight between her thighs was almost comforting. Or it would have been if she wasn't so desperate to get him inside her. Teague didn't seem in any sort of hurry, though. He kissed her as if he had all night, as if he didn't have an inferno of desire inside himself demanding more.

Callie hooked her leg around his waist, angling her hips so his cock notched in her entrance. He pulled back a little, giving her a look, but she needed him too desperately to keep playing this teasing game. Another time, perhaps, when it didn't feel like they were living on borrowed time that could be stolen from them without warning. "Please, Teague. I don't want to wait anymore."

He pushed into her in one smooth move, bringing them as close as two people could possibly be, stealing her breath and her heart along with it. "Anything for you, angel." He moved, drawing out almost completely and then starting that slow slide back to completion. All the while, he cupped the back of her neck, and slid his other arm beneath the small of her back, bringing them impossibly close. Every stroke brought her closer to the edge, rubbing against her clit even as he filled her in the most perfect way possible.

She clung to him, wanting to draw this out forever. But her body wasn't listening. Her orgasm crested, and it was all she could do to ride it out in his arms. He kept moving, drawing out the feeling until she was sure she couldn't take it any longer.

Then, and only then, did his strokes become staggered and he followed her over the edge, burying his face in her neck as he came. He slid to the side and tucked her against him. "I'll never get tired of that, either."

Against all reason, a laugh escaped. "I'd say that's a good sign since you just married me." It wasn't real yet, probably wouldn't be for some time, but she liked the way the words sounded. She liked the idea of Teague as her husband even more. She lay with her head on his shoulder and listened to his heartbeat as their bodies cooled. "Will you tell me now?"

He glanced at her. "The tattoos? Sure."

She shifted off him so she could see the tree in its entirety. She'd seen it before, of course, but it was different now. Now there was time to truly *see* it. She traced the twisted branches that tangled from the trunk and over his shoulder. "Oak?"

"Good eye. It's family. Strong and rooted deeply."

That sounded sweet, but she stopped on the scar bisecting the tree. "And this? Did this come before or after the tattoo?"

He hesitated, and she once again wondered if it was his father who had hurt him. From everything she'd learned of Seamus O'Malley in recent weeks, she didn't doubt he was capable of it. But…to raise a hand to his son? Let alone what must have been a blade? It took a special kind of monster to deal out that kind of violence. She curled her hands into fists, trying to quell the sudden anger coursing through her system. You don't hurt the helpless and innocent. You just don't. For someone who supposedly held family above all things to do it…She wanted to hurt that man. She wanted to hurt him badly. "You don't have to tell me."

"No, I want to." He covered her hand with his own. "My father isn't a good man. He didn't like the fact that I mouthed off to him when I was thirteen, so he decided the best way to deal with my attitude was this." A shadow passed over his face. "It was just one cut, and not a deep one at that, but I never forgot. That's the other side of family. It can be strong enough to stand in the face of any enemy that arises, or it can be the rot that eats away at your insides, weakening you until you're little more than a shell. Both tattoo and scar are reminders of that."

Oh, Teague. She kissed the scar, because there was nothing else to do. If a time machine existed to allow her to save him from the hurts he'd experienced at the hands of the man whose one purpose in life should have been to protect him, she would have taken it in a heartbeat. But it didn't.

There was nothing she could change but the future, and even that wasn't a sure thing.

"The ones on my knuckles are my siblings." He waited for her to look up before he pointed to each in turn. "Aiden, Carrigan, me, Cillian, Sloan, Devlin, Keira."

Her gaze landed on the one representing him. A flame.

She knew that specific flame. She'd seen it before. "Saint Jude?"

He grinned. "Yeah."

Which meant the other symbols represented saints as well. She touched each in turn. It was such a different way to go about representing a family that he obviously had very conflicting feelings about. But he loved them. That couldn't be any clearer. She stopped on his bare ring finger. "This one?"

"Well, angel, I left that one blank because I figured someday I might meet a woman I cared about enough to marry." He rolled back on top of her, grinning. "That one's yours."

Mine. She kissed him, the riot of emotions in her chest only getting worse. She loved him so much it hurt to breathe. He took the kiss deeper, his hands sliding over her skin in a way designed to make her lose her mind. As he slipped a finger inside her, she had one last thought before pleasure bore her away.

Maybe he's right. Maybe things really will be okay.

CHAPTER EIGHTEEN

The phone ringing brought Teague out of a delicious dream about being wrapped around Callie. He opened his eyes and smiled because the dream wasn't far off from reality. She was curled up against his side, her head pillowed on his shoulder. He touched her hair, smoothing it back, marveling that she was his wife. It had been an impulsive move, but he didn't regret it in the least.

The phone rang again, snapping him out of it. He reached blindly for the nightstand and answered without looking at the screen. "What?"

"Where the hell are you?"

Aiden. He almost snapped that it was none of his brother's fucking business, but the panic in Aiden's tone gave him pause. "My apartment. What's going on?"

"Get your ass back here now. Carrigan's gone."

For one breathless moment, Teague thought he meant

dead. Then the actual words penetrated through the fear. "Gone."

"That fucking piece of shit Halloran has her." Aiden paused, and when he spoke again, he sounded forcibly less panicked. "He said we have twenty-four hours to turn over Brendan Halloran's murderer, or they'll kill her like they killed Devlin."

Teague sat up. His first instinct was to deny that James would go to those lengths, especially when he knew Teague was already looking for the woman who shot Brendan. But, as much as he wanted to like James, he couldn't trust the man with his sister's life. The years had a way of changing people. He hadn't expected the Hallorans to gun down Devlin. He couldn't afford to underestimate them again.

"I have some leads." He slipped out of bed and yanked on his pants.

"What?"

"You might be totally okay with putting our family in jeopardy in a grab for power, but I'm not. I started looking into Brendan's death as soon as I saw which way the wind was blowing." He stepped out of the bedroom, closing the door softly behind him. "I know it's a woman. She was dressed as a stripper, but none of the other girls in the club knew her."

"That's not enough."

"No shit." He closed his eyes. "Devlin…" His voice cracked and he cleared his throat. "Devlin managed to get his hands on security tapes from the gas station across from the back entrance. I haven't had a chance to look at them—"

"Bring them. We'll look at them together."

Teague released a breath he hadn't realized he'd been holding. He hadn't wanted to touch those tapes. Not alone. They felt like his last link to Devlin. It was a stupid feeling. His brother's life was about more than just computer work. But it was the last thing he'd done before he died. The wound was too new, too raw, for Teague to be able to poke at it without hurting.

But he could do it with Aiden.

"Okay." Teague never thought he'd stand with his older brother after learning Aiden wanted this god-damn war. The time for finger-pointing and the blame game was over. They'd both lost a brother. It didn't make what Aiden did right, but there was only one man who ordered that hit. Halloran. He might as well have pulled the trigger himself. It didn't matter if it had been James or Victor or even that little shit Ricky. That hit wouldn't have gone down if one of them hadn't given the go-ahead.

"Aiden..." It was harder than it should have been to say what he needed to say. "This isn't your fault. I know I said it was, but—"

"Teague."

He stopped. "Yeah?"

"As much as I appreciate the thought, it's not up to you to absolve me of this. It's not something *anyone* can." The guilt was so thick in Aiden's voice, it was hard to make out his words. Teague wanted to comfort him. He wanted to say that it was bullshit and that Aiden couldn't have known what would happen.

He didn't.

Because his brother was right. Aiden had known the risks in putting Teague forward as a candidate to marry

Callie, and he'd still gone ahead with the plan. Maybe their father had been the deciding factor, but Aiden had supported him. He bore the guilt for that. Hell, they all bore guilt over this. If Teague had been faster with the investigation, maybe he could have stopped them from killing Devlin. If Aiden hadn't helped orchestrate an O'Malley-Sheridan alliance...If anyone had stopped to think that Victor Halloran might not take the insult lying down...If, if, if...

No one could go back in time and save Devlin, no matter how much they all wanted to.

But they could save Carrigan.

"I'll be home in twenty."

"Good."

Teague hung up and turned to find Callie standing in the doorway to the bedroom, dressed in only his sheet. The concern on her face said she'd heard enough to be worried. "What's going on?"

It was tempting to tell her that nothing was wrong and keep her from worrying, but she deserved to know. She was as much a part of this as he was. "Carrigan's been taken by the Hallorans."

She went pale. "Have they...?"

"She's alive." Aiden hadn't said what kind of condition she was in, and Teague had been afraid to ask. He knew the reputation the Hallorans had as well as the next man. The thought of his sister in their hands...Fuck. He'd failed Devlin. He wouldn't fail Carrigan. "I'm going to save her. I have to."

Callie nodded. "Of course. If they haven't...They must want something."

"The identity of Brendan's killer." He scrubbed a hand

over his face. "They gave us twenty-four hours to do damn near the impossible."

If anything, she got paler. "So if you find his killer, it will put a stop to this?"

"That's what they claim. I don't know if I believe them, but I'll do whatever it takes to save Carrigan."

She crossed to him and wrapped her arms around him. "She'll be safe, Teague. I promise."

They seemed to be making a whole hell of a lot of promises that neither one of them were capable of keeping. That didn't stop him from hugging her close and kissing her forehead. "I've got to go."

"I understand. Go. I'll shower and call a cab."

She started to step back, but he wasn't ready to let go of her yet. He couldn't shake the feeling that if he walked away now, it would be the last time he ever saw her. Teague grimaced. All the bad shit that had happened lately was skewing his perspective. Callie would go back to the Sheridan residence, where she was as safe as she could be. He cupped her face. "Don't make any stops along the way."

Her smile was as bittersweet as the feeling taking up residence in his chest. "Go take care of your family, Teague. I'll do what I have to."

He kissed her. "I'll see you soon."

"Definitely."

He walked back into the bedroom, threw on a shirt, and grabbed his keys. "Call me when you get home safely."

"I will."

There was something off in her tone. He hesitated, searching her face, but all he saw was a soul-dragging sadness that mirrored what he'd felt for the last twenty-four hours. A small voice warned that this was a mistake, that he should drive her home himself, but with the clock ticking down, he couldn't afford the wasted time. No matter how much he wanted to. "Be safe." He kissed her one last time and walked out the door.

* * *

Callie took her time dressing. She moved on autopilot as she called a cab and waited for it to arrive. All the while her thoughts circled in upon themselves. She kept coming back to one hard truth.

I am the only *one who can save her.*

If she turned herself in, it would put a stop to everything. No one else in Teague's family would be hurt. He'd never be put in a position where he had to choose between her and them. Callie climbed into the cab and closed her eyes as it lurched into motion. It might kill her father to lose her. That was one of the many factors that had bought her silence on this. But Papa's feelings weren't enough to hold her back now. There were too many people at risk. What was one life when weighed against five? Or ten? Or twenty? Not enough.

Not even when it was hers.

"Ma'am?"

She opened her eyes to find the cabbie parked out in front of her house. She must be more out of it than she'd thought, because time wasn't passing correctly. She paid him and stepped out onto the sidewalk. The air was clean and brisk and made her think of home. This was the house she'd grown up in. All her good memories were rooted here, and no small amount of bad ones, too.

And this was the last time she'd walk through the door.

It was tempting to get back in the cab and go straight to the Hallorans. Too tempting. She couldn't do it, though. She'd been a coward this entire time. If she was going to step up, she was going to do it right. She would say her good-byes. She would face the firing squad wearing something other than the clothes she'd had on yesterday. And she would do it with her spine straight and head held high.

It took entirely too little time to shower and change, but she refused to linger in her room. If she stopped moving, she'd falter, and that was unacceptable. She made her way down to her father's office, mentally preparing herself and going over what she'd say. She was so focused on the impending confrontation that it took longer than she'd like to admit to realize the room was empty.

There was no time to search for Papa.

She sighed and circled around the desk to write him a note. The pen was heavy in her hand, but she forced the words out. They weren't the right ones, but there were no right words for this situation.

Papa, I am so terribly sorry. I was the one who killed Brendan Halloran. This war is my fault, and it has gone on far too long. I'm going to set things right. I love you, and I hope someday you can forgive me.

There was more, so much more, but she made herself set the pen aside and walk to the door. She paused for one last glance at the room where there'd been so many father-daughter talks. Papa was strong. He'd survived Ronan's death. He'd survive hers. She had to believe that.

Oh my God, I don't want to do this. She shoved the thought down deep, wishing she could do the same with the fear making each step harder to take than the last. Turning herself in didn't mean a clean death. If it did, maybe it would be less terrifying. The Hallorans would make an example of her. She knew what that would entail, every excruciating detail of it.

Callie didn't want to die. Not when she'd finally started to *live*.

She moved through the house, pausing to touch photos here and there. The one that caught and held her attention was one of her and Ronan, taken barely a month before he'd died. He had his arm around her shoulder and they were both grinning at the camera like fools. It had been one of the last carefree moments of her life. She touched it. *I'm finally doing the right thing, Ronan. It might not be what you'd have chosen and it might have taken me far too long to get around to, but I'm going to make things right.*

Her fingers itched to dial Teague, but what would she say? That this was all her fault and she'd spent all this time with him and never told him the single damning truth that might make him hate her? That she wasn't the woman he thought she was? She didn't know if she could stand to hear the caring leach out of his voice and be replaced by a cold stranger.

And if it didn't happen?

If he somehow miraculously forgave her...

She'd be putting him in the position of having to choose between her safety and the safety of his entire family and everyone they protected. And no matter which way he chose, he'd bear the guilt for the rest of his life. She loved him. She couldn't let him shoulder any more than he already did.

No, this decision was hers and hers alone.

She walked out the back door and made a beeline to the garage. She picked the vehicle closest to the door—the Escalade she'd driven for her date with Teague. It hurt to think back to how good that had been, to how uncertain she'd been of him. And now they were married. She touched the ring on her finger. Teague would be okay, too. He might care deeply about her, but he *loved* his family. He would survive. That was all that mattered.

As long as Callie did what it took.

She took a deep breath and drove out of the garage. It wasn't a long drive into the Halloran territory, and she took the most direct route. The mix of old and new gave way to smaller and smaller homes, all sandwiched in together. She pulled up to the curb next to the pub where Teague had met James Halloran before. James was the best bet she had of the trade-off actually happening. Teague trusted his word—or at least he had before the drive-by shooting that took his brother's life. Could she trust him?

What if it's all for nothing? What if they don't let Carrigan go? What if I turn myself in and it makes things worse?

If she was going to sacrifice herself, it couldn't be for nothing. She *refused* to let it be for nothing. Which meant she needed a contingency plan in place. She took a shuddering breath and went through her phone, looking for the information she'd saved there after she graduated from college and officially stepped into a leadership role within the family. As Papa had taught her, it paid to know her enemies, and not all of them were on the same side of the law as the Sheridans were.

But first she had to say her last good-bye.

* * *

Teague waited while Aiden got the footage going. It wasn't the best quality, but it'd give them more than they'd had before. And at this point, he couldn't afford to turn away from a potential lead. He leaned over, squinting at the computer screen. "Is there any way you can clear it up?"

Aiden shot him a look. "I'm not a computer expert."

No, that had been Devlin. Grief poured through Teague. He gritted his teeth, trying to ride out the pain. Carrigan needed him to stay focused, no matter how hard it was. "Fast-forward to around one a.m. They found his body pretty quick, and I don't get the feeling she stuck around."

His phone rang as a woman stumbled out the back door. He answered without looking at the screen. "Now's not a good time."

"Teague..."

His attention sharpened. "Angel?" The woman on-screen lifted her head and, even though the video was grainy and she was in the distance, he *knew* that face. He knew every line of that body, barely covered by the skimpy dress. Teague shook his head. He had to be wrong. There was no fucking way *Callie* was the person who'd killed Brendan. He was so focused on trying to figure out who the woman really was, he forgot he was on the phone.

"I just wanted to say good-bye." Callie's voice slammed him back into reality.

"Good-bye?" Even as he said the word, he knew. "Don't you fucking dare."

Her laugh was filled to the brim with hopelessness. "I did it. I killed Brendan. It wasn't...I didn't go in there planning to do it, but I was the one who pulled the trigger. This is all my fault. Your brother *died* because of what I did."

Teague flinched. He might have been willing to lay the blame at the faceless killer's feet, but the truth was that there was plenty of blame to spread around. "If we're going to blame you, then let's heap a load onto the Hallorans because they gave the order, and my older brother because he knew war was a distinct possibility when he and my father agreed to marry me off to you. And, fuck, let's blame me, too. Because I knew what the danger was and I didn't get Devlin and the girls out of town."

"If I hadn't gone to that strip club, none of this would have happened, and you know it."

Maybe not, but *she'd* be dead. He knew enough about Brendan to know that. Maybe not right away, but he would have killed Callie at some point. "Come here. We'll talk about this."

Her sigh was so faint, he barely heard it. "I can't. You'll convince me there's another way, and I won't do what needs to be done. I won't let another person be hurt because I'm too much of a coward to step forward."

"Where are you? I'll come get you."

"No, Teague. I didn't call for that." It sounded like a car door opened and background noise whispered through the line as she must have stepped onto the street. "You'll be okay without me. This was...God, being with you was like being in a dream I never wanted to wake up from. Even though the world's been falling apart around us, I've been happier in the last two weeks than I have in a very long time. Because of you."

His throat burned, but he swallowed past it. "Callie, don't do this."

"You'll be okay, Teague. I promise. This isn't the end for you. You'll survive and your family will be safe. I'm only sorry I didn't do this a week ago."

Before Devlin died.

His brother was gone. There was no getting him back. Teague couldn't lose Callie, too. "Angel, please."

"Promise me it stops here. Promise me that you and James will sit down and do whatever it takes to make peace."

He couldn't do it. If she died, he'd set the world on fire in retaliation. "Callie, goddamn it, it doesn't have to be this way. We'll get James here. We'll figure this shit out. Just give me some fucking *time* to find a way around this."

"I—" Her voice caught. "I have to go. I love you." And then she ended the call.

Teague redialed, gripping the phone so tight he was afraid it'd crack as the call rang and rang. It went to voice mail, and he redialed again. This time it didn't even ring. "Fuck!"

"What's going on?"

He turned to find that Aiden had paused the security footage with the woman in the middle of the screen. He pointed. "That's my wife."

Aiden swung around so fast, it was a wonder he didn't fall out of his chair. "That's *Callista Sheridan*?" He shook his head. "Wait, *wife*?"

"I married her last night." He frowned at the screen. He should have seen this coming. Hadn't there been bruises on her throat less than twenty-four hours after Brendan was killed? Hadn't she been reluctant to talk about it time and time again, changing the subject every time he brought it up? *Goddamn it.* He'd thought that it was an ex-boyfriend or that she'd gotten into a rough situation. In what reality would he have connected the dots to guess that *she* was the one to put Brendan out of his misery?

Even now, with her confession ringing in his ears and her grainy image on a tape in front of him, he was still trying to wrap his mind around it. Every cell of his being rejected the idea that she could kill someone in cold blood. He dialed her again, already knowing that it'd go straight to voice mail. Her phone was off. She wasn't going to give him a chance to talk her out of this.

"I never would have guessed."

"You and me both." He stared at the image, half-sure that it'd morph into one less familiar. "She had bruises on her throat the night we announced our engagement. He choked her."

"I've heard that's how Brendan got his kicks."

Had he...Fuck, Teague couldn't think the words. Callie hadn't acted like a woman hurt in that way. Not that he was an expert. But even taking into account people dealing with that kind of assault in different ways, he didn't think she'd have let him near her if she'd been hurt like *that*. He released a breath he hadn't been aware he was holding. "What if it was self-defense?"

"Do you really think Victor Halloran cares? His son is dead, and it sounds like she's responsible."

Victor might not care but Teague cared. He looked at his brother. Aiden had aged years in the last few days. The hard exterior he presented the world was cracked and flawed, and the exhaustion was starting to leak through.

If Teague had half a brain in his head, he'd go to the FBI and throw both himself and Callie on their mercy.

But they hadn't done shit to help him before now, and he couldn't trust her life in their hands.

He never thought he'd trust Aiden again—not after what he'd done to put them all in danger—but desperate times called for desperate measures, and twenty-seven years of looking up to his older brother weren't something he could shake off in the space of two weeks. "I need your help."

Aiden didn't hesitate. "Anything."

CHAPTER NINETEEN

Callie walked into the pub even though all she wanted to do was throw herself into the SUV and drive to Teague's house. She picked up her pace, ignoring the stares of the men scattered around the tables despite the early hour. The bartender was a big man who didn't look particularly happy to see her. He coughed. "You've got the wrong place, ma'am."

Ma'am. The irony of being addressed so politely when she was here to turn herself in wasn't lost on her. She didn't bother to attempt a smile. "I'm Callista Sheridan. I'm here to speak with James Halloran. Is there some way you could convey that to him?"

He stared at her so long, it was an effort not to shift. She could hear chairs being shoved back as the men rose behind her, sharks scenting blood in the water. The bartender finally propped his meaty forearms on the faded wood. "This isn't the place for you."

God, would people please stop trying to give her an out? She was teetering on the edge of fleeing as it was. She took a deep breath, smelling stale beer and other things that she didn't want to name. "Be that as it may, I need to speak to him."

The bartender nodded as if she'd said more than she had. He narrowed his eyes at something over her shoulder. "You boys don't want to be crossing James, now do you?"

Someone cursed. Another said, "Fuck, Tommy, we was just lookin'."

"Sit your asses down before you do something that we'll both regret." He waited a long moment and motioned to a booth situated in the back corner. "Take a seat. You might have a long wait."

"Thank you." She didn't look back as she made her way over and slid into the booth. There was no telling how close those men had been, or what was truly on their minds. It seemed foolish to be grateful the bartender had warned them off when she was walking willingly into her probable death, but she was grateful all the same.

As it turned out, she didn't have to wait long.

Ten minutes later, a man who could only be James Halloran walked in through the back door. He was almost as big as Brendan had been, but where his older brother's blond hair was shorn short, James had let his grow to his shoulders and had a short beard. But the similarity was there in the breadth of his shoulders and the blue eyes that turned her way. He wasted no time walking over and taking the seat across the table. "I already told Teague the terms. He's an idiot if he thinks a pretty face will sway me."

Callie flinched. "Before we go any further, I'll need assurances. You told Teague that turning over Brendan's killer would be enough to let Carrigan O'Malley go."

His blue eyes gave away nothing. "That's the deal."

Not exactly the most comforting. *It doesn't matter. I have a contingency plan in place. It will be okay.* God, she was such a liar. But she was also stuck between a rock and a hard place. She could get up and walk out of here and back to safety, but that was guaranteed to get Carrigan killed. Turning herself in and trusting James to keep his word was a risk, but it was one she'd have to take.

Teague trusts him. That has to be enough.

Callie took a deep breath. It was now or never. "I did it."

"It was your idea? Does he even know you're here?"

God, she didn't want to say the words—what she really wanted was to go back two weeks and never set foot in Tit for Tat. But that wasn't an option and it was time to take responsibility for her actions. She cleared her throat. "I killed Brendan."

The shock on his face would have been comical under any other circumstances. "You're fucking with me."

"I'm not."

"How—" He shook his head. "I don't know what you think you're going to accomplish here, but lying isn't going to help anyone. Do you know what my father will do to you?"

He was trying to make her change her mind. Despite everything he and his family had done, apparently there was a little shred of honor left inside James Halloran. It was almost a shame that she was going to reward it with a truth that would crush them both. "I'm not lying. I went to Tit for Tat to talk to Brendan—to corner him, really, since he'd been resistant to speaking to me. He mistook me for one of the working girls and..." She hesitated, and then forced herself to continue. "He wouldn't take no for an answer. And so I shot him."

Disbelief slowly turned to something else. James sat back. "You're serious."

"I wish I wasn't. God, you have no idea how much I wish I wasn't. I didn't want to kill him, but I'm the one who pulled the trigger. Carrigan shouldn't suffer for my sins."

The expression slowly left his face, leaving him as cold as ice. "You're going to have to come with me."

"I assumed as much."

She rose and turned for the front door, but he caught her arm. "No, this way."

She didn't understand the change until she saw the faces of the scattered men around. They'd obviously either heard or gathered enough information to connect the dots. All wore the same look, as if they were all too happy to fall on her and rip her limb from limb. It was enough to make Callie shrink back against James, even though he was no better.

What had she gotten herself into?

She shoved the thought away. This wasn't a surprise. It didn't matter what happened to her, because this would put a stop to the war. She just had to remember that and hold fast. She folded her shaking hands, doing a really horrible job of convincing herself that she wouldn't break down and beg for mercy. Even the most highly trained soldiers broke under torture eventually.

She was hardly on their level.

James held the car door open for her, and his courtesy in the midst of their situation made her laugh softly. She ignored his sharp look and slid into the seat, also ignoring the presence of her phone in her purse. She'd turned it off when it'd become clear Teague wasn't going to stop calling. Not that Callie could blame him. If their situations were reversed....Well, she'd move heaven and earth to keep him safe.

Which was part of the reason she was in her current situation.

The ride passed quickly, but not nearly quickly enough for her tastes. James's anger seemed to soak into the air between them, his agitation growing the closer they got to their destination. He took a corner too fast and slammed on the brakes hard enough to throw her forward against her seat belt. She glanced at him, and froze.

All that anger was gone as if it'd never existed. There was nothing on his face or in his body language to indicate anything other than an icy control that raised the small hairs on the back of her neck. He turned those cold blue eyes on her. "Get out."

She scrambled to obey. Whatever had brought about this change, she didn't want him touching her again when he looked like *that*.

Like Brendan.

She followed him to the front door, her heart inching closer to her throat with each step. The house had been built sometime in the last ten years, and took up four times as much space as the others on the street. If she didn't miss her guess, they'd demolished half the block to put this in, as well as planting large trees around the perimeter. The pale blue exterior was actually quite nice, and wasn't remotely what she'd expected of the Halloran home. Her mistake.

She barely got through the door when James's hand closed around her upper arm. He jerked her forward hard enough that she stumbled. If she expected him to parade her around his family or throw her to the wolves immediately, she was sorely mistaken. Instead, he dragged her upstairs and practically threw her into a room. She shoved her hair out of her face and gasped when she saw Carrigan cuffed to a bed. Callie spun to face him. "You have me. Let her go."

"No."

It took a full five seconds for the word to penetrate. "That was the deal. You *said* that was the deal—you have Brendan's killer, and you'll let her go."

"I lied." James slammed the door shut, and the sound of the lock clicking into place filled the room.

Callie stared at the closed door. He'd…lied. All her careful planning and he'd *lied*. Frustration built up, clawing its way through her stomach and throat, tearing past her lips in a scream that shook her very being. It felt so damn good that she screamed again, grabbing the closest thing to hand—a heavy lamp—and flinging it at the heavy wood. It hit with a meaty thump and fell to the floor with a clang.

"Been there, done that. It won't change anything."

She turned to find Carrigan watching her. The hopelessness that had been threatening since she walked into that pub got stronger, eating away at the edges of her vision. *No. I am Callista Sheridan, and I will not give up without a fight*. She smoothed her hair back. *This is why contingency plans exist.* Though with the way things were playing out right now, she wasn't willing to trust *that*, either.

So be it.

She'd just come up with a contingency plan for her contingency plan. "Then we'll just have to find another way."

* * *

James walked down the stairs like a man on his way to the hangman's noose. Goddamn Callista motherfucking Sheridan. It was bad enough when he thought the woman who'd pulled the trigger that ended Brendan's life was some poor, defenseless girl pushed beyond her limit. Bringing so-called justice to someone who was just another victim would taint his soul almost beyond repair.

But he could have lived with it if it meant the O'Malleys and Sheridans were no longer gunning for him and his.

Now...now he was in an impossible situation. To bring justice to Brendan's killer meant taking out Sheridan's heir. He'd heard the traces of fear in her voice when she'd confessed. She was no assassin, sneaking into that club to cold-bloodedly kill his brother. Brendan had mistaken her for a stripper, and knowing the way he treated the strippers...A traitorous part of James's mind didn't blame her for defending herself.

Why the fuck had she gone there in the first place?

Because that was lose-lose no matter how he spun it. Either things ended the way they did—with his brother dead and her running off—or Brendan would have done irreparable harm to her and they'd be in the same fucking spot they were now.

If Callista Sheridan died, it would bring all the might and righteous fury of both the O'Malleys and the Sheridans down on their heads. He'd seen the look on Teague's face when he mentioned her. The man was out of his damn mind for the woman, and he wasn't going to take this lying down, no matter how much he wanted his own people safe. And removing Sheridan's heir would also remove the last thing holding Colm Sheridan back from going out in a blaze of glory and taking them all with him.

This shit was well and truly fucked.

He strode into his father's office, flinching at the heat from the roaring fireplace. It didn't matter if today was particularly hot and sticky. The old man had a chill in his bones that he never quite shook. The rest of them just lived with it. His gaze landed on his little brother sitting next to his father. What the fuck was going on here?

Victor raised gnarled hands. "I hear you've found the little bitch who killed your brother."

James narrowed his gaze at his brother. Someone from the pub must have called Ricky. His idiot brother just smirked like he'd done something smart. It was enough to have James's fists clenching. He hated that Ricky saw the movement and paled before setting his jaw and raising his chin.

He had to approach this right. There would only be one chance to keep this from going completely tits up, so he couldn't fuck this up. He straightened. "Things are more complicated than we expected."

"I don't see the complication. We'll skin the little—"

"It's Callista Sheridan."

Victor frowned. "Sheridan's daughter?"

He took a deep breath. "It was an accident." Lie. "She was meeting Brendan, and there was some confusion and the gun went off." Lie. "She's been too afraid to come forward." That, at least, he suspected was partly true.

"Hmmm."

Before James could relax—his father was actually considering changing his course—Ricky bolted upright. "You can't be thinking of letting that bitch go."

"Sit down, and shut your fucking mouth."

Ricky ignored him and turned to their father. "She shot Brendan. She *killed* him. That's unforgivable. Or am I the only one who cares that he's dead?"

James saw the exactly moment his brother's words tipped their father over the edge and into a madness that would get them all killed. Victor pushed to his feet, his whole body seeming to rattle with his shakes. "Your brother's right."

"But—"

"Justice must be served, James. Unless you think your brother's killer should walk free because the little bitch has some connections?"

There was only one right answer to that question. To do anything else would get him thrown into the same boat as the women upstairs. He gritted his teeth. "No. Of course not."

"We do it tomorrow. The boys deserve a spectacle."

Jesus Christ. "Yes, sir." He turned, but his old man's words stopped him the second his hand touched the door. "The O'Malley whore, too. Make examples of both of them."

Well, fuck. This situation had just gone from bad to catastrophic.

* * *

It took an hour for Teague to convince his mother to take Sloan and Keira to their house in Connecticut. An hour wasted, but he couldn't move on the Hallorans with his family vulnerable. It would be horrible to come home victorious only to find out that they'd lost two more.

He refused to let another member of his family be hurt—or worse.

He ducked into a side room and pulled out his phone. There was one person who could put a stop to this before any more blood was shed, but it was a long shot. Teague dialed from memory, and impatiently waited for the call to connect.

"Well, well, well," Finch drawled. "I was wondering if I'd hear from you today." He sounded far too pleased with himself. It set Teague's teeth on edge.

"I'm assuming you're up to date on the current cluster-fuck? The Hallorans have my sister and my wife."

"Wife, huh? You sure move fast."

"Cut the shit, Finch." He made an effort to keep his voice low. "You can put a stop to this right now. You damn well know that they're behind the shooting that killed—" He choked on the name, but finally forced it out. "That killed Devlin. Do something."

"There's no conclusive evidence and you know it."

It was an effort to keep from beating his head against the wall. "They're going to kill the women."

"I heard something along those lines."

It couldn't be clearer that this piece of shit wasn't going to do a damn thing. Teague had betrayed his family time and time again, telling Finch things he never could have found out on his own, and for what? To be left hanging in the wind repeatedly. That shit stopped now. "Then I'll take care of it myself."

"Now, Teague, don't go and do something stupid. We have things under control."

Fat fucking chance of that. They were playing him the same way they'd been playing him from the very beginning. "This thing between us is over. Find another rat." He hung up, and then threw his phone against the wall so hard the screen cracked. All he wanted to do was stomp on it and find something heavy to crush it with until it was no more than pieces.

But there was still the slightest chance Callie would find a way to call him.

Cursing, he scooped it up and gingerly thumbed it on. The screen lit up despite the spiderwebbed glass. Thank God for small favors. He slipped it back into his pocket and walked down the hall, where he met his remaining brothers and father in the study. Father, naturally, didn't look pleased. "Your fiancée started this war."

"She wasn't my fiancée at the time, and *you're* as much to blame for this war as she is. She was defending herself." He refused to believe anything else. Callie would only take a life if she had no other choice. He hadn't known her long, but he knew that to the very core of his being. Of course, his father didn't care about that.

So he had to give the man something that he *would* care about.

Teague kept his tone calm and even. "Beyond that, I married her last night. She's an O'Malley now, as well as being a Sheridan. The Hallorans also have Carrigan. We can't sit back and do nothing. You know what those sick bastards will do to them."

Support came from the unlikeliest of places. Cillian stepped forward. "I just watched Devlin *die*. I'm not going to lose Carrigan, too."

Even Aiden was nodding. "Father, if we let this stand, where will it end?"

Seamus sank behind his desk, looking every one of his fifty-five years for the first time Teague could remember. He carefully rested his hands on the polished wood. "Then we take them back."

Thank Christ. Teague took a step back. "In that case..." He opened the door and moved out of the way to allow Colm Sheridan to enter the room. Everyone froze— though his father looked half a second from going for the gun he kept in his top drawer—so Teague kept talking, "He has a stake in this, same as we do. Or was all that talk of alliances bullshit?"

"By all means." His father motioned the other man to the chair across from him. "Shall we get our girls home safely?"

"Yes." Colm sank into the indicated spot. Teague noticed bags under the older man's eyes that hadn't been there last time. But Sheridan was here, and they were planning like allies instead of enemies. That was better than he dared hope when he'd invited Callie's father to this meeting.

Callie.

God, he wanted to reach across the distance and shake

her until some sense popped into that gorgeous head of hers. She'd been so determined to protect him and martyr herself, she hadn't once stopped to ask him what he thought of the whole thing. No, she'd apologized like she expected him to turn on her like a junkyard dog.

She'd said she loved him.

He rubbed a hand over his mouth and turned to face the window. Out of everything that had come out of her mouth during the phone call, *that* was the thing that burrowed into his mind and wouldn't let go. She was doing this for *him*—so that he wouldn't see any more people he cared about hurt. Totally missing the point that she was numbered among those people.

If something happens to her . . .

He fought down panic at the thought. The Hallorans had barely had her three hours. Even if James couldn't convince his father to spare her—and Teague was starting to doubt his former friend remained an ally—she shouldn't be hurt yet. If there was one thing Victor Halloran loved, it was a spectacle. Since it was becoming increasingly clear that he hadn't released Carrigan as promised, it was only logical to assume he was going to do something dramatic.

But that shit took planning.

Which meant they had a small amount of time to act.

He turned back to the room to hear his father say, "Then it's settled. We'll attack at nightfall."

"No." The word was out before he could think better of it. Teague crossed his arms over his chest. "They're already planning on killing both women. If we attack, what do you think is the first thing they'll do?"

"If you have a better plan, now's the time to speak up."

Aiden sounded like he actually hoped Teague had a better plan.

"I'll go in first. Then you attack, and while the Hallorans are rushing around, trying to figure out where the bullets are coming from, I'll get them out."

Colm frowned. "How do you plan to get in there without being caught?"

"I've done it before." Not in a very long time, and he'd been sneaking *out* then, but he doubted much had changed since. He ignored the glare his father sent him and focused on Colm. "James Halloran and I used to be friends."

"Hmm." He finally nodded. "Then it's a plan."

Father looked like he wanted to argue, but he finally nodded as well. "You have an hour. After that, we go in with guns blazing."

CHAPTER TWENTY

No, not like that. Twist it the other way."

Callie glared at the other woman. "Forgive me if I'm not as adept at picking my way out of handcuffs as you are."

"You would be if you were better at taking directions." Carrigan glared right back. "Twist it the other way."

With a sigh, Callie obeyed, twisting the bobby pin she'd bent out of shape to the other side. A little jiggle later and she was rewarded with a click. The cuff opened and Carrigan's wrist slipped free. "Fucking finally." She snatched the makeshift pick out of Callie's hands and went to work on the other side.

In the two hours she'd been fighting with the cuffs, she'd managed to keep the fear at bay, but now that her hands were idle, it came rushing back—with interest. Getting Carrigan's hands free was only the first—and easiest—of the hurdles they had to clear. She glanced at the sky, the beauty of the setting sun completely lost on her. It wasn't a gorgeous sunset. It was a mark of too much time passing.

"Don't freak out." Carrigan stepped out of the bathroom, where she'd retreated after she was freed. "We can't get out of here until it's dark anyhow."

How in the world did she manage to be so confident? Callie snapped the curtains shut. "Then let's get started."

They went through the room from top to bottom, looking for anything they could use as weapons or tools to scale the outside of the house. While she was certain she could survive a fall from the second story, she didn't like their chances of doing it without some kind of injury that would prevent them from being able to run.

Because escape was the only option now.

James had made it perfectly clear that he wasn't going to honor the promise to release Carrigan now that he had Brendan's murderer. If he wouldn't do that, there was no reason to believe the Hallorans would call off their dogs, either. And with each passing hour, her faith in her contingency plan diminished. The war would continue whether she died or not.

So she was going to do her damnedest *not* to die.

She opened the closet. "There's other clothing in here if you want to change." Considering Carrigan must have been wearing that dress for two days now, she was surprised when the woman shook her head.

"I'm good."

"You're going to scale the side of this house in that dress?"

Carrigan turned a sharp look at her. "I'd rather keep this dress on than change into something of *his*."

That brought Callie up short. His? She must mean James, but there was a wealth of rage in her voice that seemed significantly more personal than this situation warranted. Not that she was an expert on such things but...She spoke without turning from the closet. "He didn't...hurt you?"

"No." She muttered something that sounded like *I did that all on my own*, but before Callie could question her, she said, "Fuck. Fine. Grab me those sweats."

She obeyed because she was pretty sure if she said anything else, Carrigan would turn on *her*. She went to hand them over, but the woman indicated that she should drop them on the floor on the side of the bed furthest from the door. When Callie raised her eyebrows, she shrugged. "No guarantee that he's not going to come check on us. If I'm wearing his clothes, that's a sure sign that we're up to no good."

"Good thinking." It was something she should have considered on her own. Callie rubbed a hand over her eyes. They still didn't have a way out of the room. While tying bedsheets together worked well enough in the movies, James only had a fitted sheet on his bed. That wouldn't get them anywhere near the ground on its own.

She moved to the window again, and muscled it open. The cooling air was heaven against her face, and she spared a brief moment to close her eyes and just breathe it in. They would figure this out. They had to. She leaned out the window a little, careful to keep an eye out for anyone below. As she'd suspected, it was a straight shot to the rocky ground. There was no way they could jump without turning an ankle—and that was the best-case scenario.

She leaned out a little further, angling to get a view of the windows on either side of them. Both had the same setup. Damn it. A little further. *There*. Three windows down on the right, the garage cut out from the house. It would still be a drop, but seven feet was better than twenty. Callie ducked back inside and carefully closed the window. "I have a plan."

"I'm all ears."

They both froze at the sound of a heavy tread coming down the hall. Carrigan kicked the sweats under the bed. "Hurry!"

She tossed Carrigan the cuffs and she threw herself onto the bed and slipped them loosely around her wrists in the approximate spot she'd been in before. For her part, Callie spun in place, trying to figure out if they'd moved anything or if there was any indication that they had no intention of sitting here and waiting to be murdered. Nothing. Or, at least, she didn't think so. Damn it, she couldn't be sure.

But it was too late to do anything more. The footsteps stopped outside the door.

She dropped onto the bed next to Carrigan, hoping she could shield any inconsistencies with her body. They both looked over as the door opened, and Callie's stomach lurched into her throat. *Brendan*.

The man moved fully into the room, and the image shattered. Not Brendan. But they were close enough in looks that this had to be another brother. He eyed them, his gaze lingering too long on Carrigan's bare legs for Callie's peace of mind. She shifted, trying to draw his attention, even though his creepy blue eyes gave her chills. "What do you want?"

"So you're the bitch who killed my brother." He leaned against the wall, but she wasn't fooled. His body was tensed, ready to spring into motion at a second's notice. "You're prettier than I expected."

It sounded like a compliment, but she couldn't shake the instinct demanding she go for his throat. So she stayed silent. That didn't stop him, though. He shifted closer. "You're going to die for what you did. But not for a long, long time." He grinned. "Baby, I'm going to enjoy breaking you." His gaze moved back to Carrigan. "Both of you."

"Ricky."

Callie jumped, but the man didn't. Obviously he'd heard James approach. He didn't turn. "Yeah?"

"Get the fuck out of here."

"Yeah, sure." He tipped an imaginary hat. "I'll be seeing you two again real soon."

James waited for his brother to walk out of the room before he turned his attention on them. "Make whatever peace with God you can. You only have tonight."

Then he was gone, too, shutting the door behind him. Callie sagged, adrenaline beating against the inside of her skull like she'd just been in the middle of a fight. Carrigan sat up, the cuffs dangling from her hands. "It's almost a shame those two are going to miss out on their entertainment tomorrow."

How could the woman joke at a time like this? Callie kept her mouth shut, because she was afraid if she opened it, she'd start screaming and never stop. So she held very still and watched the minutes tick by on the clock; the slow movement of time, much steadier than her heartbeat, grounded her. She finally took a breath and made an effort to unlock her muscles. "I don't suppose you can pick a door lock as well as your handcuffs?"

"Old doors? Not so much. But the ones they have in new houses like this?" Carrigan motioned to the heavy wood door between them and the rest of the house. "Piece of cake."

She certainly was a woman of unexpected talents. Callie moved to the window and glanced at the sky. They were well on their way to dusk, but it would be a good hour yet before they could make a move. "How did you learn to pick locks?"

"Aiden taught me." She smiled, though it was a touch bittersweet. "He convinced one of the men to teach him, and he passed it along to Teague and me. Though Teague never quite picked it up. I have a natural skill for it, I guess." She shook her head. "And a tendency to want to be where I'm not supposed to."

"It sucks being shut out for your own protection." She'd dealt with that time and again growing up. Even as young as ten, Ronan was considered mature enough to sit in on meetings with Papa, while she was told to go play with her dolls. She'd resented it then, but that resentment only grew the older she got. Even when she'd stepped up to take over the legitimate side of the business, Papa had done his best to shield her from the uglier sides of what being a Sheridan meant. And then Ronan was gone, between one breath and another, and it was left to her to fill the shoes he'd left behind. She didn't feel guilty about that early resentment, really, but most days she wished she could go back to being that naive girl who didn't know any better.

"So-called protection. They blind us and then are sur-

prised when we're gunned down because we had no way
to keep ourselves safe." Carrigan looked away, her shoulders bowing in. "That didn't help Devlin."

"I'm so sorry." *My fault.* God, wouldn't she ever learn
that apologizing after the fact wasn't worth the words that
came out of her mouth? "I know that doesn't mean much
now, but I was trying to make it right by coming here."

Carrigan snorted. "Is that what you were doing?"

"I killed Brendan." It shouldn't get easier to say those
words, but they still flowed off her tongue. "This is all my
fault."

The woman turned on the bed to face her fully. "That's
a crock of shit."

"Excuse me?"

"You're worse than Teague is with playing the martyr."
Carrigan sighed. "No wonder he's head over heels in love
with you."

She'd known he cared. Of course she'd known he
cared. He wouldn't have acted the way he had, or touched
her with such tenderness if he didn't care on one level.
But that didn't matter now. "Even if he did before, he
won't now. Not when Devlin was killed because of a war
I started."

"You didn't kill my brother."

"I might as well have. They were out for vengeance for
Brendan's death."

Carrigan rolled onto her stomach and propped her chin
on her hands. "I can't say I'm sorry to hear that you're
the one who put that monster into the ground. My father
was considering selling me off to him before your engagement was announced. I would have put a bullet in his
brain before I walked down the aisle, too."

"It wasn't like that." She wouldn't have done it if she had any other choice.

"Who cares? It's done and the world is a better place for it. Teague knows that, same as I do."

"But—"

"Boston has been a powder keg waiting to be lit for years. With the patriarchs getting older and the heirs a few short years from taking over, there's a flux coming. That scares people. If you weren't the match that set it off, someone else would have been."

"That's easy for you to say when *I'm* the one who set it off."

Carrigan sighed. "How about I put this another way? Do you think for a second that my father, proud asshole that he is, would sit back and let your family and the Hallorans create an alliance through marriage?"

She hadn't really thought about *anything* beyond her panic at the thought of being married to a man known for his mistreatment of helpless women. Callie sank onto the chair and actually thought about it. By all accounts—and she'd seen nothing to disprove it in her direct interactions with the man—Seamus O'Malley was just as prideful and violent as Victor Halloran. Judging by how Halloran was reacting to her and Teague's marriage, it wasn't outside the realm of possibility that Seamus would have done something similar. "We can't know that for sure."

"Sure we can. I'm an expert on my father. The insult alone would have him out for blood, and the possibility that your two families would crush ours in the middle? Yeah, he'd come gunning for both of you—and he'd strike first, before you had a chance to." Carrigan rolled on her back. "Or, take it a step further. Maybe if your fa-

ther had refused the marriage offer, *that* would have made
Victor Halloran declare war all on his own."

"But—"

"Really, there's more than enough blame to go around.
No matter which way you swing it, this started before you
pulled the trigger. If Brendan's death hadn't been enough
to start a war, then something else would have happened
and *that* would have been an inciting incident."

Callie opened her mouth to argue, but stopped. The
more she thought about it, the more Carrigan's argument
solidified in her mind. She tried to come up with a scenario that didn't end in war...and came up short. She
frowned. "You're wasted as a pawn in marriage."

Carrigan laughed. "Try telling that to my father."

It was a crying shame for such a calculating mind to
be relegated to such an archaic role. Callie might have
agreed to an arranged marriage, but it had ultimately
been her choice. Carrigan didn't even have that. "I'm
sorry."

"You have a nasty habit of apologizing for things that
you have no control of."

"That doesn't make me any less sorry. You deserve
better than that." She didn't have to like the woman to
recognize that. But it put Carrigan's actions in a completely new light. Callie compared herself to a caged
bird when she was feeling melodramatic, but she had a
lot of freedom. And, one day, she would run the Sheridan empire.

Carrigan truly was caged. If her father was really forcing her to marry a man of his choice—and Callie had
no reason to believe otherwise—then she couldn't blame
the woman for escaping every chance she got. Speaking

of . . . "Where did you go the other night? I mean, I assume
something went wrong because you ended up here." She
motioned to the room they were currently locked in.

"I went out for a bit of air, and that jackass James
grabbed me."

Callie started to ask about the man the bartender had
seen her with, but changed her mind at the last minute.
Carrigan was entitled to her secrets. She glanced at the
window. "I think it's dark enough."

"Thank God." She stood and walked to the door. "Just
give me a minute to change and I'll have us out of here."

She pressed her ear to the door as Carrigan changed into
the sweats—she had to roll them four times and knot the
drawstring to keep them from falling off— and crouched
next to the keyhole, holding her breath. If they were found
out now, there was nothing stopping James or whoever
caught them from killing them on the spot. They'd been
promised death, after all. There was nothing but silence on
the other side of the door.

She closed her eyes, listening harder. Was that a rustle?
Was there someone standing right on the other side, listening just as hard as she was, knowing exactly what the
soft clicks of Carrigan's tools in the lock meant?

*This is the only way. You die now, or you die how the
Hallorans choose.*

When she looked at it like that, there wasn't really
any choice at all. She couldn't just sit here and wait for
the ax to fall, proverbial or otherwise. Now was the time
for action.

"Got it." Carrigan's words were barely more than a
whisper.

"Just a second." Callie padded over to grab the lamp. It

was unwieldy, but any weapon was better than no weapon at this point.

Carrigan nodded. She took the other lamp and then cracked open the door.

They waited, but no one burst into the room and no sound of alarm went up. Apparently James was confident in his people's ability to keep them contained in the house without a guard. Well, he was about to be proven wrong. Callie slipped into the hallway, followed by Carrigan, padding on bare feet. She would have liked to get the other woman a pair of shoes that weren't heels, but James's were almost comically too large. So bare feet it was.

She silently counted the doors as they moved past them. One. Two. Still no one in the hallway but them. Three. She pointed to the third door. Carrigan tried the handle and it opened with only the slightest creak.

Footsteps in the hallway behind them had them both spinning around. James stood at the top of the stairs, his eyes narrowed. Callie tensed, waiting for the moment he'd sound the alarm. Even with two of them against one of him, she doubted they'd win in a fight. He walked to them slowly, his gaze flickering over her and landing on Carrigan.

She raised her chin. "Come to drag us back to our cage?"

"No." He snagged the back of her neck and dragged her against him. The kiss was quick and brutal and left Callie feeling like the worst kind of voyeur. James stepped back, easily evading Carrigan's left hook. "You and me, lovely, we're not fucking finished. Not by a long shot." Then he turned around and walked away.

Callie stared after him, unable to believe what just happened. "Did he just—"

"I'm going to *kill* him."

She grabbed Carrigan's arm. "Let's go. I don't want him to suddenly change his mind." Though the look on his face made her think he wouldn't. Obviously things between him and Carrigan were significantly more complicated than the woman had let on.

After a slight hesitation, she nodded and let Callie lead her through the door. The room wasn't a bedroom. It looked sort of like a study, but the shelves were mostly empty, and the few pieces of furniture all had a light coating of dust across them. She moved immediately to the window and pushed it open. "It's only a short drop to the garage roof." When no one answered, she turned to find Carrigan holding a book, frowning at it. "What?"

"Nothing." She shut the book. "I'm bringing this with me."

It would make it more difficult to maneuver with her carrying something, but Callie didn't point that out. Whatever that book was, the other woman thought it important enough to set her lamp aside and tuck it against her chest. She motioned to the window. "The coast looks clear, but there's no way to know what we're walking into."

"Anything's better than staying here."

"Then let's not waste any more time." Callie sat on the windowsill and shifted one of her legs outside. She waited for one breathless moment, but only the distant caw of a crow answered her. So far, so good. She set her lamp on the floor, climbed the rest of the way out, and dropped the few feet onto the garage roof.

Instantly, she crouched down, trying to minimize the chance of someone seeing a human-shaped shadow where it shouldn't be. The yard below her was as empty as the street beyond it, but she couldn't afford to assume that the Hallorans had no guards set up. He'd be a fool to assume there wasn't the potential for attack. No, they were there. Somewhere.

Carrigan joined her on the roof with a light thud. She looked to Callie, obviously willing to follow her lead. It felt strange after the woman had basically ripped her a new one on two different occasions, but she didn't hesitate to shuffle along the roofline, keeping as low as she could. The pitch was steep, but the newish roof gave them plenty of traction. She aimed for the part of the slant closest to the ground—and furthest away from the bright floodlights positioned strategically around the back. They'd have to brave those to get to the street, and even then it was a long ten blocks to territory that wasn't owned by the Hallorans—not including skirting the warehouses surrounding the highway.

One step at a time.

"You hear about the entertainment boss has scheduled for tomorrow?"

She froze on the edge of the roof, tucked up against the body of the house. God, how hadn't she noticed the man standing down in the shadows, the bright red spot of his cigarette burning in the darkness? A second ember rose. A second man. *Damn it.*

"Pretty girls. Almost a shame."

The first man laughed, the harsh hack of a longtime smoker. "Only a shame if he doesn't share." He kept laughing, joined by the other speaker.

Callie looked over at Carrigan, but she couldn't see anything beyond the pale shape of the woman's face. Did she feel as sick as Callie did hearing that? Because, right now, she was torn between the urge to descend on these two monsters like an avenging Valkyrie, and the need to expel the meager contents of her stomach.

She managed to resist both impulses.

They needed to get out of here alive. That meant not attacking anyone unless there was no other choice. And throwing up was for the weak. If she got out of this, there would be plenty of time to be sick. Right now, she had to hold it together.

So she waited and tried very hard not to listen to all the things Halloran had planned to do to them. It was cold comfort to know that Brendan—and apparently Ricky—came by his monstrous side honestly. Sins of the father and whatnot.

Eventually the men finished their smoke break and wandered off. Callie counted to one hundred mentally before she moved. She touched Carrigan's arm and motioned to the same nook the men had stood in. Then she slid down the side off the roof and lowered herself to drop to the ground. She moved to the side as Carrigan followed her, once again scanning for someone who might catch them. Once the other woman stood, she leaned in. "I think we can get to the street around this corner. The lights are pretty bright, but there are trees that we can use as cover."

"Works for me."

Callie sidled along the edge of the house, took a deep breath, and leaned out a little to look around the corner. Nothing. She glanced back to nod the all clear. Her heart tried to pound its way out of her chest as she took that first step into the yard. Even though they'd been at risk before, she felt significantly more vulnerable without a wall at her back. Another step.

When no one shouted at her to stop, she picked up her pace, aiming for the closest tree. She was almost there when a dark shape stepped into her path and a hand slammed down on her mouth, cutting off her scream.

CHAPTER TWENTY-ONE

Teague held Callie as she struggled. "It's me. Don't scream, angel. It's me." She finally went still, and he allowed her to turn in his arms to face him.

"Teague?"

Carrigan slipped next to them. "You're about an hour too late, but I'll forgive you if you get us out of here without anyone being shot." She turned as Aiden ghosted up next to them. "You too?"

"Contrary to what you believe, I do care."

"Whatever."

If he let them, they'd end up in a full-out argument right here in the middle of Halloran property. "Let's go." Teague turned without waiting for an answer. The trees weren't spaced closely together, but they were large and cast strange shadows. If they were careful, they should be able to get out of here before his father and Colm Sheridan attacked.

Even as the thought crossed his mind, gunfire sounded from somewhere close by. He spun on Aiden. "We're supposed to have another hour."

"Don't look at me. I didn't know shit about this."

He realized he was still holding Callie and forced himself to let go. "We do this quick and quiet. I'll take the lead. Aiden will bring up the rear. You move when I move."

Both women nodded, which was a token of just how scared they were. Fuck, he was scared, too. If he got this close and lost either one of them? It was unthinkable. He checked the surrounding area, but there wasn't a bit of movement, though the sounds of fighting were growing by the second. It was now or never. He squeezed Callie's hand and then darted out into the open area, nearly sprinting to the next tree.

Silence.

He turned back as Callie followed his movement exactly—a quick rush from one tree to the next. And then Carrigan. Teague moved as soon as his sister reached him, rushing to the next tree.

Again, silence.

This is too easy. Why aren't there more guards out back? If I were Victor Halloran, I'd—

Gunshots, this time far too close.

He whirled around in time to yank Callie to his chest as a spotlight shone on the gap between the two trees she'd just run through. A man yelled, "I see you, you little bitch. You're not going to make it to the property line." Teague didn't recognize the voice, but Callie flinched. Obviously she knew who spoke. He wanted to ask her, to reassure her that she wasn't being taken back there again, but it was false comfort at best.

Instead, he leaned around her. The harsh light gave him a clear view of his siblings despite their cover behind the tree. They couldn't stay here. It was only a matter of time before men came to flush them out—right into the path of that gun.

Aiden knew that as well as he did. He jerked his thumb in the opposite direction. All those childhood games of hide-and-seek in their Connecticut home, teaming up against the girls, came in handy now. He and Aiden had been speaking without words for years. His brother would take Carrigan in the opposite direction, splitting the enemy. It didn't magically make their odds good, but bad was still better than suicidal.

He nodded. *God go with you, brother.*

With effort, he put the fate of his siblings aside. He couldn't afford to be distracted right now—not with Callie's life in his hands. Teague pulled a second gun from his ankle holster. "I trust you know how to use this?"

She checked to make sure it was loaded, and slammed the clip back into place. "Your sense of humor is suspect."

"That's what everyone keeps telling me." Despite the situation, he grinned. "I missed you, angel."

"I...I missed you, too."

"And if you ever think of trying some shit like this again—"

She pressed her fingertips to his lips. "Can we talk about this when we aren't in danger of being killed?"

"If you insist." He kissed her, light and quick, and then turned to survey their options. The fence was a few short yards away. There was every chance that there were more men on the other side of it, but as long as they were on this side, they were sitting ducks. He motioned. "I don't suppose you can climb that?"

"Give me a boost and I can."

It would slow them down, but there wasn't any other option. "Okay. Count of three."

A shout went up behind them and someone opened fire. He glanced back to find Aiden and Carrigan pelting away from them. "Three!"

She flew next to him, keeping up easily. He hit the fence first and went down on one knee. "Up." She didn't hesitate to put her foot into his cupped hands. He lifted with all his strength, regretting her startled yelp as she soared over him, but there was no time for courtesy. He barely waited for her hands to disappear off the top of the fence when he jumped, grabbing the rough wood and hauling himself to the top.

Pain blazed through his side, almost sending him toppling back into the Hallorans' yard. He clung to the fence, gritting his teeth. *Fuck, fuck, goddamn it, that hurt*. It took all his strength to fall on the right side—the street side. Teague hit the ground hard enough to drive what little air he'd retained from his lungs. He wheezed out a breath and rolled onto his back, his entire world made up of a red haze of pain.

Instantly, Callie was next to him, concern in every line of her body. She lifted a hand and gasped. "You're bleeding."

"I think...I was shot." He managed to get a breath in, but the sheer agony of it made him regret his decision. Did he really need to breathe?

Voices sounded on the other side of the bushes shielding them. "They came over around here somewhere."

"They couldn't have gotten far."

He tried to keep his harsh breaths quiet, but it was nearly impossible. He was vaguely aware of Callie shifting her stance on the gun in her hands. She touched his chest, though whether it was in comfort or warning, he couldn't say.

The bushes in front of them parted, and she raised the gun. The man's startled yelp was cut off halfway through, the shot knocking him back. She looked sick but determined. "You can't run, but you need to move. I'll draw them away—"

He grabbed her arm with all the strength he had left—a pathetically small amount. "Don't you fucking dare. You did the noble thing once..." An agonized breath. "No more."

"They will finish what they started and kill you."

He wasn't sure what clued him in. It might have been a scuff of a shoe on pavement. Or maybe the slightest shifting somewhere below the level of consciousness. It didn't matter. He yanked Callie down on his chest a second before shots fired, biting the fence where her head had just been.

She rolled off him almost immediately, aiming once again, but she didn't pull the trigger. "What if I kill someone in the building across the street?"

"Empty," he gasped.

"You're sure?" Her voice wasn't anywhere near calm, but her hands were steady.

"Yes."

She didn't ask again. She shot once, twice, a third time, and whoever was on the other side of the bushes gave a pained cry and sounded like he crumpled to the ground. She glanced at him. "We need to move."

"I know." But he suspected he couldn't. His thoughts were fuzzy, and he wasn't sure if that was the pain level or the blood loss.

She knew it. Damn it, he could see it in her eyes. Callie dropped the gun and yanked her sweatshirt off. He didn't have the strength to cry out when she pressed it against his side with all her might. "Don't you dare die on me, Teague O'Malley."

Spots danced in front of his eyes that had nothing to do with it being night. "I love you." Then the blackness swallowed him whole.

* * *

Callie knew the moment he passed out. She wasn't sure if it was because of the pressure she was putting on his still-healing ribs or because of blood loss, but she dearly hoped it was the former. As long as they didn't puncture anything, broken ribs wouldn't kill him. A gunshot wound surely would.

A car pulled up on the street near them. She cocked her head to the side, tracking its movement as it stopped and the doors opened. This was it. There was no escape for either of them. By her count, she only had five or six shots left, and to grab her gun, she'd have to take her hands off Teague's wound. Since the fabric was already wet with his blood, she couldn't afford to do that.

She closed her eyes. *I don't know if you're listening, God. I've made a grand mess of this. But spare Teague. He never asked for any of this.* A silly, foolish prayer.

"Callista Sheridan?"

She tensed. Of course they knew her name. That

wasn't as surprising as the fact that they were yelling at her instead of shooting first. But then, they'd want their entertainment, wouldn't they? Couldn't have that if she was dead.

"Ms. Sheridan, my name is John Finch. I'm with the FBI. You placed a call to my office earlier today."

She blinked. There was no way the Hallorans could know that...but was it a risk she was willing to take? They could be lying, waiting for her to run out into the open and then gunning her down. She looked at Teague. It was hard to tell in the shadows, but he looked scarily pale. He needed a doctor, and quickly.

So she took a leap of faith. "I have an injured man here. He's been shot."

"We're coming to you." He hesitated. "Please try to resist shooting any of my men."

She highly resented the amusement in his voice. There was nothing amusing about this situation. Nothing at all. "Get in here."

The bushes parted and two men rushed to her. She tensed, waiting for the bullets to tear through her flesh, but they just shouldered her aside and knelt next to Teague. "Bullet wound to the upper chest. He'll need surgery and an immediate transfusion."

The other turned to her. "We have an ambulance en route."

This turn of events was nearly impossible to wrap her head around. She'd hoped her contingency plan would work—God, of course she'd hoped—but it was still too good to be true. A third man appeared and offered her a hand. "If you'll come with me, please?" He sighed when her gaze tracked back to Teague. "Mr.

O'Malley will get the best medical care the government has to offer."

That didn't mean a damn thing if he died before they could get him to the hospital.

The man sighed again. "I can see there'll be no talking to you until he's off." He turned around and disappeared through the bushes, leaving her to sit just out of reach while the other two men went to work on stabilizing Teague.

Sirens cut through the night. The *silent* night. She turned to look back at the Hallorans' property. Where were the gunshots that had been peppering around them since Teague showed up? She frowned. "It's not safe here."

"It's as safe as anywhere." The paramedic spoke without looking at her. Or at least she hoped he was a paramedic. "We've secured the situation."

They'd secured the situation.

She didn't get a chance to ask more questions, because the sirens' volume increased before abruptly shutting off. Red and white lights played along the fence line. The ambulance was here.

It happened so fast. Too fast. One second she was struggling to her feet, and the next they were shutting the doors between her and Teague and tearing off down the street. Callie stood on the sidewalk, staring after the ambulance. She was supposed to be there, with him.

"Now, we really do need to talk, Ms. Sheridan."

Talk. This man wanted to talk when the life of the man she loved—her *husband*—hung in the balance. She realized she was still holding a gun and turned it on him. "I don't think so."

Finch's eyebrows rose. "Do you really think it's wise to add to your body count tonight?"

No, but there was no room for wisdom when Teague needed her. She didn't lower the gun. "Please take me to the hospital."

"Ms. Sheridan—"

"You misunderstand me. That wasn't a request." There were other men around them, men who didn't look too happy with her pointing a gun at what she suspected was the man in charge. She didn't care. They hadn't saved her just to gun her down in the street. "Where is your car?"

He pointed to a black sedan behind him. Typical. She motioned that she'd follow him. A few seconds later they were in the car and he turned on the engine. "Now, we'll talk."

"Drive." She didn't want to talk to this man. She didn't want to talk to *anyone*. But she had the feeling Finch would get his way one way or another. "Why are you so eager to have a conversation?"

"You're a very interesting woman. I'm kicking myself for overlooking you previously."

She didn't like the sound of that—at all. But she lowered the gun and leaned back against the car door. She could still shoot him, but that had never been the goal. All she wanted was to get to the hospital. "Why did you conveniently show up in time to save the day, but not earlier when you knew I'd been taken?"

"The wheels of bureaucracy turn slowly, my dear." He glanced at her out of the corner of his eye. "Your new husband is very important to me and my friends. I hope you understand and respect that."

Shock and exhaustion and just plain old trauma made

her slow, because it took her several long minutes to realize what he meant. *Oh Teague, why didn't you tell me?* She wasn't surprised, though. She hadn't exactly been honest with him. It was only expected that he'd kept some things back as well.

But working with the FBI?

Then again, she didn't exactly have room to talk. *She'd* put in a call to them for help. She found herself speaking without having any intention of doing so. "As much as I appreciate the assistance, stay away from my people, John Finch. Whatever arrangement you have with my husband is between the two of you, but if I hear about you sniffing around where you shouldn't, I doubt either of us will like the results."

He laughed, startling her. "Got some steel in your spine, don't you? No wonder he was willing to throw it all away to save you."

She didn't ask what he meant. He was trying to bait her, and she wanted no part of it. "Do we have an understanding?"

"Oh, we do, indeed." He turned muddy brown eyes on her, shifting between one breath and the next from the nonchalant jokester to something infinitely more dangerous. "Keep your people on the right side of the law, Ms. Sheridan, and we won't have a problem." He stopped the car. "Now, go see to your husband."

She looked out the window to find them in front of Massachusetts General Hospital. "Thanks for the ride." She reached for the door, but his hand on her arm stopped her.

"The gun, please."

The gun that linked her to the murders of two men. She

turned and met his gaze. "And what do you plan on doing with it?"

"Your sins from tonight won't come back to haunt you, if that's what you're wondering."

As if she would trust this man. Being FBI only made him *more* suspicious as far as she was concerned. "If it's all the same to you, I'll take care of it."

"If you insist."

"I do." She opened the door and paused. "May I borrow your coat, Mr. Finch?"

"By all means." He shrugged out of it and passed it over.

She slipped it on, instantly dwarfed. Callie didn't like it. She didn't like the musky scent of old cigarettes that clung to the fabric, either, but she could hardly shove the gun into the waistband of her jeans. "I'll see it's returned to you." She shut the door, and then gritted her teeth when he rolled down the window.

"Tell Teague that I'm sorry. It wasn't supposed to be this way."

If it was as she suspected and Teague was informing to the FBI on his family—and hers?—then they'd failed him spectacularly. "You should have been there."

"I know." The exhausted admission struck her to her soul. They'd all screwed up to one degree or another. This situation wouldn't have gotten so out of control without multiple people failing to put on the brakes.

She sighed. She wanted to blame this man, but there was more than enough blame to pass around. "You have a good night."

"Not likely." He pulled away from the curb before she could respond.

Callie slipped the gun into one of the deep pockets in the coat. As much as she wanted to rush into the hospital and demand to know where Teague was, she had to take care of the weapon first. She skirted the edge of the buildings, following the street down to the overpass leading to the waterfront. There were better ways to go about disposing evidence, but this would have to do. She didn't like trusting Finch not to gather evidence and press charges against her, but there was no other option. He had her backed into a corner. It was entirely possible he actually saw her shoot those two men, which meant there wasn't a jury in this country that would find her not guilty.

It was a worry for another day.

She moved through the trees at the water's edge. It was remarkably deserted, and she wasted no time wiping the gun down and flinging it as far into the water as her strength could carry it. She waited a few moments to see if anyone saw her do it, then turned around and strode back to the hospital buildings.

It took twenty minutes to get any information at all about Teague—despite the fact that she kept telling them she was his wife—and another ten to be guided to the right part of the hospital. The nurse pointed to the waiting area with the impatient air of someone who'd done it countless times before. "He's in surgery. The doctor will be out once they're done putting him back together."

One hell of a beside manner. She muttered her thanks and sank onto the faded blue chairs. Or maybe they were gray. It was impossible to say. Callie should call someone, let them know where Teague was. Or, *God*, wash her hands. She looked down at the blood crusting her palms, and the overwhelming urge to curl up and sob flowed over her like a tidal wave.

Her hands shook, the tremors working their way through her entire body. *Oh God, oh God, oh God.* Her lungs tried to close, each breath seeming to tear itself free. She bent over, resting her forehead on her knees, and closed her eyes, but that only made it worse. All she could smell was smoke and blood and something she suspected was her own fear.

She lurched to her feet and stumbled to the bathroom. The cold water felt good on her skin, but it wasn't doing a damn thing to get the blood off. She turned it hotter and pumped a bunch of soap into her hands. She scrubbed until her skin was raw and pink and there wasn't the slightest trace of blood. There was no help for her clothing, though.

With a sigh, she made her way back to the waiting room. The nurse at the station didn't look particularly happy to see her, but when she asked to use a phone, she pointed Callie to a public one down the hall.

And then the calls started. First, to her father, who didn't answer. *I'm fine. I'm at the hospital.* Then to Carrigan, who also didn't pick up. *Teague's been shot. We're at the hospital.* And, finally, to Micah, who *did* pick up. "Where the hell have you been?"

Her throat tried to close. Again. "I'm at Mass General."

"You're okay?"

"Yes. It was Teague who was shot. I'm fine." Or as fine as she could be, considering the circumstances.

"Thank Christ." He blew out a breath. "I'm on my way down to the jail. Your father and pretty much everyone he took with him to deal with the Hallorans are locked up."

Locked up was better than dead. She wasn't sure when she'd made that belief transition, but she didn't see herself going back anytime soon. "What are the charges?"

"I don't know yet. Do you need me to swing by on my way?"

As much as she was loath to stall him, she couldn't keep walking around the hospital in bloodstained clothing. "If you have a change of clothes in the car, I'd appreciate it."

"I'll be there in ten."

She hung up and leaned her forehead against the wall. Papa was locked up, Teague was in the operating room, and God alone knew where the rest of his family and the Hallorans were. It felt like she was the last person standing.

It was a horribly lonely place to be.

CHAPTER TWENTY-TWO

Teague woke up to the steady sound of beeping. He opened his eyes, squinting in the low light and feeling like he'd been run over by a truck—several times. His gaze landed on Callie's sleeping form, curled up in a chair next to his bed. "Angel." His voice was so hoarse, it was barely above a whisper.

But she heard it. She sat up. "You're awake."

He lifted his hand, and she wasted no time coming to perch on the edge of his bed. "What happened?"

"Your...friends...at the FBI showed up right in the nick of time to save you and arrest everyone."

The way she said *friends* indicated that she knew exactly what devil's bargain he'd struck with the FBI. So they'd shown up to save the day? It was almost enough to make him laugh—at least it would be if he didn't get the feeling it would hurt a whole hell of a lot. So typical of them to ride in just in time to sweep up the mess. "No one knows."

"I'm not particularly worried about it at this point."

Something inside him relaxed. That was it. The air was finally clean between them. He had no more lies, and she... "Is Brendan's death the only skeleton in your closet?"

"Yes." She didn't so much as flinch.

Fuck, he loved this woman. He reached for her hand and carefully laced his fingers through hers. "Where do you want to go for our honeymoon?"

Her eyebrows shot up. "Honeymoon?"

"Don't you think we deserve one after this?"

"Well, most definitely, but—"

"Then we'll take one." He glanced down at the bandages covering his chest. "As soon as the doctor gives me a thumbs-up on being able to do my husbandly duties."

"There's still quite a bit of mess to clean up here. Both our fathers are being charged with assault. Victor Halloran is being charged with conspiracy to commit murder, but I think the police are more excited about the evidence of tax fraud they found when they searched his house." She shook her head. "It's enough to make a cynical person wonder if they waited for the conflict to start solely so they could get access to the place."

Since Teague suspected that was exactly what they'd done, he wasn't about to jump to their defense. "And the rest?"

"I think they had their eyes on the prize, so to speak. Aiden and Carrigan are fine. They were able to slip away when the commotion started with the feds. Your mother and other sisters are back in town. They've all been in to see you already." She made a face. "Your mother wasn't impressed by our eloping. I'm nearly one hundred percent sure she's going to insist on going ahead with a giant wedding."

That sounded like his mother. He noted the dark circles under Callie's eyes. For all her attempts at being upbeat, she was obviously exhausted. "How long was I out?"

"Two days. They had a difficult time stopping the bleeding in your chest from the gunshot wound, and those bruised ribs are now officially broken, but they got you patched up."

Shit. He frowned at her. "And how much of that have you been here?" When she didn't answer, he tugged on her hand. "Angel, answer me."

"I went home to shower and get a few changes of clothing."

But she'd been by his side the rest of the time. "I don't deserve you."

"I think that's up for debate." Her smile was the barest curving of her lips, gone as quickly as it appeared. "I'm sorry I lied to you."

"Everyone lies, angel. I'm more worried that this tendency of sacrificing yourself for others is a habit of yours." He waited until she looked at him again. "I've never felt so helpless in my life. Not even when my brother died." *Fuck, that still hurt.* "Not when I found out Carrigan was taken. *Never.* Until you called me to tell me that you loved me and you're turning yourself over to the Hallorans."

"I thought it was the best way to make sure no one else you cared about was hurt by something I started." She met his gaze, her blue eyes holding so many things, he was at a loss to name them all. "It was naive to believe that, but my head isn't always on straight when it comes to you."

"Did you ever stop to think that maybe *you're* one of the people I care about?" He hesitated, but there was nothing holding him back from admitting how he felt. "I love you, too—more than I ever thought possible—and the thought of losing you... Angel, don't ever pull that shit again."

"I can't promise that."

He didn't really expect her to. He raised her hand, ignoring the pain the move brought, and pressed his lips to her knuckles. "The fact that I understand means it's entirely possible we're both too foolish to live."

"Saint Lucia."

He blinked. "What?"

This time, her smile was real and stretched across her mouth. "When you get a clean bill of health, I'd like to spend a week down in Saint Lucia drinking ourselves stupid and making love all over the house."

"Sounds like one hell of a honeymoon."

"Yes." She leaned down and kissed his forehead. "And when we get back, we'll start putting things right."

The sizzling saga of the O'Malleys
continues...

Beautiful Carrigan O'Malley has a parade of
potential suitors but the only man she wants
is the head of a rival ruling family. To be
with Carrigan, James Halloran will fight all
his enemies—and his own blood.

Please see the next page for a preview of

The Wedding Pact.

She wasn't here.

James Halloran drank his beer and did his damnedest not to look like he was searching the dance floor below for someone specific. Just like he hadn't shown up here five nights a week for the last four months, even though he was needed elsewhere. With his old man in the slammer and his little brother causing more problems than he fixed, all of James's attention should have been on getting his people back onto stable ground.

Instead, he couldn't get *her* out of his head.

Carrigan O'Malley.

He didn't know what he would say to her if he *did* see her. Apologize? Considering the last time they'd seen each other, he'd kidnapped her, tied her to his bed, and his father had sentenced her to a horrifying death... Yeah, there wasn't a fucking Hallmark card that covered that.

And she'd taken something of his, something irreplaceable. The last link he had to his mother. It was a stupid sentiment, but he'd never been able to fully pack away the old photo album. To know it had been in her possession for the last four months...It left him feeling edgy and strangely vulnerable. He couldn't admit to anyone that she'd taken it without admitting what it meant to him, and that was handing a loaded gun to the O'Malleys. No fucking way was he going there.

He reached for his beer, only to realize it was empty.

"Want another?" The short bartender didn't look old enough to drink, but she was good enough at her job not to give him shit for showing up, having a single drink, and leaving. Over and over again.

"No, thanks." *She* wasn't coming tonight, just like she hadn't come any night since the one where she'd blown his fucking mind in a supply closet. Before he realized exactly whose ear he'd been spilling filthy words into. Before she said her name and everything changed. Before he made the decision that labeled him just as cold a bastard as his old man.

Carrigan O'Malley. The daughter of the enemy. The one woman he sure as hell needed to keep his hands off.

Her absence made sense. If he had sisters, he would have gotten them the hell out of Dodge before shit hit the fan, and he would have kept them somewhere safe while things played out. The power situation wasn't stable in Boston—not like it had been a year ago—but it was evening out. It *had* to. He was all too aware that war among the three families was the least of their concerns if some outside threat decided to take advantage of the power fluctuation. He knew the Sheridans and

O'Malleys—knew how they thought, knew what they wanted, knew how they'd react to a given threat.

Better the devil he knew than the devil he didn't.

He'd been in talks with Colm Sheridan and his daughter, Callista, about securing peace. She, at least, wasn't willing to let the past get in the way of the ultimate good. The reluctant admiration he'd first felt when she turned herself over to him, admitting to be the one who pulled the trigger that ended his older brother's life, had bloomed into full-fledged respect. Teague was a lucky son of a bitch—and so was everyone under Sheridan protection. Callista Sheridan was a force to be reckoned with.

Somehow, James didn't think Carrigan would be as willing to let the past go. She was prickly and prideful and had a furious temper—and he knew that after having been around her for less than three days.

That was enough of that shit.

He pushed to his feet and headed for the spiral staircase leading down to the main floor. Since it was a Tuesday night, the place was far from packed, but there was still a cluster of dancers sweating and grinding in the middle of the floor, and plenty of people standing around the lower bar, waiting for drinks. He scanned their faces out of habit, not really expecting anything but disappointment.

His gaze landed on familiar green eyes, and he stopped short. He had to be seeing things. It had happened before—he'd been sure it was her, only to approach and realize he'd been projecting her image on some other pretty brunette. But then she shook her head, like she was trying to dispel his image, and he *knew*.

James took a step toward her, still having no fucking idea what he was going to say.

She turned tail and bolted.

He was giving chase before making a decision to do so. The voice of reason piped up to point out that running her down wasn't going to do a damn thing to reassure her that he wasn't up to no good, but it wasn't like he had another option at this point. She wasn't going to sit there and let him approach her.

That didn't stop him from hauling ass through the doors and out into the street. He looked left and then caught sight of her further down the block, making impressive time considering the six-inch spike heels on her feet.

But he had the advantage on open ground.

James poured on more speed, closing the distance between them. She cast a panicked look over her shoulder, and it was almost enough to make him stop. Only the knowledge that he wouldn't get another chance like this again kept him moving. That and something inside him that he was reluctant to put a name to. It felt a whole hell of a lot like the conscience he'd thought was dead and gone.

She was less than six feet in front of him. It was now or never. "For fuck's sake, *stop*."

"Leave me alone."

He put on a burst of speed and hooked an arm around her waist just as they reached the corner, jerking her to a stop. "Hold on for a second."

She drove her elbow into his stomach, and then slammed her heel into his toe. Even through his boots, he felt it. "Get off me." Her struggles increased. "Let go!"

He let go, holding his hands up and gritting his teeth against the throbbing in his foot. "I'm sorry, okay. I just wanted to talk."

"You have a funny way of showing it." She glanced over her shoulder, checking to see if he had other men with him, or maybe looking for an escape route. "Goddamn it, I knew better than to come back here."

"I'm not going to hurt you." *I never would have let them hurt you.* But the words wouldn't come. He might have stood back and let her and Callista Sheridan escape that night, but he could have done more. He'd taken the path that resulted in the least risk to him, and something horrible could have happened to either of them as a result.

She laughed, a low, broken sound. "You know, considering our history, I find that hard to believe."

What could he say? She was right. In her position, he would have done more violence than an elbow to the stomach. Hell, he would have drawn a gun and put an end to the threat once and for all. But things with them were different. She damn well knew that he didn't want her hurt, abduction or no. "No one laid a hand on you."

"No, you just threw me in a trunk, and then tied me to a bed and—" She shook her head, drawing his attention to her mass of dark hair. "I don't know why I'm still standing here. Stay the hell away from me."

This was it. She would walk away, and it was entirely likely that he'd never see her again. He'd never see his album again. *That's the reason you're here, dipshit. You're not fawning over some woman, no matter how hot she is. She took something from you and you want it back.* "Where is it?"

She stopped, but she didn't turn back. "Where is what?"

"Don't play dumb, lovely. It doesn't suit you." He took a step closer, close enough to see the way her shoulders tightened, as if she could sense his proximity. "That album wasn't yours to take."

She gave him an icy look over her shoulder. "Even if I did take something—which I didn't—I wouldn't have kept it."

She was bluffing. She had to be. He made himself hold perfectly still, all too aware that one wrong move would send her fleeing into the night. "Liar."

"Whatever you have to tell yourself to sleep at night."

It struck him that maybe she'd gotten rid of the album. She had no reason to keep it. It was nothing to her—less than nothing. He strove to keep his thoughts off his face, but from the curiosity flaring in her green eyes, he did a piss-poor job of it. "I'll make you a deal."

"That's rich. You have nothing I want."

Maybe not, but he wasn't above playing dirty. Not in this. Not in anything anymore. James closed the distance between them in a single step and grasped her chin tightly enough that she couldn't pull away. "Give back what you stole, and you'll never have to see me again."

"And if I don't?"

"Well, lovely, then I'm going to have to take that as a sign that you still want me as much as you did four months ago. Which means you want to see me again—and again, and again."

Her eyes went wide. "Are you seriously offering *not* to stalk me if I give back this thing I supposedly stole? What kind of deal is that? It's bullshit."

She wasn't afraid anymore, which was a goddamn relief. Instead there was a spark of anger vibrating through her body, and she was eyeing him like she wouldn't mind taking a chunk out of his hide. He preferred this Carrigan to the frightened one. As long as she was focusing on where she wanted to hurt him, she wasn't thinking about the threat he potentially posed. "I said you and I have unfinished business, and I damn well meant it."

"Wrong." She snorted. "Finished business is the only kind we have—ancient history. For the last time, get your big paws off me."

He released her for the second time. "I'm not bluffing."

"Neither am I." She turned around and walked away.

This time he let her go. He had no goddamn right to threaten her, but the thought of never seeing the album again—it sure as fuck wasn't the thought of never seeing *her* again—made him twitchy. It wasn't a threat he'd have made six months ago, but he wasn't the same man he'd been then. He'd given up trying to be better than the rest of the Hallorans. That same violence and aggression that ran through their blood ran through his, too.

No matter how much he hated it.

Things had gotten out of control after his older brother's death five months ago. Even now, knowing what he did about the monster Brendan was, his absence was still a weight in James's stomach. He didn't choose his family, and half the time he didn't like them, but they were all he had. The Halloran empire in Southie. All the death and unforgivable shit, and for what? A few square miles of land in the part of Boston no one else wanted?

He waited until he saw Carrigan climb into the back of a cab before he turned and headed for his car. He wasn't quite thirty yet, and he was so goddamn *tired*. It never ended. The power games, and the unforgivable acts, and the compromises on what he used to think of as his honor. There was nothing left of it anymore, and hell if that didn't send a pang of loss through him.

Not for the first time, he wondered what his mother would think of the men her beloved sons had turned into. He couldn't shake the belief that he was failing her. But she was dead and gone some fifteen years, and his old man was very much among the living. The only link James had to her was the album Carrigan had taken—a shrine to the man he might have been in different circumstances.

That man was dead and gone as surely as his mother was.

Now it all fell to James. The responsibility of keeping the Halloran name from disappearing the same way other enemies of the Sheridans had. People still talked about what Colm Sheridan did to the MacNamaras, though the details were sketchy now, thirty years later. All anyone knew was that it was horrific enough that no one had challenged him since.

James couldn't let that happen to his people. And they were his, whether he wanted the responsibility or not. The only other option was walking away and letting his idiot of a younger brother take over, which was as good as signing the death warrant of everyone who depended on the Hallorans to keep shit in check in their territory.

Besides, where would he go? This was his life.

He slid into the driver's seat of his cherry red '70 Chevelle and sighed. His life would be a whole lot less complicated if he could let the specter of his night with Carrigan O'Malley go. She hated his ass, and for good reason. Spending more time chasing her was courting more problems than he had resources to deal with. Life was too tenuous right now to throw something like this into the middle of it—the whole thing could erupt like a bonfire at the first spark of trouble.

"I'm going to leave that woman alone." Even as he spoke the words, he knew he was a damned liar.

* * *

Carrigan huddled in the back of the cab, trying not to shake. James motherfucking Halloran. She should have known better than to risk going back to the same club he'd taken her from, but it had been a test. Avoiding that location meant she was afraid. Carrigan had learned a long time ago that every time she refused to face her fear, it got more powerful. A fear left unchecked took away her control.

And control was one thing she didn't have nearly enough of as it was.

Why the hell was he there? In months and months of her frequenting that club, she'd never once seen him there. And she *would* have seen him there. James was the kind of man who stood out, even in a crowd. She'd bet what little freedom she had left that he'd never been there at the same time she had. As tempting as it was to chalk it up to a coincidence, it was too damn much to believe he'd been there tonight by chance. Which meant he'd been there looking for *her*.

She shivered. Taking the album was a mistake. She'd known the second she opened it and saw its contents that he wouldn't rest until he had it back in his possession.

If she had half a brain in her head, she'd send the thing back to him and good riddance. Even as the thought crossed her mind, she shook her head. As questionable as it was, she wasn't ready to give up that pawn—especially since it was important enough for him to seek her out.

He said he'd been thinking about that night.

He lied.

He *had* to have lied. The sex obviously didn't mean shit to him since he'd thrown her in a trunk less than ten minutes afterward. Not to mention that every remaining member of his shrinking family had been all too happy to threaten to kill her—and worse. They would have done it. She wasn't naive enough to think they wouldn't have.

Hell, her own father did worse than that to people who crossed him. There was no reason to believe James would have suddenly developed a conscience and played white knight to her damsel in distress. Yes, he'd stepped aside and let her and Callie go when they were sneaking out. Her body burned at the memory of how he'd kissed her, of the look in his eyes when he'd growled that they had unfinished business. *Stop it.* He might have let them escape, but that didn't mean he wouldn't have stood by and watched her tortured and killed if his father commanded it.

Which was why the fact that her brain kept circling back to him in the intervening months was so incredibly unforgivable. She could claim Stockholm syndrome until she was blue in the face, but it wasn't the truth.

The cab pulled up in front of her family's home, saving her from following that train of thought any further down the rabbit hole. James Halloran was the enemy, and she'd be every bit the stupid bimbo her father thought she was if she forgot that.

Carrigan paid the driver and climbed out of the cab. She made it all of three steps when she realized what she'd done—she'd come home wearing her clubbing clothes when she was supposed to have been at church, praying for her father's immortal soul. *Goddamn it.*

"Rough night?"

She startled, nearly tipping over her heels, and spun to face the male voice. It took all of a second to recognize whom it belonged to. "Cillian? What the hell are you doing lurking out here?" The middle child of seven—and third boy—Cillian had lived as much a charmed life as possible under their circumstances. He'd always been kind of an idiot, but he'd never had to face the same things she and her sisters had. Or even that Teague and Aiden had. There had been no one requiring him to grow up, and so he'd happily played at being a Lost Boy.

Until Devlin died.

It seemed like so much of their lives centered on that one tragedy. Things had been a certain way. Before Victor Halloran lost his mind and declared war. Before things escalated to the point of no return. Before a bullet from a Halloran man snuffed out the life of the best and brightest of their family. Now life had been divided into Before Devlin and After Devlin. She rubbed a hand over her chest, wondering how much time it would take to dull the edge of pain thinking about him brought.

As Cillian moved closer, the toll the last few months had taken on him was written all over his face. Even in the shadows, his eyes were haunted. He glanced at the intimidating front door to the town house, the trees lining the street making the darkness feel more absolute despite the lights peppered between them. "I wasn't ready to go in."

To face their reality.

Was there anyone in their family who didn't want to run as far and fast as they could to get away from the hell they lived in? Carrigan didn't think so. Six months ago, she would have put Cillian on that short list. Maybe even Devlin, too. Now? Now Devlin was gone and everything was different.

Devlin was the one who had still maintained an aura of innocence despite everything. The one who might have escaped the net their father was so intent on tangling them in. Family.

She almost laughed. Who was she kidding? No one escaped. Not Devlin. Not Cillian. Sure as hell not her.

Carrigan looped her arm through his. "I'm not ready, either. Want to go for a walk?"

He glanced down the street. The same direction he'd been coming from—the direction of the pub where her brothers had all been walking back from the night everything went to hell. "It's not safe."

She could argue that it was as safe as it ever was, that they were supposed to be back to peacetime relations with the Hallorans, and that Teague marrying the heir to the Sheridans had made sure that they'd be fine on that end as well. But the memory of James waiting for her in that club was still too fresh. It wasn't safe. It might never be safe again. "The park?"

He hesitated, and she thought he might refuse. "Sure."

They made their way down the block, her heels clicking in the darkness. There was so much to say, and nothing at all. What could she say that would make anything okay? It wasn't okay.

"I thought you were at Our Lady of Victories."

It wasn't really a question, but she answered anyway. "Sometimes I need a break." A break that no church could give her, despite what her father believed. She'd tried when she was still in high school. They spent every single Sunday morning at Mass, and she'd thought that maybe the salvation she was looking for could be found inside those four walls. So she'd spent hours on end there, praying with every ounce of will her sixteen-year-old heart could muster up. Praying for someone to save her.

Silence had been her only reply.

So she'd gone looking for salvation in other places.

In all the years since, the closest she'd come to salvation was what she felt that night in James's arms.

Fall in Love with Forever Romance

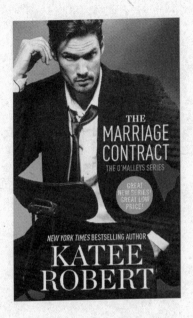

THE MARRIAGE CONTRACT
by Katee Robert

New York Times and *USA Today* bestselling author Katee Robert begins a smoking-hot new series about the O'Malley family—wealthy, powerful, dangerous, and seething with scandal.

Fall in Love with Forever Romance

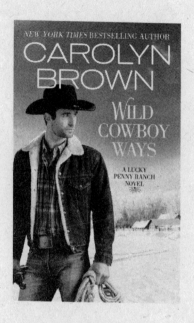

WILD COWBOY WAYS
by Carolyn Brown

New York Times and *USA Today* bestselling author Carolyn Brown begins a hilarious and heartwarming new series with Lucky Penny Ranch, where the wild Dawson brothers might finally be looking to settle down.

Fall in Love with Forever Romance

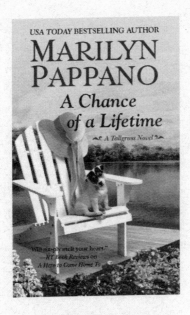

USA TODAY BESTSELLING AUTHOR

MARILYN PAPPANO

A Chance of a Lifetime

≈ A Tallgrass Novel ≈

"Will simply melt your heart."
—RT Book Reviews on
A Hero to Come Home To

A CHANCE OF A LIFETIME
by Marilyn Pappano

In the tradition of *New York Times* bestselling author Robyn Carr comes the fifth book in Marilyn Pappano's Tallgrass, Oklahoma, series. Calvin Sweet is back from the war and Benita Ford's husband has died in combat. Can the two find love and chase away Calvin's demons?

Find out more about *Forever Romance!*

Visit us at
www.hachettebookgroup.com/publishing_forever.aspx

Find us on Facebook
http://www.facebook.com/ForeverRomance

Follow us on Twitter
http://twitter.com/ForeverRomance

NEW AND UPCOMING TITLES

Each month we feature our new titles
and reader favorites.

CONTESTS AND GIVEAWAYS

We give away galleys, autographed copies,
and all kinds of exclusive items.

AUTHOR INFO

You'll find bios, articles, and links to personal websites
for all your favorite authors—and so much more.

GET SOCIAL

Connect with your favorite authors, editors, and
other Forever fans, and share what's important to you.

THE BUZZ

Sign up for our monthly romance newsletter,
and be the first to read all about it.

VISIT US ONLINE AT

WWW.HACHETTEBOOKGROUP.COM

FEATURES:

**OPENBOOK BROWSE AND
SEARCH EXCERPTS**

•

AUDIOBOOK EXCERPTS AND PODCASTS

•

AUTHOR ARTICLES AND INTERVIEWS

•

**BESTSELLER AND PUBLISHING
GROUP NEWS**

•

SIGN UP FOR E-NEWSLETTERS

•

**AUTHOR APPEARANCES AND TOUR
INFORMATION**

•

SOCIAL MEDIA FEEDS AND WIDGETS

•

DOWNLOAD FREE APPS

Bookmark Hachette Book Group
@ www.HachetteBookGroup.com